Praise for *The Ex Hex*

"A spooky romantic-comedy treat that had me sighing at one page, laughing out loud at the next. *The Ex Hex* is the perfect book for fall."

—*New York Times* bestselling author Tessa Bailey

"Sterling casts a spell on her readers."　　　　　—*USA Today*

"The book perfectly hits the same sweet spot as the 1998 cinematic classic *Practical Magic*, without the dark plot elements about the abusive ex; it's got a hint of *Bell, Book and Candle* charm without the casual midcentury sexism. It's cozy and cute and Halloween appropriate, and Rhys is *extremely* attractive. *The Ex Hex* was, in short, a blast."

—Jezebel

"A delightful and witty take on witchy mayhem."

—PopSugar

"If you like seasonal fall reads but don't want to jump full into horror, this is the perfect October book for you. . . . It promises *Hocus Pocus* vibes, but with a lot more heat. So curl up with a pumpkin spice latte and *The Ex Hex* for a perfect autumnal reading experience."

—Book Riot

"Humorous, magical, and sexy."　　　　　—The Gloss

"This festive rom-com has it all!"　　　　　—*Woman's World*

THE
KISS
CURSE

THE KISS CURSE

a novel

ERIN STERLING

AVON

An Imprint of HarperCollinsPublishers

THE KISS CURSE. Copyright © 2022 by Rachel Hawkins. All rights reserved. Printed in the United States of America. No part of this book may be used or reproduced in any manner whatsoever without written permission except in the case of brief quotations embodied in critical articles and reviews. For information, address HarperCollins Publishers, 195 Broadway, New York, NY 10007.

HarperCollins books may be purchased for educational, business, or sales promotional use. For information, please email the Special Markets Department at SPsales@harpercollins.com.

FIRST EDITION

Designed by Diahann Sturge

Title page and chapter opener art © Kuznetsova Darja / Shutterstock, Inc.

Library of Congress Cataloging-in-Publication Data has been applied for.

ISBN 978-0-06-302751-0 (paperback)
ISBN 978-0-06-327523-2 (international edition)
ISBN 978-0-06-327181-4 (hardcover library edition)

22 23 24 25 26   LSC   10 9 8 7 6 5 4 3 2 1

For Merlin and Bosworth. I'm glad y'all don't talk.

THE
KISS
CURSE

PROLOGUE

Thirteen Years Ago, Penhaven College...

Given that the spell had been "Turn this leaf into something else," and Gwynnevere Jones had indeed *turned that leaf into something else,* it seemed extremely unfair that everyone was now screaming at her.

Okay, so it was less that they were screaming *at* her, more they were just screaming in *general,* and yes, all right, *maybe* the leaf now resembled some kind of small dinosaur with very pointy teeth currently clamped around the toe of her professor's pointy boot, but had the spell been specific?

It had not!

Had everyone else made completely boring shit like a pen or a slightly bigger leaf?

Yes!

Was Gwyn's the only spell that had this deeply cool locomotion effect, and therefore they should all be thanking her and telling her what a badass witch she was instead of saying things like "Make it stop!" and "What the fuck?"

Honestly, Gwyn thought so!

This, she thought as she once again tried to gather enough power to turn her bitey creature back into an oak leaf, *is why I didn't even want to come here.*

Penhaven College in Graves Glen, Georgia, taught both regular students and witches, the witchcraft classes secretive and hidden from everyone else who just thought the kids who went to those weirder buildings on campus were pursuing esoteric degrees in Folklore or something. Advanced Hedge Making, maybe.

Gwyn had grown up in Graves Glen, but it had never occurred to her she'd actually be sent to Penhaven. Her mom was cooler than that, she'd thought, way less traditional than most witches—or moms for that matter—and Gwyn had assumed she'd end up at some normie school, drinking beer in red Solo cups and practicing magic on her own.

But no. On this *one thing,* her mom had decided to get super traditional and insisted she go to Penhaven.

Gwyn's mom, Elaine, was pretty much the least traditional person Gwyn knew. She'd raised Gwyn all on her own, making a living selling bath salts and special teas at various festivals and Ren Faires, reading tarot cards in the cozy kitchen of their cabin. Gwyn had loved that life, had assumed she'd get to follow in her mom's footsteps, doing her own thing, and then, as high school had wound down, Penhaven had reared its ugly head.

"It'll be good for you," Elaine had told Gwyn, her blond hair glowing in the sunlight in their kitchen, her eyes kind, looking like a saint, or, even worse, like Stevie Nicks, because how were you ever supposed to say no to Stevie Nicks?

That's how Gwyn had ended up at Penhaven, taking classes like Ritual Candles and Phases of the Moon.

And Simple Form Conversion, a class she had already been suspicious of due to how math-y it sounded.

"Miss! Jones!" her professor shouted, and Gwyn shook her head, still trying to pull together as much magic as she could. It was hard, though, seeing as how she'd really put her back into it, magically speaking, to turn the leaf into the very thing now chomping Dr. Arbuthnot's admittedly fierce boot.

You don't always have to be a show-off, you know.

Gwyn's cousin, Vivi, wasn't there in the classroom with her—she still had two more years of high school to go before Elaine, no doubt, sent her off to do this same thing. But Gwyn knew that's exactly what she would've said, and at the thought, she screwed up her face, trying to concentrate harder.

Her hands were placed flat on the table in front of her, the surface trembling slightly, the ends of her long purple hair pooling next to her palms.

The dye had been a flash of rebellion before she'd started classes, her normally red hair turned deep amethyst, but of course her mom had only smiled and smoothed a hand over the back of her head, telling her it suited her.

That was the problem with having a Cool Mom.

"Have you got it?"

Gwyn's concentration broke for the barest of seconds as her lab partner, a pretty brunette named Morgan, edged closer, dark eyes wide.

"Yeah," Gwyn said, making herself smile even though she very assuredly did *not* have it. "Almost there!"

The thing had, thank the Goddess, let go of Dr. Arbuthnot's boot.

Except that now it seemed to be looking kind of hungrily at her dangling scarf, and Gwyn gritted her teeth, her sparkly blue nails digging harder into the table's surface. She was *not* going down as the first student in Penhaven College history to accidentally get a teacher eaten.

All right, so when she'd done the spell, she'd placed her hands on the leaf and just thought very hard that it needed to *change*. She hadn't given it any more direct instructions than that. Maybe that was the issue?

Lifting her head, Gwyn focused on the scene at the front of the classroom.

There were no windows here, everything lit with sconces against the wall, the heavy wooden tables the students sat behind all on a slightly raised platform, almost like they were in a Victorian operating theater or something.

At the front of the room, Dr. Arbuthnot stood behind an old-fashioned wooden lectern. Well, she normally did. Right now, she was in front of it, holding on to the edge as she sent blue bursts of light from her fingertips toward the thing currently crouching and growling at her feet.

But Gwyn's little leaf monster was clever, darting out of the way, and if Gwyn hadn't been worried this whole thing was going to get her expelled or burned at the stake—if they still did that—she almost would've felt . . . proud of the little guy.

Like Gwyn, he was scrappy.

Dr. Arbuthnot could, Gwyn knew, decimate the thing with a simple spell, but she wanted Gwyn to be able to control it or, better yet, turn it back into a leaf. That was the point of the class, after all, and Gwyn was determined to get this right.

She might not have wanted to come to Penhaven College, but she'd be damned if she became the Class Screw-Up.

Determined, she focused on the creature, lifting her hands, and she could feel it start to shift.

Start to change.

Almost there.

Her fingers flexed just as the leaf creature jerked its head toward her.

At the same time, the classroom door flew open, banging against the wall.

Gwyn didn't pay that any attention, her gaze locked on the front of the room, her power building, and then—

There was a sudden flash of light, and a smell that reminded Gwyn of campfires and autumn nights filled the room.

At the lectern, Dr. Arbuthnot suddenly stood up straight, and Gwyn watched as little bits of smoke and flaming debris—fiery bits of leaf—drifted up toward the ceiling.

Gwyn's hands dropped, her mouth falling open. Shit.

Shit.

She'd overdone it somehow. She'd put too much power behind the spell and instead of transforming the thing back into a leaf, she'd just . . . obliterated it.

And then she heard Morgan sigh just as Dr. Arbuthnot looked toward the door.

Gwyn followed her gaze.

A boy stood there.

No, a man. Older than Gwyn, but not by much, his dark hair shaggy, his blue eyes bright even from a distance. He was dressed all in black, his hands still raised toward the front of the room, and Gwyn had no doubt that whoever he was, his ancestors had absolutely once stared down the business end of a guillotine.

You didn't get cheekbones like that without oppressing some peasants.

"Penhallow," Dr. Arbuthnot said, adjusting her scarf, and Gwyn's gaze sharpened.

She'd called it, all right. The Penhallow family basically ran this town even though they didn't even live here. But one of their ancestors founded Graves Glen—and the college itself—so every once in a while, a Penhallow deigned to join the lowly citizens of Gwyn's hometown for a summer or so.

"Is everyone all right?" he asked, his eyes sweeping the classroom as he reached up to push his hair back from his face.

Gwyn opened her mouth to tell him that they were *more* than all right, that she'd been seconds away from having the whole thing in hand, and doing a very basic spell that just blew shit up wasn't all that impressive, really, but Dr. Arbuthnot beat her to the punch.

"Fine now, yes. Thank you, Penhallow."

"I was passing by," he explained, "and heard the commotion. I thought I could help, so—"

"We're fresh out of both medals and cookies," Gwyn interrupted, flexing her fingers. "And you didn't actually help. You just blew the thing up. *I* could've blown the thing up."

The Penhallow guy looked over at her, one brow crooked. "Then why didn't you?" he asked, and before she could reply to that, he was gone, the door closing behind him.

At the front of the room, Dr. Arbuthnot brushed little bits of leaf ash off the front of her long skirt and readjusted her glasses. "We'll speak after class, Ms. Jones," she said, and Gwyn rolled her eyes even as she nodded.

She and Dr. Arbuthnot spoke after class at least once a week. By the end of the semester, Gwyn was probably going to have to start paying rent on her office or something.

Next to her, Morgan was still looking wistfully at the door. "That was Llewellyn Penhallow," she said on a dreamy sigh, and Gwyn snorted, gathering up her things.

"*Llewellyn*," she repeated, because when a guy had a name like that, you didn't even *have* to make fun of it. Just repeating it was enough.

Morgan elbowed her, tucking her hair behind her ear with her other hand. "You have to admit he was cute," she pressed, and Gwyn slung her bag over her shoulder, glancing back at the door.

"Cute, maybe," she said with a shrug. "Asshole, definitely. Probably has the word 'Esquire' after his name."

"Well, you won't get the chance to find out," Morgan said as she started picking up her books. "Someone told me he's not even finishing the summer semester. His dad is apparently calling him back to Wales for some family thing."

Given that the Penhallows were a very powerful, very ancient line of witches, Gwyn figured "family thing" could mean a lot of different stuff, probably none of it good.

Not that she really cared.

No, right now the main thing Gwyn cared about was that she had to talk to Dr. Arbuthnot, somehow make it on time for her next class, which was all the way across campus, and also go help her mom out at Something Wicked, the store they ran in downtown Graves Glen.

Llewellyn Penhallow, Esquire, got exactly one more thought from Gwyn as she made her way toward the front of the classroom and Dr. Arbuthnot's disapproving face.

Thank the Goddess I'll never have to see that asshole again.

CHAPTER 1

"Iff I yell 'boo-yah' when we catch the ghost, you'll get it's meant to be ironic, right?"

Gwyn whispered the words as she crept behind her cousin, Vivi, through the dark woods, a sliver of moon bright in the navy-blue sky, the small ball of light Vivi had conjured up bobbing cheerfully right above their heads. The early September air was surprisingly cool and smelled crisp, a hint of smoke tickling Gwyn's nose.

Definitely a good night for ghost hunting.

Maybe a less perfect night for joking, though, because Vivi looked over her shoulder, hazel eyes narrowed. "Gwynnevere."

"What?" Gwyn protested. "It's that or some kind of 'ain't scared of no ghost' thing that I frankly think is a little dated."

"Why do I get the feeling you're not taking this seriously?"

Gwyn, who was currently wearing a black sweater dotted with little white ghosts, gave Vivi her most serious face. "I have no idea why you would think that."

As she'd expected, Vivi's stern expression gave way to a fond smile and a roll of her eyes.

"Fine. I accept your ironic 'boo-yah.'"

"Thank you," Gwyn said, readjusting the leather bag slung across her chest. Since this was her first ghost hunt, she'd raided Something Wicked for anything that seemed like it might be useful, but the store mainly catered to tourists, not actual witches.

That meant that Gwyn currently had a bag full of crystals, a couple of jarred candles, and a velvet pouch of the bath salts her mother made especially for the store.

Vivi looked back at her again as the candles clinked against the crystals. "I told you, you didn't need to bring anything," she said. "This is more of a fact-finding mission."

"And I get that, Vivi, but I've seen exactly one ghost in my life, and it was super scary, so excuse me for wanting to be prepared."

"With chamomile and lavender bath salts?"

"The important part is the salt."

When Vivi paused again, her eyebrows raised, Gwyn waved a hand. "You know. Like in the shows."

"The shows?"

"The ones where handsome guys hunt ghosts, and they're always like"—she lowered her voice to a gruff growl—"'We're gonna need to make a ring of salt around the perimeter' or something. So." Gwyn patted her bag. "Salt."

"We're witches, Gwyn," Vivi reminded her. "Maybe we shouldn't take our cues from TV?"

"We're not *ghost-hunting* witches," Gwyn argued, dodging around a large branch as they pushed deeper into the woods. "And that show ran for, like, twenty years. I bet they got *something* right."

Vivi considered that, then finally gave a shrug. "Probably can't hurt."

The wind rattled the leaves overhead, whipping Gwyn's long red hair back from her face as she took bigger steps, trying to keep up with her cousin. "You know, if *I* had a hot husband, I would definitely find more reasons to be home, less reasons to scuttle through haunted forests."

Vivi laughed a little at that. "I invited Rhys to come with us, but he's swamped with work and trying to wrap everything up before our trip."

Gwyn made an agreeing noise at that, ignoring the little pang in her chest at the thought of Vivi being gone. It was stupid—she was only going to be gone for a few weeks, making a trip to see some magical ritual Vivi was interested in back in Rhys's home country of Wales—but it would be the longest Gwyn had been apart from her cousin in ages. And since Gwyn's mom, Elaine, was also off at a witchy retreat in Arizona, it would mean Gwyn was totally on her own.

Which was fine. She was an adult, after all, she could handle running the show without—

Overhead, an owl hooted, and Gwyn gave a little shriek, moving closer to Vivi.

Clearing her throat, she pushed back her shoulders and

moved on. "So first big trip to the homeland, how are we feeling about it?"

Vivi's smile was almost brighter than her light spell. "It's going to be *amazing*. Rhys is taking me to Snowdonia, up near where his brother lives, and—"

"Dickhead Brother or Werewolf Brother?"

Vivi shot Gwyn another look. "They actually go by Wells and Bowen, and for the last time, Bowen is not a werewolf, he just . . . doesn't shave very often."

"I don't know, Vivi, sounds like an excuse a werewolf would make," Gwyn said as she skirted around a pile of leaves.

Vivi laughed at that, shaking her head. "In any case, yes, Bowen. Wells still lives in the village where they grew up, so I'm sure we'll pass by and visit him, too."

"Cool. Maybe you can ask him what was more important than coming to his brother's wedding."

Vivi groaned. "Okay, Gwyn, seriously. It didn't bother me! It didn't even bother Rhys."

"Well, it bothered me," Gwyn replied, irritated all over again. Vivi had gotten married back in the summer, a small wedding in Graves Glen in the same meadow where she'd met Rhys years ago. It had been beautiful and simple, and even Gwyn had gotten a little teary-eyed, not that she would ever admit that, and while Gwyn really had been alarmed by Bowen's facial hair and the fact that he looked like he might actually die if he ever had to smile, at least he'd shown up.

Rhys's father and other brother, however, hadn't come.

Gwyn couldn't imagine not being there for Vivi on her wedding day, and it wasn't like Wells hadn't been invited. He had. Rhys had even talked to him a couple of days before the wedding, but when the actual day arrived, he hadn't been there.

No excuse, nothing. Just a total no-show.

What kind of brother was that?

But then, from what Gwyn remembered of the one very brief interaction she'd ever had with Llewellyn Penhallow, she shouldn't have been that surprised.

"Rhys says that's just how he is," Vivi went on now. "His father wouldn't come, so he wouldn't, either. He's . . . I don't know, loyal, I guess. And I think that pub keeps him busy."

It was still bizarre to Gwyn that Llewellyn Penhallow, who'd practically been famous for what a powerful witch he was that one semester at Penhaven, ran a *bar* back in Wales instead of doing some kind of Impressive Witch Shit, but Gwyn had never really cared enough to ask just why that was.

"My job keeps me busy, too!" she said now, crossing her arms over her chest. "The other day, I was organizing grimoires in the back room at Something Wicked, and then I was, like, 'You know, "grimoire" is a weird name, where did that even come from?' and the next thing I knew, I had, like, twelve Wikipedia tabs open, and it was dark outside."

Vivi smiled at that, shaking her head as she continued trudging uphill, and Gwyn followed.

"But I still came to your wedding is the thing," she added, and Vivi reached out, brushing Gwyn's hand with hers.

"And I appreciate it. Just like I appreciate you checking this out with me."

Gwyn had been so caught up in righteous indignation that she almost forgot where she was and what they were doing.

Right. Ghost hunt. Spooky woods.

"Maybe there won't be a ghost?" Gwyn offered, really, really hoping that was the case. She'd had plans for tonight, plans that involved trying out a new tea she'd ordered and taking an ob- scenely long bath. Plans that in no way involved hiking through the woods late at night all because Vivi had overheard some of her students at the college talking about strange lights and noises in this part of the forest.

"It's probably just kids with flashlights, drinking beer and making poor romantic choices," Gwyn said now, her mouth a little dry as she looked around her. Even with the help of Vivi's light spell, the darkness felt intense, heavy. She got the sense that there could be anything watching her just outside of this warm circle of light, a thousand eyes in the trees, and she shivered, pull- ing the sleeves of her sweater over her hands.

"Maybe," Vivi acknowledged, toeing a pile of leaves with one booted foot. "But we have a responsibility to the town to make sure it's nothing more than that."

"Responsibility" was not a word Gwyn was a huge fan of, but she had to admit her cousin was right: It was the Jones women's magic that fueled Graves Glen, and that meant if there was magical fuckery happening, it was up to Gwyn and Vivi to stop it.

Linking her arm with her cousin's, Gwyn tugged Vivi close. "I really hate when you're right. It's one of your most obnoxious qualities."

Vivi grinned at her. "Rhys says the same thing."

"The rare subject on which your husband and I agree," Gwyn said on a sigh, and Vivi bumped her hip, still smiling, the light floating over them glowing brightly on her face.

Too brightly, Gwyn suddenly realized.

Because it wasn't the only light around them now.

Gwyn turned her head slowly, her arm still locked with Vivi's as she took in the . . . thing drifting through the forest toward them.

The one ghost Gwyn had seen had definitely looked like a person. Glowy and floaty like whatever this was, but definitely person-like.

This wasn't that. It was almost like a cloud, shifting and undulating, emitting this weird green light, and the magic coming off of it . . .

Gwyn shivered even harder now, her teeth nearly chattering. She'd always been more sensitive to magic than Vivi or Elaine, able to feel its presence sooner than they could. This thing had sneaked up on her, but now that it was here, she could tell that whatever had made it, there was something wrong.

Big-time wrong.

She reached into her bag just as Vivi moved closer, her brows drawn together. "I've never seen anything like this before," she said, raising one arm out toward the thing.

"Vivi, maybe don't touch the scary blob?" Gwyn offered, pushing away the candles and the crystals, her fingers brushing the velvet pouch holding the bath salts.

Vivi kept walking toward it, that hand still outstretched. "Rhys and I spent all that time researching curses last year, and we didn't come across anything that even remotely looked like this," she went on. "I can't even tell what it's made of."

"My nightmares and a bit of hair gel?" Gwyn suggested, finally managing to get a handful of salt. "Anyway, it's bad and I hate it, so *duck.*"

CHAPTER 2

W ait!"

Gwyn whirled around to see three figures standing just at the edge of the bubble's glow, their faces a sickly green. Salt was still clutched in her fist, ready for launch, when Vivi said, "Sam?"

A young woman stepped forward, her hair bright turquoise, the bubble reflected in her glasses. Gwyn recognized her now. She was a witch at the college who also worked at the Coffee Cauldron, the café just down the street from Gwyn's shop. The girl next to her, shorter with long black hair caught back in a braid, worked there, too, Gwyn realized. The third kid was unfamiliar, but looked just as freaked out as the other two, dark eyes wide.

Vivi clearly knew them, though, and as she moved closer, they all quailed a little bit.

"What are you three doing out here?" she asked before turning to Gwyn and saying, "This is Sam, Cait, and Parker. They're in my History of Magic class at Penhaven. And they're *usually* good students who certainly wouldn't be in the woods, messing around with dangerous magic."

"Okay, so I know this looks bad," Sam said. "And admittedly, things are . . . not going to plan, but this spell is harmless, I promise."

"It was my idea, actually, Dr. Jones," Cait offered. "We're all in Dr. Arbuthnot's Simple Form Conversion class this semester, and she was teaching us about how to turn one thing into another, like, you know, a leaf into something else."

Gwyn barely managed to keep from rolling her eyes. The college witches never strayed from their classics, did they? Why bother figuring out anything new and innovative in witchcraft when you could do the same boring lessons year after year?

"And anyway," Cait continued, "it made me think about Halloween coming up, and we could maybe use magic to, you know, level up a little bit. For the tourists."

"So you decided to magick up a ghost?" Vivi asked, frowning as she crossed her arms over her chest.

Gwyn went for a similar pose, hoping she looked as stern and authoritative as Vivi did, but knowing that her ghost sweater was *probably* undermining it.

"It isn't a ghost!" Sam insisted. "Seriously, it's just a little bit of glitter, glue, and water that we magicked up into *looking* like a ghost." She nodded at the third member of their little party. "It was actually Parker's idea. They're really good at this kind of stuff."

Parker preened a little, flicking their brown curls back. "It's really not that hard," they said. "You just—"

"Nope!" Vivi lifted a hand, cutting them off. "This might seem harmless, but this is exactly why we *don't* do real magic for the tourists. The kids in my non-witch classes have been talking all week about this glowing thing in the woods. We're supposed to be a little more discreet than that."

The three witches looked a little crestfallen at that, and Gwyn could tell Cait was about to argue. And honestly, she got it. What was the point of having magic if you couldn't have some fun with it?

But Gwyn knew she needed to have her cousin's back here, so she stepped closer to Vivi and said, "Vivi's right, y'all. Trust me, magic that *seems* like a little bit of fun and not all that serious can very easily blow up in your faces. And if you want to try something like this, you need to have a more experienced witch supervising at the very least."

She and Vivi had had Elaine, after all.

But Sam only looked glum, shaking her head. "Dr. Jones, you know how strict the college is. There are all these rules about when and where we're supposed to do magic. We never get the chance to just . . . improvise. Try new things."

"Yeah, those rules are actually there for good reasons, and I say that as someone who hates rules on principle," Gwyn replied, then glanced over at Vivi.

Vivi *loved* rules. Rules were her favorite.

But instead, Vivi was watching the trio of witches with a thoughtful expression. "I guess the college is a little formal on that kind of thing," she said slowly. "And part of developing your skills does come from practice . . ."

Now she turned to Gwyn, who frowned. "Don't do thinky face at me," she said, and Vivi's brow furrowed.

"I don't have a thinky face."

"You do! You're thinky facing at me right now, and I don't like it!"

"I was just thinking—" Vivi started, and Gwyn pointed at her. "See?"

Ignoring that, Vivi went on, "—that maybe this is also part of our responsibility now. To the town. To mentor young witches. Give them a safe space to try out magic that isn't connected to the college."

There was that word again, and Gwyn was going to remind Vivi that they had plenty of responsibilities as it was—Gwyn had the store, Vivi had two jobs, *and* Halloween was next month, which meant things would get even more hectic. Now she wanted them to set up some kind of Girl Scout troop for Baby Witches?

But then Gwyn looked over Vivi's shoulder and saw that Sam, Cait, and Parker's faces were practically glowing at the thought, their eyes going the full puppy dog, and when she glanced back at the "ghost," she had to admit, it was a pretty impressive bit of magic. The luminescent effect alone was tough to create, even tougher to maintain, and they'd done it.

And, if she was honest, she could admit that there was something kind of fun about the idea of being an Elaine for a new generation of witches.

"Fine," she said on a sigh. "But only because I think it would really piss off your bosses at the college."

Vivi shook her head, smiling, and then turned back to her students.

"All right, so Gwyn and I will work with you if you want to start trying out spells. *But.* No more skulking around in the woods at night, and absolutely *no* 'improvising' without talking to one of us first, okay?"

The three of them nodded so fast it was a wonder their heads didn't snap off, and Vivi dusted her hands together, clearly pleased with herself.

"So now the only thing to do is get rid of this," she said, gesturing back to the hovering blob, and Parker frowned.

"Yeah. That's . . . kind of why we were out here. We're not really sure how to *un*make it?"

Gwyn turned back to the shimmering mass, now significantly less scary since she knew what it was made out of and who had made it.

Without giving it too much thought, she reached back into her bag, grabbing that handful of salt again.

Vivi frowned. "Gwyn, I don't know—"

"Oh, come on," Gwyn said. "Couldn't hurt!"

And with that extremely ill-fated pronouncement, she threw the salt.

"HAS ANYONE TOLD you you're a wee bit impulsive, Gwynnevere?"

Gwyn glared across the table at Rhys, Vivi's husband, as she scrubbed her wet hair with a towel. She'd taken a twenty-minute shower when she'd gotten back to her cabin, but she still felt like she was covered in ghost goop. How could something technically made out of glue, glitter, and magic be so disgusting when it exploded?

There probably wasn't a shower strong enough to make her ever feel clean again, a sentiment Vivi clearly shared because she still hadn't emerged from the upstairs bathroom.

"As a matter of fact, they have," Gwyn answered Rhys now. "Teachers, several exes, and one particularly mean traffic court judge. And now you."

"What glorious company I keep," Rhys replied, moving to the counter where an electric kettle was bubbling away.

Vivi appeared, wrapped in one of Elaine's robes, her damp hair leaving spots on the peacock-blue silk. "I feel like that was the first of many showers I'm going to take tonight," she said, and Rhys smiled at her, handing her a mug of tea.

"As long as I get to join in on at least one, I see no problems there, my love."

Vivi smiled at that, stepping closer, and as they wrapped their arms around each other, Gwyn rolled her eyes. She was happy for them, really, and Goddess knew the two of them had been through it before finding this happily ever after, but honestly, there had to be *limits*.

"I am sitting right here," she said. "Zero desire to be privy to any of this!"

"Hey," Vivi said, pointing a finger at Gwyn. "Do you know how many times I had to sit on the couch and watch you full-on make out with someone while I pretended to look at my phone? This is payback."

"Fair," Gwyn admitted, even as she realized just how long it had been since she'd made out with anyone. Months, really.

That was depressing.

Rhys chuckled, pressing a quick kiss to Vivi's forehead before pulling away and turning back to the tea, Vivi coming to sit across from Gwyn at the table. This tended to be the place they all gathered these days even though Vivi had her own apartment over the store downtown, where she and Rhys currently lived. Technically Rhys had his family's place higher up the mountain, but given that the house was like something out of a Tim Burton movie, it usually sat empty.

Rhys walked back to the table, handing Gwyn a mug, and since he'd used her favorite tea blend, she decided to forgive him for making her think about shower sex.

"I have to say, I like this part where we go out to do witch things and you stay here and make tea," Gwyn said, blowing over the top of her mug as her cat, Sir Purrcival, leapt up onto the table. Gwyn had tried shooing him down over the years, but the fact that he now had a very cozy cat bed right in the center of things was proof of who'd won that fight.

He blinked at her, his eyes a bright yellow green against his black fur as Rhys snorted, pouring hot water into his own mug. "I know my strengths," he told her before coming to sit down next to his wife.

"And, spell explosion aside, it seems like you had a productive night," he continued. "Found out the source of the ghost rumors, steered some local youths back onto the correct path . . . "

"That was all Vivi," Gwyn assured him. "She made thinky face at me, and I was helpless to resist."

"I do not have a thinky face," Vivi objected, but Rhys smiled, shaking his head.

"You absolutely do, my love. It's one of my top favorite faces of yours. Something sort of like this."

Rhys furrowed his brow just the slightest bit, his eyes taking on a faraway expression, and Gwyn slapped the table with her free hand.

"That's it! God, that's uncanny."

Vivi scowled as she glanced back and forth between them. "You know, it was much better for me when you two didn't like each other."

"I've always liked Gwyn," Rhys protested, and Gwyn shrugged.

"I didn't like you."

"Dickbag," Sir Purrcival said sleepily from his spot in the middle of the table, and Rhys scowled at the cat.

"Still no luck on reversing the whole talking spell thing, I take it?" he asked Gwyn, and she shrugged.

"Not really a priority." Thanks to some witchery fuckery last year, Sir Purrcival could speak. It turned out a cat's thoughts were mostly about food and insults, but Gwyn had gotten used to it.

She leaned forward, petting Purrcival, and he lived up to his name, purring happily as she stroked his back. Across the table, Rhys's hand went to the back of Vivi's neck, and she leaned into his touch just the littlest bit, probably unconsciously.

Gwyn felt it again, that weird little feeling in the pit of her stomach that could *not* be jealousy or longing or anything like that, because those were feelings Gwyn very much did not have.

But it was . . . something, and she didn't like it.

To distract herself from possibly feeling feelings, Gwyn reached across the table for the little jar of lavender honey, adding some more to her tea as she asked, "So big trip rapidly approaching?"

"Yes, it is," Rhys said, "and it will shock you not at all to learn that Vivienne already has a very thorough packing list. I, on the other hand—"

"Maybe we shouldn't go."

Vivi said the words hesitantly, glancing back and forth between Rhys and Gwyn. "Just . . . tonight reminded me that now that our magic is fueling the town, we have—"

"Vivi, if you say 'responsibilities' one more time tonight, I am going to create another ghost blob just to explode on you all over again."

"Well, we *do*," Vivi said. "And Halloween is coming up."

"In over a month," Gwyn reminded her, and Rhys took his wife's hand, nodding.

"And we'll be back in time."

"*And* you deserve a long-delayed honeymoon."

"And that," Rhys agreed, pointing at Gwyn. "Plus you've wanted to take this trip for ages."

Vivi bit her lower lip, thinking. "It would be really helpful with my research."

"Go," Gwyn urged her now. "Everything here will be fine. The store is doing great. It practically runs itself this time of year anyway, and to be honest, I've been craving some alone time."

Both of those were lies—the store wasn't doing so hot right now despite their being so close to Halloween. And Gwyn was actually slightly allergic to being alone, but she gave her cousin her brightest smile.

"Besides, I want souvenirs. Little Welsh flags, maybe some kind of stuffed dragon situation . . . ooh, and if you see Rhys's brother, you can kick him in the nads for me!"

"Which brother?" Rhys asked, then held up a hand. "I mean, I'll happily kick either one, I just need to make sure I've calculated the appropriate defense strategy once they've gotten up."

"She means Wells," Vivi said, smiling a little at last. "She's still holding a grudge about the wedding."

Rhys pulled a face. "*I'm* not holding a grudge about the wedding, and it was *my* wedding. And my brother, for that matter."

Gwyn shrugged. "Don't seek to question my grudge-holding ways, Rhys. I'm a Taurus."

She didn't bother to add that her grudge against Wells Penhallow had existed since long before the wedding, that it had its roots in her college days, but if a girl could hold a grudge, she could also keep some secrets.

"Fair enough," Rhys replied. "Welsh flag, stuffed dragon, emasculated brother, all for you upon our return."

Vivi finally laughed, leaning her head briefly against Rhys's shoulder.

"Okay, I can't beat you when you team up," she said. "You're right. Everything's fine, the town will be fine, and we will totally go to Wales as planned."

"Thank sweet Christ," Rhys said on a sigh, flopping back in his chair, and Gwyn smiled, reaching across the table to squeeze Vivi's hand.

"Look, we've already dealt with an entire cursed town, a talking cat, and now an exploding ghost, and we've handled all of it. What could possibly happen that would be worse than any of that?"

CHAPTER 3

When the door opened to The Raven and Crown, Wells actually let himself believe—foolishly—that he might have a customer coming in.

It was a rainy evening after all, the mid-September weather typically cool and blustery for this tiny corner of Wales, and the pub was warm. Cozy, even. There was a fire crackling merrily away in the hearth, there was ancient dark wood everywhere, and, most important, if you'd been out in the rain on a cold autumn night, there was alcohol.

Lots of it, given how rarely Wells actually got to pour a drink in this place.

So when he heard the creaking of the door, heard the rain slapping against the side of the building as someone pushed their way in, he situated himself at the taps, ready to pull a pint or pour a dram, whatever was needed.

The figure at the door muttered to himself, pulling off a hooded greatcoat, and an older version of Wells's own face stared back at him.

Bollocks.

Not a customer after all, merely his own father.

Simon Penhallow didn't often make his way down into the village of Dweniniaid, preferring the confines of their slightly ghastly manor on a hillside just outside of town. In fact, Wells knew for a fact that his father had only been in The Raven and Crown twice in the thirteen years since Wells had taken it over.

Once had been Wells's first day in charge, and his father had only stayed long enough to grunt, glance around, give a nod that passed for approval in the Penhallow family, and stomp back out.

The second time had been last year, after Wells's youngest brother, Rhys, had informed his father that the Penhallow magic that had once fueled the town of Graves Glen, Georgia, was no longer present, driven out by a powerful coven of witches.

One of those witches was now Rhys's wife, something Simon had not taken particularly well. Privately, Wells thought it was the best thing for his brother, settling down with a woman who seemed to be sensible enough aside from falling in love with his idiot brother, but that was something best kept to himself.

So now, as Wells watched his father unwind his scarf, hanging it alongside his coat, his disappointment that this wasn't an actual paying customer slowly began to bleed into something else.

Suspicion.

What on earth would bring Simon from his books and his spells and his various plots on a night like this?

"Evening," Wells called out, already searching behind the bar for the one brand of whisky his father would deign to drink. He kept it on hand just in case a moment like this should ever arrive, and given that it hadn't in nearly a year, when he did locate it, the bottle was dusty enough that he had to surreptitiously wipe it with the damp towel hanging from his belt loop.

"Not much of one in here," Simon commented, glancing around as he took a seat at the bar.

"Rain is probably keeping everyone at home tonight," Wells said, and even to his ears, it sounded absolutely ridiculous. Since when had *rain* kept anyone from a pub in Wales? In all of the United Kingdom, for that matter?

But his father let him have the lie, nodding absently to himself as he accepted the glass Wells had poured for him, and then, to Wells's absolute shock, turning the glass up and draining it dry in one go.

When he thunked it back to the bar with a nod and a gruff "Another," Wells complied, then grabbed himself a glass and sloshed a measure in as well. Whatever it was that had his father in this mood, it would soon become Wells's problem, too.

Such was life as the eldest son.

Rhys, his youngest brother, would tell him he secretly loved this, being their father's right-hand man, and while Wells tried never to give Rhys credit for anything if he could help it, he had to admit there was a time in his life when that had been . . . not entirely untrue.

It had been easy, after all, being the Favored Child. Rhys had made it his mission in life to irk their father, and Bowen, the middle brother, had always seemed to operate separately from all of them, an island unto himself. So yes, Wells had enjoyed the way his father's stern gaze naturally fell on him when there was something to do, some responsibility to shoulder.

But after thirty-four years of it, the past thirteen spent running this dismally unsuccessful pub, Wells had to admit he was a bit tired of the whole dutiful son thing.

And yet . . .

Here he was, pouring his father whisky, waiting to hear what had to be done.

Christ, he was hopeless.

Simon sipped the second whisky more slowly, looking over at the fire before turning his face back to Wells. Shadows played along his severe bone structure, making him look more sinister than he was.

"It's always like this," Simon said, then gestured around the pub in case Wells hadn't caught his meaning. "Dead. Isn't it?"

For a moment, Wells thought about lying again, insisting that it was the storm or maybe there was some important game on the telly—Goddess knew his father would have no idea if *that* was true or not—and that's why there was no one bellied up to Wells's bar.

Instead, he dropped the towel onto the bar with a wet slap, bracing both hands on either side of it. "Actually, given that you've shown up, this is a busy night."

His father made that sound somewhere between a grunt and

a huff, the noise that passed for a laugh for him. Wells had heard himself make it just the other day on the phone to Rhys, and he wasn't sure which one of them had been the more horrified.

"So the pub my great-great-grandfather opened is a failure, and the town that my great-great-uncle founded no longer carries a drop of Penhallow magic."

Simon lifted his glass in a sort of ironic toast, but given that Wells had not until this moment known that his father even understood the concept of irony, that was a bit alarming.

"The point of the pub was never to make money," he reminded his father now. The Raven and Crown had been built on the site of the first settlement of Penhallow witches in Dweniniaid, and there was still a flicker of that ancient magic there, magic Wells tended to rather like a gardener with a dwindling potato patch.

It had been his ancestors' hope that building a pub in the spot would keep that magic strong, the land feeding off the energy of all the people who drank and laughed and fought and sang in a village pub, and in the early days, it had.

But now, no matter the daily spells Wells did, he could feel that little flame of magic slowly flickering out, a candle in a gale.

"I know that," Simon said on a sigh, sitting up a little as some of the melancholy faded from his face. "It's simply that . . . it's as if it's all slipping away. We anchored ourselves here, and we did the same in America, and what have we come to? An empty pub and . . . and *this*."

With a flick of his hand, Simon conjured up an oval of gray

smoke that gradually grew bigger and clearer, resolving itself into something resembling a mirror.

Wells knew immediately he was looking at Graves Glen. He'd only been there once, the summer he'd taken the traditional classes at Penhaven College, but while that had been thirteen years ago, not much had changed. It was still a quaint little pocket of serenity tucked into the gentle blue mountains of Georgia with an old-fashioned main street running through its downtown, streetlights casting a soft glow over everything.

Something in Wells's chest gave a rather painful kick looking at it. He'd only stayed in Graves Glen for a semester, just a handful of months, but the place had always stuck with him. He'd liked it there. Moreover, he'd liked *himself* there. In Graves Glen, the Penhallow name was a source of awe and interest, not fear. There, he'd actually been actively practicing his magic instead of just passively channeling it through this place. But his uncle Colin, the guardian of the pub up until then, had died, and it was important that a Penhallow witch be the keeper of the flame, as it were, and somehow years had gone by with him stuck in one place.

Wells shook off those melancholy thoughts, focusing on the picture in front of him.

It was late afternoon in Graves Glen now, so those streets were relatively busy, people enjoying the perfect, golden autumn day, and in the middle of it all, Wells spotted a bold shop window, a giant papier-mâché witch grinning at him as bright purple lights over her head spelled out . . .

"'Practice . . . safe . . . hex,'" he read out carefully, and his father's glare nearly ignited the little bit of whisky left in his glass.

"This is what's become of Gryffud's dream," Simon said darkly. "This place, once a haven for our kind, a seat of . . . of learning and, and erudition, and the perfecting of our craft is now run by these women hawking their cheap Halloween souvenirs and making ridiculous puns."

Another flick of Simon's hand, and the entire picture disappeared.

As far as puns went, Wells didn't think that one was *particularly* odious, but since his father was already reaching for the bottle of whisky, pouring his own glass this time, Wells thought it might be best not to mention that.

Instead, he started to say, "Graves Glen—" but off of Simon's look, quickly amended to the Welsh.

"*Glynn Bedd*," he corrected, "isn't completely free of Penhallows. Rhys is still there."

Simon gave Wells a look that said *exactly* what he thought about that, and Wells raised his hands in defense. "I'm just saying. We haven't been driven out altogether."

Snorting, Simon pushed his half-full glass aside. "Once your brother married that Jones woman, he became one of them. Make no mistake, boy, he has chosen their family over ours. The Penhallows are finished in Glynn Bedd just as we seem to be finished in Dweniniaid."

He heaved another sigh, as outside thunder rumbled through

the sky. If his father stayed in this mood, the whole bloody village would flood before too long.

It was almost unbearable, all of a sudden, thinking of spending days behind this bar while rain poured from the sky and no one walked in that door. Wells killed his time with reading up on spellcraft, strengthening the runes and spells put into this place to preserve the original spark of Penhallow magic, but there was only so much of that a man could do, really.

Wells thought again about that feeling he'd had when Simon had conjured up Graves Glen.

Not quite longing, but not far off, and suddenly, his heart began to beat harder, his mind racing, and the words seemed to slip out of his mouth before he even had time to think about them.

"What if I went to Glynn Bedd?"

CHAPTER 4

Wells was careful to keep his expression neutral, his voice calm, but the second he said it, he knew that's exactly what he wanted to do, where he wanted to be.

Finally a chance to be of use *and* get out of this dreary place.

Simon watched him from underneath heavy silver brows, his face giving nothing away, and Wells couldn't help but rush in, leaning across the bar.

"I know the pub is a family tradition, but maybe it's time for something new, eh? I could . . . I could set up some kind of shop there in town. Something for serious witches, not this silly touristy nonsense. I can make sure our name is remembered there even if our magic is gone."

Simon took that in, turning the glass in his hands. "There's been a Penhallow running The Raven and Crown for over a hundred years," he said, gruff. "To see it closed . . . "

"Da, look around. It's closed in spirit if not in name. And all the spells in the world aren't going to keep that last little bit of magic hanging on forever. Not with the place this empty."

Wells reached forward, grabbing his father's arm and giving it the slightest shake. "Let me do this. Let me help."

"Glynn Bedd is the more important family legacy, true," Simon admitted begrudgingly. "And I can't trust your brother there."

He looked up at Wells, and for the first time, there was actually a hint of softness in the old man's face. "I've always been able to trust you to do what's best for this family."

"And I will," Wells promised. That was the thing about their father that Rhys and Bowen had never understood. Yes, he was strict and emotionally distant, but he did love them in his way. They were his sons, and family mattered more to Simon than anything else. Why else would he care so much about this godforsaken pub or some little town in the mountains of Georgia?

Because they'd been built by family, and that meant Simon saw it as his duty to safeguard them.

Wells had watched over this pub for over a decade, and now he would do the same for Graves Glen.

Heaving another sigh, Simon pulled his arm from beneath Wells's hand.

"You're a good lad, Llewellyn," he said, and then he reached down, tugging a heavy silver ring from his finger.

Wells had never seen his father without this particular ring, the stone in the center a deep purple that almost looked black, Penhallow dragons etched on either side of it.

He pressed the ring into Wells's palm now, placing his other hand on Wells's shoulder as he pulled him in.

"All right. Go to Glynn Bedd. Protect our legacy there."

And then, shocking Wells even more, he gave him a brief hug. "I'll miss you, son," he said, and Wells was surprised to feel his throat tightening up a bit.

"I'll miss you, too, Da."

His father gave his back a rough pat, then straightened up with a huffed, "Well."

"Well," Wells echoed, and then, with a nod, his father was walking back out into the night. As the door opened, Wells noticed the rain had stopped.

The pub was still technically open for another hour, but he locked the door behind Simon, turning off the main lights.

He'd leave tomorrow, first thing, but for now, he spent a little extra time wiping down tables, stacking the chairs even as he thought, *Good fucking riddance.*

His mind was already churning with ideas, none of which involved ever pulling a pint again. In that brief glimpse he'd gotten of the town, he'd seen what appeared to be an empty storefront, and he was already imagining what he might do with such a space.

The opposite of whatever it was Rhys's in-laws did, clearly. To each their own, of course, but surely there was a market for something a little more tasteful, something a little more *real.* A place where witches from the college could gather, discuss spells and techniques. A place that would ensure the Penhallow name was still associated with magic in the town, no matter whose power now flowed through it.

Opening a small door behind the bar, Wells was so caught up

in this fantasy of his new life that he was halfway down the stairs to the cellar he'd converted into a flat before he realized he wasn't alone.

The hair on the back of his neck rose, and he could feel magic heavy in the air. Whoever it was down here, they were a witch as well.

A powerful one.

"Who's there?" he called, even as he began moving his fingers at his side. It had been a long time since he'd had to do any kind of spell like this, but luckily, the memory hadn't left him. "What the hell are you doing in my pub?"

He was just about to lift his hand, let the stun spell he'd worked up fly, when suddenly, a light flared on, making him squint, the spell sputtering out as a familiar face grinned at him from the far side of the room.

"Not the warmest welcome, big brother."

Bowen was stretched out on Wells's bed, one hand still lifted from the light spell he'd conjured, and what appeared to be a metric ton of hair on his face. Wells felt, as he often did with both his brothers, that familiar surge of irritation and affection.

"I could've killed you," he said to Bowen, flipping on the lights as Bowen's spell winked out.

"Could have," Bowen agreed with a shrug. "Didn't."

It had been over a year since Wells had seen his brother, and clearly Bowen had been using that time to get both hairier *and* more annoying. The hairier part Wells could at least understand— Bowen had spent the past few years doing some kind of magical research up in the mountains. Facial hair was probably a requirement for that kind of thing.

"How did you get down here without me or Da seeing you?" Wells asked, crossing his arms over his chest.

Bowen grunted. "Magic."

"Hmm," was Wells's only reply, and then he glanced down and frowned.

"Get your bloody boots off my bed," he said, smacking at Bowen's feet, and his younger brother smirked, swinging his legs down and sitting on the edge of the bed.

He looked tired, Wells noticed now, and a little on the pale side. Wells had no idea what exactly it was Bowen did out there in the wilderness, but whatever it was, it was taking a toll, clearly.

"Do you want something to drink?" he asked, and Bowen waved him off.

"Nah, I'm not sticking around long. I have to make my way up to the house eventually, I just . . . " He paused and blew out a long breath. "Wasn't quite up to it yet."

Wells knew both his brothers had a very different relationship with Simon than he did, but it was, in his opinion, slightly ridiculous that they acted as though talking to their father were some sort of monumental feat. He did it nearly every day, after all, but then maybe it was one of those things where you had to build up a tolerance.

Like exercise. Or poison.

"How've you been?" he asked Bowen as he crossed the room

to the small bar cart he'd set up and poured himself a finger of whisky. Not nearly as fine a brand as his father preferred, but the smoky warmth helped ease the tension in his shoulders, chased away some of the lingering chill.

"Fine," was Bowen's only reply. Wells sometimes wondered how it was that he was the only one of them who knew the appropriate amount of words to use in a sentence. Rhys talked entirely too much, Bowen too little.

Then Bowen jerked his head in the direction of the stairs. "Heard you're going to Glynn Bedd."

"Ah, so sneaking in *and* eavesdropping. Lovely," Wells said, and then, when Bowen just kept watching him, relented with a nod.

"Yes. Someone from the family needs to be there now that we've been magically driven out, so to speak."

"Rhys is there."

"Rhys's loyalties are . . . conflicted. Or so Da thinks."

Bowen rubbed his chin, then nodded. "Makes sense. He's arse over tit for her."

"Seeing as how they're married, one would hope so."

Tilting his head, Bowen studied Wells for a beat, then asked, "Why didn't you come? To the wedding?"

Guilt still tugged at Wells for that. He'd wanted to go, had planned to go, but in the end, he'd followed Simon's lead. Rhys hadn't taken it badly, so it had probably been for the best.

Still made him feel like a bit of a shit, though.

"Couldn't get away," was all he said now, and Bowen gave another one of those laconic shrugs.

"Well, now you'll be living in the same town, so I guess you'll get to see plenty of each other."

Right.

Wells hadn't really thought of that yet, how Rhys might take to him in Graves Glen. They got along well enough, but Rhys didn't trust their father, and Wells doubted he'd believe Wells was coming to town of his own volition. He had a tendency to always think the worst of both of them.

Something Wells would deal with later. For now, he just smiled at Bowen, leaning back against the wall. "Exactly. Plenty of time for fraternal bonding."

"And Da's just letting you go?" Bowen asked, his brow wrinkled.

Wells snorted as he threw back the last of his whisky.

"You make it sound like he's been keeping me prisoner here."

Bowen didn't say anything to that, but the expression on his face as he glanced around Wells's small room—which, all right, he could admit was perhaps a bit cell-ish—was eloquent enough.

"I chose to stay here," Wells reminded Bowen now, pointing at him with the hand holding his glass. "Just as you chose to do whatever it is he has you doing up there in the mountains, and Rhys chose to do . . . well, Rhys chose to fuck off, mostly, but point is, I stayed because I wanted to. And now I want to go to Graves Glen."

Rhys would've pressed him on that, but Bowen, Goddess love him, accepted it, nodding as he rose from the bed, slapping his hands on his thighs.

"Fair enough. Waste of a good witch, keeping you here anyway."

"Thank you," Wells replied, because he knew that, coming
from his brother, that was practically a fawning compliment.

"I'll leave you to it, then," Bowen said, moving toward the
stairs.

"Thought you'd never leave," Wells replied, wry, and he
thought he saw the hint of a smile beneath all that beard.

Then Bowen paused, turning to study Wells before saying,
"Watch yourself. In Glynn Bedd."

Wells raised his eyebrows. "Why? Am I in danger from being
smothered beneath a pile of Halloween candy and tacky masks?"

Bowen made a grumbling sound that might have been a laugh.
"Always a possibility. But no, it's just . . . whenever there's a magical transference of power, like what happened there last year, shit
can get weird."

Wells waited, and when nothing more was forthcoming,
asked, "Would you care to elaborate on that, or is this new cryp-
tic thing something you've picked up from the sheep?"

Bowen grunted again, rolling his shoulders. "I'm just saying.
Places like that, they're vulnerable for a while. Start acting like
magnets for some fucked-up magic. And with Samhain on the
way, it's something to think about."

"I—" Wells started, but before he could even finish his sentence, Bowen had vanished.

CHAPTER 5

The Penhallow house, just up the mountain from Gwyn's own cozy cabin, was, if you were being charitable, kind of weird.

If you weren't being charitable—and Gwyn very rarely was—it looked like someone had been a massive fan of the Haunted Mansion ride at Disney World and decided to re-create that in their own house. There was velvet, there was damask, there were heavy chandeliers made of iron and antlers, and there were paintings of long-dead ancestors scowling beneath centuries of grime.

Complete nightmare of a place, and Gwyn didn't blame Vivi and Rhys for choosing to live in Vivi's apartment downtown even though it easily could've fit in the kitchen of this house.

However, she had to admit that if you were throwing a witchy-themed bachelorette party, the Penhallow house was pretty freaking perfect.

"Did I use too much lavender?"

Gwyn looked up from her own mix of bath salts to see the bride, Amanda, holding up a net bag that *did* look awfully purple, but she just smiled and shook her head. "No such thing as too much," she said brightly, adding another scoop of rosemary to her salts. "That's the fun of these kinds of projects."

"Right, and isn't lavender supposed to be calming?" That was the maid of honor, Leigh, currently sitting to Gwyn's left, sparkly witch's hat slightly askew as she pointed at Amanda. "Girl, you could use that."

The other women laughed and Amanda gave a cheerful shrug before gulping the last of her wine and setting her goblet down on the massive oak dining room table. She had her own glittery witch's hat, but Gwyn had added a black tulle veil to hers as well as a sash proclaiming Amanda *HEAD WITCH IN CHARGE*.

Not that Amanda was actually a witch. The six women currently gathered around the Penhallow dining room table were all thoroughly normal and assumed Gwyn was, too. But when in Graves Glen . . .

The bachelorette parties—and the birthday parties, and the holiday parties, and one kind of weird retirement thing—had been one of Gwyn's more brilliant ideas to make a little extra money for the store. It made sense to really lean into the whole Halloween vibe of the town, a vibe that seemed to be lasting longer and longer these days, so why not take advantage?

"So what are we doing after this?" Amanda asked, leaning her chin on her hand. "Ouija board?"

Gwyn suppressed a shudder as she tied off her bath salt bag with a little piece of ribbon. "I was thinking a tarot reading," she said. "Ouija's vibe is a little darker."

"That's true," one of the bridesmaids, Mel, said, nodding. "No one's making horror movies about tarot cards, Amanda."

The others all hummed in agreement as Gwyn got up from the table, moving to the sideboard where she'd set up snacks and, as a centerpiece, a giant cauldron filled with a bright green liquid that looked dangerous and slightly noxious but was really just a mix of fruit juice, champagne, a little vodka, and a lot of food coloring. So far, it had been a big hit, so much of a hit that Gwyn was glad she'd already arranged for the women to get rides home tonight.

In fact, as she looked back at them, giggling over their plastic goblets, their faces a little pink, their voices getting louder, she wondered if she should skip the tarot altogether and just let them chat. The cards were never as clear when you were reading for someone who was drunk, and the last thing Gwyn wanted to do was accidentally kill the vibe because she pulled Death for someone getting married in two weeks.

Tarot was out, then, she decided as she turned back to the punch, giving it a stir.

"Ladies, what are our feelings about crystals?" she asked, but when she turned back around, none of the party was looking at her.

They were all staring at the door to the dining room or, more specifically, at the man standing in the doorway.

Gwyn couldn't blame them.

He was tall, dark hair curling over the collar of a navy wool peacoat, a neatly trimmed beard accentuating the sharp angles of his face. He was holding a large leather bag, his expression somewhere between wary and baffled as he took in the scene before him, and Gwyn's eyes narrowed. He was older, and the beard had thrown her for a second, but she knew exactly who she was looking at.

"Is he . . . a stripper?" one of the women tried to whisper, but since her bloodstream was probably about 60 percent alcohol, it might as well have been a shout.

"He doesn't look very strippery," someone else replied, and the man kept staring around the table, his gaze finally settling on Mel, the one bridesmaid who had decided to go the traditional route when it came to headgear and, instead of a witch's hat, was wearing a bright pink headband, two plastic penises bobbing like antennae over her blond hair.

Gwyn watched his eyes follow those penises for a beat before he finally looked up and seemed to notice her for the first time.

The scowl deepened. "May I ask what is going on here?"

His voice was rough, his accent a slightly thicker version of Rhys's lilting tones, deeper than it had been thirteen years ago.

Gwyn folded her arms over her chest. "Party," she said succinctly, and just as she'd anticipated—just as she'd *hoped*—his posture somehow went even more rigid.

"This is the Penhallow house," he said, shoulders going back even as his eyes once again dropped to Mel's headband.

"It is, yeah," she said. "But we're using it tonight."

The man lifted his gaze to hers again, brows drawing together. "With whose authority?" he asked, and Gwyn smirked, leaning back against the sideboard.

"Well, first of all, 'authority' is not one of my favorite words, and secondly, I'm not sure that it's really your business, but Rhys is letting us use it tonight."

His expression cleared at the mention of his brother, but before he could say anything else, Gwyn pointed at him. "Ladies, this is Llewellyn Penhallow," she told the bridesmaids. "Rhys's brother. Who didn't come to Rhys and Vivi's wedding, I should add."

She heard a slight gasp from the bridesmaids but didn't look over at them as she moved closer to Llewellyn.

He was scowling now.

"Not that it's any of your business, but there were reasons I was unable to attend the wedding."

"As I was the maid of honor, it was *extremely* my business," Gwyn countered, and Llewellyn's brow furrowed.

"You're Vivienne's cousin. Gwyn."

"The one and only," she replied, wondering if he remembered her from Penhaven. They'd only ever seen each other that one time, and her hair had been purple back then, plus he'd seemed more interested in showing her up than anything else.

"Are we trespassing?" That was Amanda, looking a little more sober and a lot less happy than she had just a few minutes ago. Gwyn threw a dirty look at Wells.

"No," she said, making herself smile, the perfect hostess again. "No, we have the owner's permission to be here, this is just a . . . a family mix-up. You know how that goes. Llewellyn here is leaving, aren't you?"

"I am not, actually, given that this is my house."

Okay, this was getting ridiculous. The happy, silly mood of the bachelorette party was quickly dissipating, the women muttering to each other and looking between Gwyn and Wells, and she was pretty sure she could forget about any future bachelorette parties if she didn't nip this in the bud *right* now.

"Let's chat in the other room!" she said with forced brightness and then, wrapping her hand around Wells's arm, practically dragged him out.

That wasn't easy to do, either, given that he was surprisingly solid, but Gwyn was determined, an unstoppable force that had never given way to an immovable object.

"Look," she said in a low voice once they were in the living room, a truly horrifying chandelier of antlers overhead. "If you don't want us being here, take it up with Rhys later. But for now, let me talk a little astrology with these ladies, maybe teach them about moon phases, and send them on their happy and well-paying way, okay?"

Wells was staring down his nose at her, probably because that was his default expression, and now his eyes flicked past her, back toward the party. "Is this something you do often?" he asked. "Throw . . . these kinds of parties?"

He said that like he'd caught her running some kind of brothel/casino out of his family dining room, and Gwyn gritted her teeth.

"Trust me, there won't be any more if you don't find somewhere else in this eldritch horror you call a house to hang out while I finish up here."

Now it was his turn to clench his jaw. "My father built this house. Everything in it was either created with his magic or brought from our home in Wales."

"I feel like you think that's a flex? It is definitely not a flex."

A trio of grooves deepened on his forehead, and then he pinched the bridge of his nose, closing his eyes and taking a deep breath.

"I was prepared for Rhys," he muttered to himself. "How is this actually worse?"

Then, lifting his head, he fixed her with a steely gaze. "Fine," he said. "Finish your party, and I'll stay out of your way. But let this be the last one thrown in this house."

With that, he turned away, heading for the stairs, and Gwyn couldn't help but call out, "I mean, there won't be another one while you're visiting, but once you're back in Wales, all bets are off!"

Pausing, Wells turned back to her. In the dim light, she realized he looked almost exactly like the portrait on the wall behind him. Take away the powdered wig, trade the breeches for a pair of dark jeans, and it could basically be the same man.

"I'm not visiting, Ms. Jones," he said, and Gwyn doubted his aristocratic ancestor there behind him could've sounded frostier or that anything in this house was scarier than that pronouncement.

"I'm staying in Graves Glen. For good."

CHAPTER 6

S o I can only assume you've come here to ruin my life."

It was later in the morning than Wells normally woke up, the effects of magical travel not as rough as jet lag but still noticeable, and he had just poured himself a very needed mug of tea, which he was now quite grateful for.

Taking a fortifying sip, he turned to face Rhys.

His youngest brother stood in the doorway between the kitchen and the living room, hands in the pockets of a very nice coat, his customary half grin on his face but his eyes wary.

It had been almost a year since Wells had last seen Rhys, and there were changes there, but subtle ones. He seemed a little more comfortable in his skin, a little steadier. No doubt the work of Vivienne Jones, and Wells was grateful for that even if it was slightly surreal that Rhys might now be the most settled of all of them.

Bracing one hand on the counter behind him, Wells lifted the mug and drank again before answering. "Life Ruination of

Youngest Brother *is* on the agenda, yes, but it's at least ten steps down. You have time to prepare accordingly."

Rhys snorted at that, moving more fully into the kitchen and leaning against the refrigerator. "Was step number one Annoy the Living Piss out of Gwyn Jones? Because you can definitely tick that one off, mate."

Wells frowned, glancing back toward the dining room.

That had been . . . unexpected. *She* had been unexpected. He knew about Gwyn vaguely from Rhys, but he'd been unprepared for a tornado disguised as a beautiful woman, especially when his head was still muddled from travel.

There was no trace of her or her party in the house now. She'd cleaned up well before she'd left last night, but he had a feeling he'd still be finding stray bits of glitter and lavender in the rugs for quite some time. "No, that was an unfortunate side effect of the *actual* step one, which was Come Into My Family's Fucking House and Not Find It Filled With Strangers."

Rhys lifted one shoulder. "Funny thing is, if you'd made maybe a *pre*-step that involved, oh, I don't know, giving me any sort of bloody heads-up that you were coming to town, all of this could have been avoided. You could've come in completely unbothered and lit a candle to Da's picture or whatever it is you do when you arrive in a new place, and *I* would not have had my delightful wife woken up by a phone call that seemed to involve the words 'high-handed' and 'complete asshole.'"

He threw Wells a wink. "That's how I knew she was talking about you."

Wells was thirty-four years old, so it was probably bad form to wonder if there was anything handy he could throw at his brother, but old habits died hard. He settled for flipping him a two-fingered salute with his free hand, and Rhys smirked before pushing himself off the fridge to stand in front of Wells, his arms folded.

"Seriously, Wells," he said, and while Rhys was very rarely anything remotely resembling serious, Wells had to admit he looked it now. "Gwyn told Vivi you said you were staying for good. Why?"

"The pub was dying, and there didn't seem much point in running it anymore. I wanted . . . I don't know, a change of scenery, I suppose. Made sense to come back here."

It wasn't a lie even if it wasn't the full truth of it, and for a long beat, Rhys just watched him.

Wells was alarmed to realize he had no idea what his brother was thinking. He was used to Rhys's quips and comebacks, his jokes and deflections, but clearly the last year had changed him if he was actually weighing what he wanted to say.

And then what he said was, "You utter bastard."

Wells blinked. "Beg pardon?"

"Da sent you here," Rhys said now, pointing. "Because he couldn't stand it that we no longer run this town. So now he has to make sure he has a foothold here, and Goddess knows it can't be me. So he sends you, the favorite, to save the day."

It stung a little even as Wells had to admit to himself that he could see why Rhys would jump to that conclusion. He was the loyal one, after all. The obedient one.

"Actually, it was my idea," he told Rhys now, keeping his voice calm as he took another sip of tea.

Rhys tilted his head, his lips pressed together. "Your idea," he repeated. "To leave Wales and come live in a small town in Georgia."

"Yes," Wells said, setting the mug back on the counter. "Believe it or not, I *do* occasionally think for myself, and I was tired of running a pub no one ever bothered to come into. Believe it or not, I *also* happen to be a fairly talented witch, and *perhaps* I wanted to use those skills. Perhaps I wanted to do a little bit more in my life. Perhaps—"

"Christ, are you going to start singing now?"

This time, Wells did throw something at his brother, but since it was only a teaspoon, it clattered harmlessly off the fridge as Rhys laughed, holding his hands up.

"Fair enough," he said, and here was the Rhys Wells knew—slow to anger, quick to drop it. "But seriously, if you're going to live here, can you try not to make my new family long for your head on a platter? I only just got Gwyn to start calling me by my name and not an insult."

"Well, I wish that I'd known that last night. Ms. Jones and I could've bonded over the one thing we apparently have in common."

Not that Wells actually thought that would've worked. Maybe he had been . . . well, not a *prick* but not at his best last night. But then that woman had seemed to radiate dislike for him the second he'd walked in the door, and he'd felt a bit back-footed about the whole thing. Strange women in his house, the cloying smell of lavender and rosemary mixed with vodka and fruit juice, the little pointy hats . . . it had been quite a lot to take in.

A reminder that this was not his family's town anymore.

But that would change, and soon. Gwyn Jones could have her silly Halloween things, her American mall version of witchcraft. There was a space for him here, too, and he was going to carve it out.

Rhys frowned now, tilting his head to one side. "I did not realize you also had a thinky face, Wells," he said, and Wells scowled.

"What the hell does that mean?"

Rhys shook his head, waving it off. "Never mind. So I take it you're planning on living up here?"

"Is that a problem?"

"No," Rhys said, then gave a little shudder. "I sure as fuck don't want to, and if I asked Vivi to, I'm pretty sure she'd divorce me. The Haunted Mansion is all yours."

Wells wanted to object to that description, but he had to admit the house was a bit more . . . Gothic than he remembered.

Eldritch horror, Gwyn had called it last night, which Wells thought was overly harsh.

Still, he might want to do a bit of redecorating if he was going to make the place his.

"Good," Wells said, then turned and placed his mug in the sink. "You live downtown, right? Above Gwyn's shop?"

When Rhys nodded, Wells smiled and fought the urge to rub his hands together. "Excellent. I need a ride in that direction."

HALF AN HOUR later, he found himself on Main Street, staring at the building he had seen there in the pub. It was indeed empty and, according to a sign in the window, available to rent.

It was a little down at the heel, the glass dirty, the awning sagging, but there was potential there. Wells could see it. And unlike most business owners, he *literally* had tricks up his sleeves.

There were plenty of people milling about, and the sky overhead was a bright blue with just a few puffy clouds drifting slowly across. A breeze ruffled the little orange and black flags already hung above the street, and in the distance, the mountains were just beginning to show hints of orange and red amongst all the green.

Wells felt his spirits lift just standing there.

This was it. Where he was supposed to be.

On his left hand, his father's ring sat heavily, and he absentmindedly rubbed the silver band with his thumb before reaching into his pocket for his mobile to dial the number on the sign.

He'd just punched in the first number when there was a cackle from across the street.

Turning, he watched as what appeared to be a large mechanical witch, its head moving back and forth in jerky motions, emerged from the front door of Something Wicked.

It bumped and slid over the sidewalk, still cackling, and Wells spotted three people, one of whom had violently turquoise hair, attempting to navigate it into place.

Just behind them, her red hair blowing in the breeze, was Gwyn.

She was so focused on directing the other three where to put the witch that she didn't notice him, which gave him a chance to study her.

Looking at her like this, without the film of irritation, magic-drunkenness, and exhaustion that had been clouding his mind last night, he realized just how pretty she was. Oh, he'd noticed it last night, but in a sort of distant way, a simple classification, really. *This beautiful woman does not like me.*

Now, though, she was smiling, laughing as the turquoise-haired girl launched into her own impression of the witch, robotic movements and all, and Wells found himself smiling, too.

Which, of course, was the moment Gwyn saw him.

That smile dropped off her face almost immediately as she shaded her eyes with one hand, clearly wondering what the hell he was doing in front of this building.

Well, Wells thought, turning away and continuing to dial, *she'll soon find out.*

CHAPTER 7

L lewellyn Penhallow, Esquire, was up to something.

It had been nearly a week since he'd arrived in town, and while Gwyn hadn't spoken to him, she'd seen him several times, coming in and out of the building across the street from Something Wicked. Sometimes he was carrying boxes, and once, she was pretty sure she'd caught a glimpse of him dragging in a suit of armor just before the front door closed, but the windows were covered with paper, and there was no outside sign of what might be going on inside.

Rhys swore he had no idea what his brother was up to. "He's being secretive about it," he'd told Gwyn just the other night when she'd stopped by Rhys and Vivi's for dinner. "Probably building some sort of museum to our dead ancestors or something. I wouldn't worry about it."

And Gwyn was *not* worried.

She was just . . . curious.

After all, Wells was already her neighbor. She'd passed him on the road up the mountain just the other day, her in her red truck, lovingly restored over the years, him in a completely ridiculous new BMW he'd apparently purchased.

Good luck with that this winter, she'd thought as she'd given him the barest of waves and he'd grimaced at her from behind the wheel, almost like he knew what she was thinking.

But if he had rented the space across the street, that meant they would *also* be work neighbors, and that was, frankly, way more neighborly than she wanted to be with Wells.

And! As one of the head witches of this town, wasn't it important that she have a good sense of what other witches were doing on *her* turf? Wasn't that, to use Vivi's favorite word, her *responsibility*?

Now, Gwyn knew she could use magic to figure out exactly what Wells was doing, but the thing is, a witch had to have *standards,* and for Gwyn, using magic to spy on someone was a little on the sketchy side of things.

Which meant that she was just going to have to wait, and given that she *hated* waiting, Gwyn had been in a cranky mood all week. And having to stop by Penhaven College on a Saturday?

Well, that increased The Crank to truly nuclear levels.

"This really feels like a thing you could've done on your own," she told Vivi now as the two of them walked toward the library. It was a sunny day, the sky clear blue, and the leaves were just beginning to turn. Had Gwyn not been basically allergic to Penhaven, she might've admitted that it was . . . kind of pretty. Idyllic, even, all the red brick and green grass.

"I need your help," Vivi insisted. "I'll end up picking something too academic or too dry. You'll understand what kinds of stories visitors might actually be interested in."

The two of them were on a mission for the Graves Glen Tourism Board. When your town's main industry is Halloween, you milk it for all it's worth, and that meant there were three official events during October, starting with what had once been Founder's Day.

That had been a celebration all about Gryffud Penhallow, the man who'd founded the town and—not that the non-witchy residents of Graves Glen knew this—set up the magical ley lines that gave Graves Glen its power. But last year, Vivi and Rhys had discovered that Gryffud had actually stolen magic from Vivi and Gwyn's ancestor, Aelwyd Jones, killing her in the process. Needless to say, none of them were big fans of Gryffud after that, so Vivi and Rhys had managed to talk the town's mayor into something a "little less patriarchal."

This year would mark the first annual Graves Glen Gathering. That was on the thirteenth, and it was all about the town's history (and selling stuff to tourists). Then a week after that, there was Fall Festival, which was more of a carnival thing with costumes and food (and selling stuff to tourists).

And then of course, just eleven days after *that,* it was Halloween proper, which was haunted houses and corn mazes and candy (and selling the *most* stuff to tourists).

They'd always spent October busy, but this year, she and Vivi were actually on the planning committee headed up by the mayor, Jane Ellis. Jane was also Gwyn's ex, but since their breakup hadn't been all that bad, Gwyn had let Vivi talk her into joining the committee, too. Gwyn had thought that would mean the occasional evening meeting, though, not digging through a dusty library on a Saturday.

"You don't even have to find a real, official story about the town," Gwyn reminded Vivi. "You can literally make something up. 'One interesting fact about Graves Glen is that it was briefly taken over by bats in 1976.' 'Graves Glen is the world's leading producer of grape gumdrops.' 'Every March, citizens of Graves Glen fight each other in the Hunger Games.'"

Vivi laughed, swatting at Gwyn's arm. "No. Jane specifically asked me to find some interesting *real* facts in the Penhaven archives we can share now that we're not talking about Gryffud anymore. And I'm hoping to find some great old pictures of the college back when it was first founded. This is the first Graves Glen Gathering, so we want to go all in."

Sighing, Gwyn tossed her hair back over her shoulders. "And you feel guilty you won't even be here for Triple G, so you're going extra hard."

"You know Jane really wants everyone to stop calling it that, but yes."

Grinning, Gwyn bumped Vivi's shoulder with her own. "Fine. But once we're done here, you're buying me lunch."

"Deal."

They had nearly reached the steps of the library when Gwyn saw a flash of turquoise out of the corner of her eye.

Sam was coming around the side of the library, Cait and

Parker in her wake, and Gwyn noticed the three of them were practically chasing after Dr. Arbuthnot.

"What's she doing here on a Saturday?" Gwyn asked, and Vivi sighed, folding her arms over her chest.

"She practically lives in her office."

The woman never aged as far as Gwyn could tell, every bit as beautiful and commanding and terrifying as she'd been thirteen years ago, and as she watched, Dr. Arbuthnot came to a stop, scarves fluttering around her as she turned to face the three witches.

"For the last time," she said, her voice carrying to the library steps. "The assignment was very straightforward. The three of you have undoubtedly chosen to make it more difficult than it needs to be, which is why you're now asking for more time."

"We're not making it more *complicated*," Sam said, her voice slightly pleading. "We just want it to be . . . sophisticated."

"Evolved," Parker added, and Cait nodded.

"Right, with just a little more time, we can give you something *really*—"

"What you will give me," Dr. Arbuthnot interrupted, "is what I asked for. On Monday, no later."

With that, she turned and walked away, sparing the briefest glance in Gwyn and Vivi's direction.

"Vivienne," she said, nodding at Vivi, who waved back.

"Gwynnevere."

Gwyn might have been imagining it, but she was pretty sure the temperature dropped at least ten degrees as Dr. Arbuthnot looked at her, but she made herself give a nod of acknowledgment anyway.

A few feet away, Sam, Cait, and Parker looked decidedly glum, their heads close together as they murmured and whispered, and Vivi gave another sigh.

"They're talented," she said. "I've worked with them a couple of times in my office over the past few weeks. But Dr. Arbuthnot is right. They make everything harder than it needs to be so that they can show off."

"Or," Gwyn countered, "the spells Dr. Arbuthnot assigns are boring and too by the book, and they want to be a little more creative."

Shooting Gwyn a wry look, Vivi quirked an eyebrow. *"Orrrr,"* she drawled, "someone's projecting a little bit?"

Gwyn scowled at her cousin, but she didn't argue. She'd spent all her years at Penhaven chafing against the rules, the requirements, the whole "we do it this way because this is the way we do it" style of thinking that drove her crazy. And yes, maybe that meant she'd occasionally screwed up, but at least she'd been *trying*.

Just like these kids were trying.

Ugh, she was going to have to be responsible, clearly.

"I think you're on your own with the archives this afternoon," she told Vivi, and then, grumbling to herself, Gwyn made her way over to the three witches.

All three of them looked up as she approached, their faces hopeful, and okay, that was kind of adorable. They *were* good kids. Talented witches who just needed a little guidance from the right witch, a witch who'd screwed up just as often as they had, a witch who got them and what they were trying to do.

"So," she said, placing her hands on her hips. "What's the spell y'all are supposed to be doing?"

THREE HOURS LATER, Gwyn had a newfound and grudging respect for Dr. Arbuthnot.

The spell Sam, Cait, and Parker had been assigned was indeed a pretty straightforward and simple one. It involved creating a basic glamour that would change their appearances, but subtly. Brown hair instead of blond, a few inches taller, that kind of thing.

Gwyn agreed that was fairly boring, and she'd thought their idea—combining it with a bigger jolt of magic for much bigger results—was a great one.

That was before she'd had to figure out how to right a nose that had been turned upside down, how exactly you got rid of five extra elbows, *why* the spell had created five extra elbows in the first place, and if her hair was going to be green forever.

Smoke was still hanging in the air as Gwyn took a deep breath and looked at herself in the mirror hanging over the living room couch in her cabin.

Her hair was once again red, thank the Goddess, and when she turned back to Parker, their once-brown hair was a sandy blond, but their nose was very much in place.

Likewise, Sam's elbows were back down to her normal two, her turquoise hair black, her eyes slightly rounder, nose thinner.

Cait was frowning at her fingernails, but that was only because she'd been trying for red polish, and her nails were purple instead.

"Okay," Gwyn said slowly, rising to her feet. "That was . . . well, I'm not gonna lie, that was awful and took at least five years off my life, *but* I think we've nailed it and gotten y'all ready for Monday. And we learned a valuable lesson about magic we find on the internet, haven't we?"

Dusting her hands off on the back of her jeans, Gwyn looked around the living room. That scorch mark on the rug was unfortunate, and Sir Purrcival was probably never coming back downstairs, but at least the fire had been fairly contained?

Was that something to be proud of?

"When can you help us again?" Sam asked, getting to her feet as next to her Parker and Cait stood as well, and Gwyn laughed, shaking her head.

"Honestly, Baby Witches, y'all are probably better off listening to Vivi and Dr. Arbuthnot. I feel like their help will lead to good grades and safe spells and just . . . far fewer elbows, really."

But all three of them shook their heads at that.

"No way," Parker insisted. "You actually listened to us. You let us *try* to do something cool."

"And then when we fucked it up, like, *so* much, you helped us fix it!" Cait added, bouncing on the balls of her feet. "You're totally Glinda the Good Witch, and we need you."

"Yes!" Sam said, coming forward to grab Gwyn's arm and give her a little shake. "Be our Glinda!"

"I don't look good in pink, and I haven't traveled by bubble in at *least* six months," Gwyn said, but they were giving her the puppy dog eyes again, and if Gwyn was honest, even with the smoke and the fire and the elbows and all of it, it had felt good, helping them out. Letting them practice magic without telling them it was too much or too weird or too advanced.

Which was probably why she heard herself say something stupid like "Okay, fine. We can try again next week."

CHAPTER 8

I just keep pulling the Five of Swords."

Gwyn was sitting at a back booth at The Cider Shack, a new restaurant in Graves Glen that had opened last summer. It had quickly become one of her favorite haunts and had seemed like a safe spot to take the Baby Witches for their second magic lesson.

They were a little disappointed, she suspected, no doubt hoping for something a little more mystical than a place that served pumpkin chili and something called Macbeth Mash, but after Saturday, Gwyn had decided they might need to start a little slower and with magic that could safely be done in public.

Hence a tarot lesson.

And if she'd made the focus of that lesson "See if you can get a read on, oh, I don't know, what Wells Penhallow is building across the street," so be it.

She'd sworn she wouldn't use magic to get to the bottom of Wells's project, but he'd been at it for over a week now, and the curiosity was finally getting to be too much.

Besides, using someone *else's* magic wasn't all that bad, right?

Now, Gwyn put down her Broomstick Burger and tapped the card in front of Parker.

"And what does that mean to you?"

Parker sighed, tilting their head back even as Cait scooted closer to them and said, "You know this one." She looked up at Gwyn. "They totally know this one, Glinda."

"There's no right or wrong answer," Gwyn reminded Parker now. "It's intuition based."

Screwing up their face, Parker thought. "Swords are air. Air is thought, intellect."

"Good," Gwyn said, nodding. "And?"

"Fives are in the middle of the suit, so conflict . . . "

Sam started singing "Bad Blood," making Cait laugh, and Gwyn rolled her eyes even as she smiled at them. They really were good kids. All three of them had been helping out at the store as a kind of exchange for these sorts of lessons, and Gwyn saw what Vivi meant about them being talented witches.

"You keep working on it," Gwyn said, wiping her hands on her napkin, "while I go grab a cider."

Sam scooted out so that Gwyn could leave, and as she walked toward the bar in the back, she could already hear them arguing over which card was worse, the Tower or Death.

The Cider Shack was crowded for a Wednesday night, and Gwyn saw several familiar faces. One of her regular customers at the shop, Sally, was at the bar with her husband, and there was Elaine's friend Nathan.

Over at a table in the corner, Gwyn spotted Jane. She was there with her fiancée, Lorna, and she and Gwyn did the same little awkward wave they did every time they bumped into each other. Which, given that Graves Glen wasn't a very big town, was fairly often.

The breakup hadn't been bad, and Gwyn genuinely liked Lorna and was happy for Jane, but it was a reminder that her romantic life had been fairly dead for almost a year now.

She'd dated a little after Jane, gone out a few times with Daniel, the guy who ran the Coffee Cauldron, and Vivi had set her up with one of her history teacher friends, Beth, but that hadn't really gone anywhere, either.

Honestly, she blamed Vivi and Rhys. Seeing her cousin that happy, that . . . *right* with someone had made her pickier. She didn't just want someone to have a casual conversation and some hot sex with. She wanted . . . well, she didn't know.

To catch someone's eye and know what they were thinking. To be in a room full of people and know that that person was *yours*. To not just enjoy someone, but enjoy the person she was with them.

Gwyn shook her head slightly.

Yeah, all Vivi and Rhys's fault, making her this mushy out of nowhere.

What she needed was some obnoxiously named cider and to get back to her students, so she moved forward and placed an order for something called The Wicked Queen's Poisoned Apple.

Gwyn had just gotten her glass when she spotted a familiar figure moving toward her.

Wells was holding a bottle of plain lager rather than one of the bespoke ciders, and in a sea of T-shirts and jeans, the man was wearing neatly pressed trousers, a button-down, and, Goddess help her, a *vest*.

No, this wasn't a vest, she amended as he got closer. This was a *waistcoat*. Surely that's what he called it.

He didn't seem to see her until he was almost on top of her, his mind clearly a million miles away, and when he did, he visibly startled.

"Ms. Jones."

"Llewellyn Penhallow, Esquire," she replied, and his lips drew together in a thin line.

See, that was the thing. He was too easy to tease, and it was too fun to stop.

"What brings you to The Cider Shack?" she asked him. "You seem more like a . . . I don't know, a Champagne Chateau kind of guy."

Gwyn thought he might have considered smiling at that, but if he had, the impulse was gone pretty quickly. "You certainly have a lot of opinions about me given that we only met two weeks ago, and you've spent maybe five minutes in my company."

Smirking, Gwyn folded her arms over her chest. "We didn't meet two weeks ago," she said, and he frowned at her, confused.

"What? No, I'm certain we never met before. I would have . . . "

His eyes moved over her face briefly, and Gwyn felt a sudden prickle of awareness, a slight bit of heat sliding up her spine.

Okay, no, she told her treacherous body. *I know I was just thinking about how I've neglected you lately, but please get a grip.*

He was handsome, she could admit that. And he had very nice eyes, and she'd always liked a man with a beard, but he was still *Llewellyn Penhallow,* total snob and Non-Attender of Weddings.

Now he took a sip of his beer and shook his head. "If you say we've met before, maybe we have, but I certainly don't remember it."

"Maybe you'll figure it out," she suggested with a one-shouldered shrug, and there it was again, those pressed lips, those hard eyes, that barely perceptible stiffening of his spine.

"Indeed. Nice to have seen you again," he said, even though it was very clear it had been anything but. "Now, if you'll excuse me, I only popped in for a quick drink. I still have work to do tonight."

"Oh, right," Gwyn said, casual as possible as he moved past her. "I thought I saw you in that dingy building across the street. What are you working on?"

She thought she'd been subtle, but then, Gwyn had never been *great* at subtle, and it was very clear from the smug smile spreading across Wells's face now that she'd failed on that score yet again.

"Maybe you'll figure it out," he said, and if Gwyn hadn't been so infuriated, she might have been a little impressed.

Then he turned and looked across the restaurant, frowning.

"Are those your employees? I recognize the one with the blue hair."

"Not employees, *mentees*," she corrected him. "Now that the *Jones* family magic runs this town, we've started working with some of the younger witches, teaching spellcraft, guiding their practices. I assume you think it's all silliness and plastic witch hats, but believe it or not, we are actually doing serious things with magic here."

"Hmm. Well, right now, they're seriously putting tarot cards on their foreheads," he said, and Gwyn whipped around.

Yes, Cait was licking the back of a tarot card and sticking it to her head as Parker and Sam tried to guess which one it was.

Great.

"That's actually a new technique for readings that they're trying out," she replied, holding her head high. "I guess it hasn't reached Wales yet."

"Hmm," he said again, and then, as he turned away, she caught the barest hint of that smile.

"Good night, Ms. Jones."

Gwyn didn't bother with a parting shot, making her way back to the table and plucking the Empress off Cait's forehead.

"Seriously?" she asked the group, and Cait gave an unapologetic shrug.

"You were taking forever and we got bored." Twisting in the booth, she looked after Wells.

"I haven't seen him up close before. He's hot."

"He's not," Gwyn lied even as Parker murmured, "Super hot,"

and Sam said, "I mean, that family has good genes, it must be said."

"His hotness," Gwyn reminded the three, "is neither here nor there. What you were supposed to be doing was figuring out what *he's* doing."

She looked at the cards still spread out on the table. The Five of Swords was still there. So was the Six of Swords. No surprise, since that card usually meant some kind of sneakiness was afoot.

A third card was slightly covered by Parker's napkin, and Gwyn pushed the piece of paper out of the way.

The Lovers stared back at her.

"I pulled that one, like, nine times in a row," Parker said, nodding at it. "We even reshuffled the deck between pulls, and still, every time!"

Gwyn picked up the card along with the others, shoving them back into the deck quickly, trying very hard not to think about that weird moment earlier when Wells had looked at her—really *looked* at her—and she'd felt . . . whatever that was.

"Clearly this lesson was a bust," she told the witches now. "So I guess we'll just have to wait and find out what he's up to over there the old-fashioned way."

She wouldn't have to wait long.

CHAPTER 9

G wyn got to the store early the next morning. She was expecting a new shipment of teas, and she wanted to get it all unpacked as soon as it came in, mostly so she could decide which ones she wanted to take home to sample. In fact, her head was so full of Tea Thoughts that at first, she didn't notice it.

It wasn't until she had unlocked the door of Something Wicked and a glint flashed in her peripheral vision that she turned around and saw it.

And when she did, she still wasn't quite sure she believed what she was seeing.

In fact, even when she'd crossed the street and was standing in front of the building, looking up at it, it didn't seem real.

Yesterday, the storefront across from Something Wicked had been completely empty, the window covered with brown paper, the deep blue paint around the door peeling.

Today, the paint was fresh and crisp, a green so dark it was nearly black, and the window showcased a display of crystals and amulets on rich velvet in the same shade.

Over the door, there was a tasteful wooden sign featuring a raven wearing a crown, and painted in discreet cursive, three words.

PENHALLOW'S MAGICAL GOODS

"Oh, I think the fuck not," Gwyn muttered under her breath and yanked open the door.

There was no cawing sound here, just the light ringing of a brass bell, and when Gwyn stepped into the shop—because that's clearly what it was, Wells Penhallow had set up a *shop right across from her shop*—she was welcomed with a wave of sage, bay, and old leather.

Dim lights encased in stained glass shades cast a warm glow over everything, and even though it had been bright and sunny on the sidewalk, Gwyn suddenly felt like if she were to open the door right now, she'd see a gray and blustery day. That was the immediate feel, like you'd just stepped into the coziest spot in the entire world, and weren't you lucky to be safe and warm inside?

She stood there for a moment, trying to get her bearings.

It was a spell. It had to be a spell, making whoever came into the shop suddenly grateful to be in there, wanting to lose themselves among the shelves of books and knickknacks, sink into one of the leather armchairs near the . . . fireplace?

That bastard literally had a *crackling fire*.

"Welcome to Penhallow's, how may I—oh."

Gwyn turned to see the bastard in question, his handsome face already going from Charming Shopkeeper to Grumpy Witch. It was really unfair that both were good looks on him, but that, Gwyn figured, was both the blessing and the curse of really good bone structure.

He looked less intimidating today, too, that stuffy waistcoat traded for a soft-looking gray sweater, his jeans the perfect amount of broken in, and if his hair wasn't quite as floppy as Rhys's, it was still swooping nicely over those blue eyes.

Not that she was noticing any of that.

"What is this?" she asked him now, and he leaned against the counter, linking his fingers with a sigh.

"Is there some new American word I'm unfamiliar with that means 'a shop'? Because I was fairly certain that particular term meant the same thing in both our homelands."

His brother would have delivered that line with a knowing sort of grin, but Wells just looked at her like he was already bored with this entire conversation, and given that Gwyn knew good and damn well that she was the least boring person *in the world,* that was particularly irritating.

Which had probably been his intent.

"Oh, I get the whole 'it's a shop' thing. The issue is, it's a shop right across the street from *my* shop, and it's clearly selling the same kind of thing."

Wells's eyebrows shot up at that, and he made a show of looking around. "Is it? Did I purchase some plastic pumpkins somewhere and forget about it?"

Gwyn rolled her eyes, stalking closer to the counter, the heels of her boots rapping sharply on the hardwood floors. "You know what I mean. This is a witchy shop. I run a witchy shop. You are stepping on my turf."

"Is this where we begin snapping our fingers and launch into a dance battle?"

Dammit, that's actually kind of a good joke.

But Gwyn refused to give him the satisfaction of even the tee-niest hint of a smile, placing her hands on her hips and lifting her chin. "I'm just saying, it's kind of a dick move to come into town and immediately become the competition."

Especially when she was barely getting by as it was these days. Not that she was going to tell him that. But Something Wicked's books were definitely trending a little more red than black, and a place like this—cozy, posh, vaguely mysterious—was not going to help matters.

Straightening up, Wells crossed his arms over his chest. "I think this town can handle having more than one 'witchy' shop, Ms. Jones. Especially given that we're going to be selling very different items to very different customers."

"There are no different customers," Gwyn argued. "Trust me. We get tourists and the occasional local looking for fancy bath salts. That's it."

"Bath salts, you say?" Wells cocked an eyebrow, then patted at his pockets. "I should write that down."

Gwyn had never thought of herself as a violent woman, but maybe, just *maaaaybe,* this man needed a good crack upside the head with one of the very fancy leather grimoires on the counter behind him.

"Also," she added, pointing one green-tipped finger at him, "I don't sell actual magic shit in my store because it's dangerous. No one coming for Halloween needs to accidentally pick up a . . . a Traveling Stone or a grimoire that actually works. That's how you end up with zombies, Esquire. You want zombies?"

His brow wrinkled, the corners of his mouth turning down. "First off, do not call me that, and secondly, nothing in here is actual magic, either. I'm not a complete idiot, you know."

Gwyn looked around her. The books lining the shelves near the door certainly looked old, but when she put out some mental feelers, she didn't get any sense of power coming off them. Likewise the jewelry in the front window and the wands lying in wooden boxes behind glass at the front counter.

"Just because these things aren't made of plastic doesn't mean they're real artifacts," he told her, moving back behind the counter to the old-fashioned black register. "I'm simply providing a slightly more . . . upscale experience."

"I will upscale your experience," Gwyn fired back, before frowning. "Okay, that didn't make any sense, and while I slightly regret the words, I do *not* regret the emotion behind them. You could have opened . . . I don't know. A tweed store. Some shop where they only sell overpriced pocket watches. Cravats R Us. Hell, didn't you run a pub back in Wales? You could have done that! But no, you opened *this,* and you did it on purpose to be an asshole."

"Has it ever occurred to you that not everything one does is in direct relation to you, Ms. Jones?"

When Gwyn didn't bother to reply to that, Wells rolled his eyes, lifting one elegant hand. "One," he said, ticking it off on his index finger, "I do not actually own any tweed. Or a pocket watch for that matter. Two, I have worn a cravat exactly one time in my life, and believe me when I say that is an experience ne'er to be repeated. And three, yes, I *did* run a pub and did not actually enjoy it very much."

"Was it because you had to talk to people and therefore pretend to be a person yourself rather than an android who runs on tea and disdain?"

He scowled, which Gwyn took as a win.

"In any case," Wells continued, "I'm running this shop because I think it's something this town needs. Regardless of what it's turned into, Graves Glen started out as a haven for witches and magic users, and it might be nice to preserve some of that history rather than cover it all in caramel and cinnamon and cartoon drawings of black cats."

Gwyn hooted with laughter at that, slapping the counter hard enough to rattle a glass jar filled with black quills. "Okay. So this is about snobbery. Got it."

"It's about tradition," he countered, and she turned away, giving him a little wave over one shoulder.

"Keep telling yourself that, Esquire. And let me know how many people want to spend . . . " She paused by the door, checking the price on the back of one of the grimoires. "A hundred bucks on something they can get at Something Wicked for twenty."

She tossed the grimoire back onto the table, already feeling a little . . . all right, maybe it wasn't *nice* to say smug, but definitely a little better. This store was beautiful, yes, and it was fancy and sort of spooky, and he was sure to get lots of people in, but there was no way he was going to make that many sales. Not for this kind of thing.

Glancing back over her shoulder at Wells, Gwyn was already smiling.

But then . . .

He was, too.

"We'll see, Ms. Jones," he replied, and that smile widened just as Gwyn's slipped off her face. "We'll see."

CHAPTER 10

W ells wasn't sure there had ever been anything he'd loved
more than the sound of the bell ringing over the door of
his shop.

And over the next few days, he got to hear his favorite sound
many, many times.

He wasn't sure if it was the ambience of the place bringing
people in—bringing them *back*—or if it was October approaching, but whatever the case, Penhallow's Magical Goods took off
right out of the gate.

It was the professors from Penhaven who started coming by
first, no doubt curious about the newest Penhallow in town.
Then, on the weekend, tourists dropped in, ooh-ing and aah-ing
over the fireplace, the leather chairs, the Welsh landscape paintings hanging on the walls. But they weren't just admiring; they
were buying.

Wells had already had to order a new shipment of leather grimoires, and he was nearly out of crystal orbs. Candles, too, he'd
realized, were popular, as was tea.

Learning that, Wells started brewing his own pots in the shop, offering them free of charge, happy to bring them over to anyone sitting near the fire as they chatted. The more relaxed people were, the more they felt a little pampered, the more likely they were to stay longer, and that meant something usually caught their eye to purchase.

It was, Wells quickly realized, much like what he'd *hoped* running a pub would be like. Friendly smiles thrown his way, hearty handshakes on the way out.

And dammit all, he was *good* at it.

He knew he was because after the first week, Gwyn had appeared in his shop again, glaring at him. "Are you serving tea in here?" she'd asked. "And not charging for it?"

She'd been wearing hot pink that day, as pink as the stripe of color she'd added to her red hair, and Wells had spent entirely too much time thinking about that pink stripe later, wondering why he had the urge to twirl it around one finger.

At the time, however, he'd simply said, "I realize Americans are naturally suspicious of tea from us Brits, but I wasn't aware that serving it for free was an issue?"

She'd muttered something dire at that before storming out again, and Wells had decided to order some more teapots.

Now it was a Saturday, which meant that his shop was pleasantly full, people chatting and browsing, and he was feeling more than a little smug when the bell rang over the door yet again.

He put on his most gracious smile as he turned around only to see that it was one of those young people who hung around

Gwyn's shop. One of her "mentees," he supposed, the girl who always wore her hair in a dark braid.

Today, she was wearing a white T-shirt with a black cat drawn on it and the words "Stay Wicked, Witches!" curling beneath. When she turned, he saw *SOMETHING WICKED, GRAVES GLEN, GA* emblazoned on the back.

Clever. Rather obvious, but not a bad souvenir item.

The girl made a show of browsing, and Wells folded his arms, rocking back slightly on his heels as he watched her drift through the store, picking up a deck of tarot cards, giving it a bored look, and putting it back.

She then moseyed over to the grimoires and literally yawned, patting her open mouth with her hand.

Wells quirked an eyebrow.

He'd expected a fight, but if this was the best Gwyn could do, he was honestly a little disappointed.

The door opened again, and now he recognized another of the college students, the one with brown curly hair and a nose ring that glinted in the dim lights of Penhallow's.

"Find anything?" he heard one say, overly loud, and the girl gave an exaggerated sigh.

"No, everything in here just seems . . . "

She fixed Wells with a look. "Boring."

He almost smiled, he really did.

And then the other person said, "I mean, we saw a TALKING CAT at SOMETHING WICKED. Everything would seem boring after that!"

The words boomed through the store, and this time, Wells couldn't hold back a snort of disdain.

Honestly.

So all Gwyn had were teenagers to come into his store, pretend to be bored, and then announce an obvious lie. As though his customers would be so easily—

"Wait, seriously?"

Wells turned.

A young witch was moving toward the pair, a woman Wells had begun to think of as one of his regulars. She was a graduate student at Penhaven and came in nearly every afternoon for tea and chat and, more often than not, to pick up a new crystal. Wells had even sold her one of the teapots when she'd asked.

Now she was standing with Gwyn's . . . *minions* and looking at something on one of their phones. Giving a startled laugh, she glanced out the door and across the street toward Something Wicked.

"Okay, this I need to see."

The bell rang again, but this time, Wells really, *really* did not enjoy that sound.

Or the many times he heard it afterward as, slowly, everyone in Penhallow's began to get up and move first toward the pair at the door and that blasted phone and then, inevitably, across the street.

Until at last, it was only the three of them left in the store, two looking very smug.

"She can't possibly have a talking cat," Wells said. "That's not a spell a person can do."

Although even as he said it, Wells wasn't sure that was actually the case. It was simply a spell he'd never *seen* anyone do. But after that lecture Gwyn had given him about No Real Magic for the tourists, surely she wouldn't break that rule for herself.

Would you? If you thought she was winning?

The next thing Wells knew, he was out the door and staring at a crowd gathered outside Something Wicked. There was literally a line out the door, and he had to make his way around it, apologizing profusely until he was inside Something Wicked and looking at . . .

A fucking talking cat.

"Happy HalloWEEEEEEEN!"

There were gasps and sighs and laughs from the crowd as Gwyn Jones, fully decked out in witch regalia, hat and all, cuddled a rather chubby black cat wearing his own little hat and a rather dashing orange bandanna.

A cat that once again opened its mouth and cried, "Happy HalloWEEEEEEEEN!"

It then turned its head to Gwyn and asked, "Treats?"

The crowd loved that, too, and as Gwyn petted it and whispered something, someone called out, "How did you train it to do that?"

Gwyn grinned, chucking the cat under the chin. "A witch never reveals her spells!" she called out, and then, winking, added, "Or where she buys ridiculously expensive props."

Everyone laughed, and Wells looked around him, amazed.

There was no doubt in his mind the cat was real, that the *magic* was real, but put something like that in front of people, tell them it's not, and they'd believe it.

The alternative was too bizarre.

In case he wasn't begrudgingly impressed enough, she then called out, "Every purchase includes a complimentary picture or video with Sir Purrcival! Be sure to use the hashtag 'Something-Wicked'!"

Diabolical.

Absolutely fiendish.

And when her eyes briefly met his, her cheek dimpling with a *Go fuck yourself* smile, Wells realized he had never been attracted to any woman more in his life.

Well, that was bloody inconvenient.

CHAPTER 11

"Exactly how much longer is this war between you and my brother going to go on?"

Gwyn was sitting at the kitchen table with Rhys and Vivi, having their traditional weekly dinner. Sometimes they did it at their place, sometimes a restaurant, but mostly, it was back at the cabin, and tonight was no exception.

And if Gwyn felt a *little* guilty thinking about Wells eating alone in that big house just up the road, she reminded herself that just yesterday, she'd found out he'd applied for a liquor license, which meant that soon that stupid, fancy store of his would start serving drinks, probably for free, and she wasn't sure even Sir Purrcival could compete with free booze.

"Until I win," she told Rhys now, reaching for more salt.

Rhys groaned, tipping his head back. "Fuck me running."

"What?" Vivi asked, and her husband sighed, sitting up straight again.

"That's exactly what Wells said when I asked him the same question."

Sipping her wine, Gwyn hid a smile behind her glass.

Business had never been better at Something Wicked. Sir Purrcival only made Saturday appearances, but that was enough. Videos of him were spreading on social media, and people who stopped in just to see him inevitably bought a few things, too. The website business had picked up as well, and she'd gone ahead and officially hired Cait and Parker to help with that.

Wells Penhallow was a pain in her ass, but she couldn't deny that competing with him had been good for business.

"He might as well pack it in, then," Vivi said, refilling her own glass. "Gwyn won't lose."

Rhys looked over at her, surprised. "I thought we were conscientious objectors in this."

"You can conscientiously object," Vivi retorted, then lifted her glass, clinking it against Gwyn's. "I'm Team Gwyn for life."

"Hear, hear," Gwyn replied, and Rhys looked between them before pulling his own glass closer.

"I think Wells is a prick ninety percent of the time, but I find I cannot toast to his failure." He screwed up his face. "Is this what familial love feels like?"

Ignoring that, Vivi turned to Gwyn. "We leave really soon. You two are going to be all right while we're gone, right? I mean, this is just some friendly competition. It's not going to lead to . . . I don't know, curses and vengeful ghosts?"

"Just for example," Rhys added dryly, and Gwyn shook her head.

"You can leave us unsupervised, I promise. Besides, I'll be too focused on teaching Sir Purrcival some new appropriate holiday catchphrases. It took *forever* to get him to say 'Happy Halloween,' but now that he knows he gets treats after it, he won't stop saying it."

As if to prove her point, Sir Purrcival sauntered up just then. "Halloweeeeen happy happy halloweeeeeen treatstreats dickbag?"

"Well, that's worth at least a thousand likes," Rhys offered, and Gwyn sighed as she reached down to feed Sir Purrcival a bit from her plate.

"We're working on it."

Next to her glass, her phone began to buzz, and Gwyn picked it up to see her mom was calling. "It's Elaine," she told Rhys and Vivi, then pointed at both of them.

"*Don't* tell her I exploited her grandchild for financial gain."

THE NEXT DAY was a fairly slow one at Something Wicked (and if Gwyn peeked out the window a few times to note it was *also* pretty dead at Penhallow's, what of it?).

That was fine with Gwyn, though. They'd made more in the last weekend than they had in the last month, and she needed to restock, plus the Baby Witches had wanted more tarot practice, so by the time a customer came in near closing, Gwyn was almost surprised.

The girl looked vaguely familiar, which meant she was probably a local but definitely not a witch. Gwyn would've been able to sense that.

"Hi!" she said brightly. "Anything I can help you with?"

The girl moved toward the counter, her long blond hair brushing the glass. "I was interested in tarot?"

Ah. Gwyn's bread and butter.

"Well, you are in luck because we have a ton of decks. What kind of vibe are you looking for? Classic Rider-Waite, something more contemporary . . . "

Gwyn reached underneath the counter to pull out one of her favorite decks to sell to humans, and just as she did, she felt it.

There was a sort of electric feeling in the air, a slight sizzle that made her hair feel like it was standing on end.

She straightened up, the cards still in her hand, and tried to focus in on that feeling. It wasn't coming from the girl. Or not *exactly* from her, but . . .

"Are you okay?"

Gwyn looked back to the girl, who was waiting for the tarot deck, and her eyes zeroed in on her neck.

There, swinging from it, was a stone on a leather cord. Just a hunk of quartz, nothing particularly special, but something must have been done to the stone because it was practically pulsing with magic, setting Gwyn's teeth on edge.

She made herself smile as she placed the deck of cards on the glass countertop. "That is such a cool necklace!"

The girl smiled back, her fingers going to the crystal. "Thanks. I bought it over there."

She gestured toward the window.

Penhallow's.

Now Gwyn didn't have to fake a smile.

Oh, I've got you now, Esquire.

Making fun of her plastic pumpkins and cartoon cats while he was selling powered up artifacts to normal people. She was going to rub this in his face so hard, he might not even *have* a face by the time she was done.

But first, she had to do her Witchy Duty.

Glancing around, she leaned forward and lowered her voice. "Okay, I don't normally do this for amulets that aren't purchased here, but that one is so pretty, I have to at least offer."

The girl's eyes lit up as Gwyn rattled off a bunch of words she knew would do the trick—"full moon," "salt," "cleansing," "powered up"—and the next thing she knew, she had the stone back in the storage room, sitting on a small silver plate.

She placed the palm of her hand on top of the crystal, breathing deep and concentrating.

After a moment, she felt the quartz stir under her hand, and then, with the faintest hissing sound, a rune rose up in front of her, wavering like smoke.

She breathed a sigh of relief. Nothing major or scary, just a simple clarity spell. *Hold this, focus on a problem, and you'd know what to do, the path opening up before you.*

For a second, she considered just leaving the crystal enchanted. Didn't normies deserve some clarity?

But no, there were rules about this kind of thing, and while

Gwyn really, really hated following rules, she broke the enchantment with some muttered words and a sprinkle of water collected from a flowing stream under a full moon.

When she was finished, the thing sat in the palm of her hand, just as pretty as it had been but no longer radiating any kind of magic.

Satisfied, Gwyn returned it to the girl with a bright grin and a coupon for 10 percent off the next time she came into Something Wicked.

Since that was her last customer and it was already closing time, Gwyn followed her to the door, locking it behind her. She only took a few minutes to straighten up the shop, clearing the register and securing cash back in the storeroom, and then she was out on the cool moonlit street, wind whipping her hair as she hurried across to Penhallow's.

Gwyn had spent the last fifteen minutes plotting exactly how she was going to confront Wells about selling real magic, and had thought she would probably start with something fittingly dramatic. Fling open the door, point a finger, maybe a nice *J'accuse!* for some flair.

She'd been waiting to have one up on Llewellyn Penhallow for thirteen years, after all; this was no time to be subtle.

But when she grabbed the handle of the door, it didn't fling at all. In fact, it was stubbornly locked, which meant that instead of storming in in a glorious, righteous whirlwind of justice, she sort of pathetically rattled the door, then tapped her fingernails on the glass while he scowled at her from behind the counter.

"We're closed!" he called out, and she put her face closer to the glass, fogging it up just to annoy him.

"I need to talk to you!" she called back, and he stood there for a beat, drumming his fingers on the counter before finally coming over and unlocking the door.

"Yes?"

Of course he didn't let her in.

Of course he just stood there in the doorway, looming, looking down that long nose at her.

And of course Gwyn shoved right past him, stepping into the dim store, one hand in the pocket of her coat.

"You," she said, pointing at him with her free hand, "screwed up."

Gwyn hadn't meant to sound *quite* that gleeful, but she couldn't help it. This was too good not to enjoy.

Wells's brows drew together, and he folded his arms tightly over his chest. "What?"

"You sold a human a magicked crystal."

"The hell I did."

"The hell you did, too," Gwyn countered. "A quartz blessed with a clarity rune. Not a bad spell, thank the Goddess, but it *could* have been. That's why we have to be so careful with what we sell."

Wells crossed over to the counter and pulled out a large black leather book, the cover flopping open as he scanned through the pages.

Gwyn watched him, her own brow wrinkled now. "What is that?"

"Every item in this store that gets sold appears in this ledger," Wells told her, not looking up. "So if I did indeed sell a quartz today, it will be in here."

"You know we have computers for that kind of thing, right? Inventory apps on our phones? I'm all for using magic, but you have to admit technology beats us occasionally."

Wells ignored that, his finger running down one of the creamy vellum pages.

It was, Gwyn had to admit, a very nice finger attached to a very good hand. Long, elegant, but still masculine, a signet ring winking dully in the dim light of the shop.

And she also had to admit, yet again, that Wells was definitely pulling off this whole . . . thing he had going on. Proprietor of a classy witch store, his white button-down neatly pressed, the deep navy waistcoat he wore accentuating his trim waist and broad shoulders.

You are checking out Llewellyn Penhallow, *girl,* please *grip yourself.*

This was why she needed to go on more dates. Too much time on her own, and she started admiring *waistcoats,* for fuck's sake.

Clearing her throat, Gwyn moved away from the counter, looking back out toward the front window. Her own little shop glowed happily in the night, the display maybe not quite as tasteful as Penhallow's—the giant broom was maybe a bit much—but cute in its own way. Unique.

Hers.

"Here it is."

Wells's voice was surprisingly flat, and Gwyn whirled around, marching behind the counter to lean over his shoulder and see for herself.

"Aha!" she exclaimed, triumphant as her finger landed on the words "Quartz (Clarity Rune)."

"I don't understand it," Wells muttered to himself, flipping back through the pages. "Everything else I've sold has been perfectly harmless; how did this *one* thing get through?"

"Maybe you didn't check well enough," Gwyn said, and then leaned closer, ignoring how nice he smelled. "Maybe you were . . . *irresponsible.*"

She gave the word a little spooky shudder, wiggling her eyebrows, and Wells closed the book so hard her hair actually puffed back from her face.

"I got a new shipment in two days ago," he said, turning away and heading for a door behind the counter. "I hadn't thought I'd put anything on the shelves, but I must have missed something. Or it got put out by accident."

"This is why you need someone else working in here," Gwyn told him as he opened the door. "You mocked my Baby Witches, but—"

"I do fine on my own," he replied, and with that, he disappeared down the dark stairwell.

CHAPTER 12

Wells wasn't sure why he'd expected Gwyn to leave quietly, but when he heard her boots thumping after him down the basement stairs, he barely repressed a sigh.

"I don't require your assistance," he called out to her as he flipped on the lights.

Such as they were. The whole place had maybe four metal sconces attached to the walls, keeping the room in a sort of perpetual twilight.

"You obviously do," she retorted. He heard a small hiss and pop, and then a globe of light floated over his shoulder, slowly climbing the shelves in front of him.

Gwyn appeared at his elbow, her head tilted up as she looked at the assortment of boxes on the shelves. The light she'd conjured up cast a warm glow over her features, her long red hair spilling down her back, and he forced himself to look away.

It would be slightly easier to stay annoyed with her if she weren't so damned beautiful.

Ever since that moment with her cat and her *smile* and her

bloody fucking *cheek*—had he always liked cheeky women? Was this new? Had someone cursed him like Rhys had been cursed?—he'd been thinking about her, and now, having her this close felt like a special form of torture.

Made all the worse by the fact that he'd clearly buggered something up royally here.

God, he'd been careful. There were a few magical items in the shop, yes. He'd wanted to keep some on hand should Penhallow's eventually become the sort of place where one could—discreetly and safely, of course—purchase that kind of thing.

But now he'd sold a magicked stone to a human, and that was a cock-up and a half.

"How hard is it to find one box?" Gwyn asked, and Wells turned around, gesturing to the sheer plethora of boxes stacked on these shelves.

Rolling her eyes, Gwyn stepped forward, those damned boots clacking and setting his teeth on edge.

From irritation, clearly.

Nothing else.

"This one is sticking out a little," she said, stretching up on her tiptoes. "Maybe it's the one?"

She tugged, but the box was just slightly out of reach, and Wells made a frustrated noise, coming closer. "Let me get that."

"I've got it," she insisted, tugging at the edge of the box, and Wells snorted, his own hand coming up next to hers. She was tall, but he was taller and able to get a firmer handle on the thing than she had.

"You demonstrably do *not* 'got it,'" he told her as he yanked, and she frowned up at him, curling her fingers in tighter, pulling harder.

"Well, if you didn't have dangerous magical shit hanging out in boxes down here—"

"One crystal with a very basic rune on it hardly qualifies as—"

"Magic is magic, Esquire."

"I've told you not to call me that. I don't even understand *why* you call me that."

They were close together now, both their hands on the edge of the box, their chests touching, the hem of her skirt brushing against his knees. Her cheeks were slightly flushed, her lips parted, and he reminded himself that it was anger causing that blush, and her lips were opening to insult him, no doubt, but that seemed hard to remember right now for some reason.

Neither of them was pulling on the box anymore.

They were just standing there, staring at each other.

A stupid, basic human reaction. She was pretty, they were close together, they were breathing hard and looking into each other's eyes. Of course he'd suddenly find himself thinking of other reasons they might be this close, other things they could be doing besides arguing.

It's just that . . . this was a side of himself he'd more or less shut down over the past few years, and feeling it roar back to life for the last woman he should be interested in was more than a little disconcerting.

"Gwyn," he said, and her eyes met his again. Had they been on his mouth? Had Gwynnevere Jones been looking at his mouth and thinking the same filthy things he had?

Wells saw the same confusion he was feeling flash across Gwyn's face, and she shook her head, almost like she was trying to clear it.

And then her hand tightened around the box, and she yanked.

It still didn't come free, but one corner of the carboard tore, something flying out of the box and hitting Wells squarely in the chest.

A pink and shimmery cloud seemed to envelop both of them, the bakery-sweet scent of vanilla filling the air. Filling Wells's mouth and lungs as he blinked against all the floating bits of glitter in the air.

It was all over Gwyn, too, a pale dusting of rose and glitter, her eyes a vivid green as she looked up at him, and if Wells had thought he'd wanted to kiss her before, it was nothing compared to how he felt now.

Now, it was like he might actually die if he didn't. Suddenly, kissing Gwyn Jones was the only thing that mattered in the entire world, and when she took a swaying step toward him, her pupils huge, her tongue darting out to wet her lower lip, Wells chased the movement with hungry eyes.

Her hand was on his chest, fingers curling in his shirt, and then somehow his hand was on her face, looking down at her as his heart nearly beat itself out of his chest.

It's a love spell, you idiot, his one last sensible brain cell cried. He'd never had experience with one, only heard they might exist, but there was no doubt in his mind that's what this was. That was clearly the box the crystal had come from, the one box in the whole bloody shop that actually contained magic, and now he was paying the price for his arrogance.

Not that he cared when she was looking at him like that.

"Wells," she murmured, and he realized she'd never called him by his name before. Always the dreaded *Esquire*. Never Wells.

He liked the sound of his name in her mouth. He wanted to taste it there on her tongue. He wanted to slide his hands into all that gorgeous red hair, and feel her body against his. He wanted . . .

Fuck, he just *wanted*.

"This is a very bad thing," he told her as he lowered his face to hers.

"Just the absolute worst," she agreed, and then she was on her tiptoes, her lips on his.

GWYN WAS NO stranger to lust. It was one of her favorite feelings, in fact. That heady rush when you looked at a person and saw desire in their eyes, how your own desire rose up to match it. The swooping in the stomach, the pounding of the heart, that shiver that raced up and down your spine . . . all of it was pretty amazing, and she had chased it whenever the opportunity presented itself.

But kissing Wells Penhallow in the cellar of his shop was on an entirely new level.

It's because you're both sex-magicked up, she tried to remind herself even as she pressed herself closer to him, arms winding around his neck as his hands slid over her back, her ribs, pulling her in even tighter.

It didn't feel like a first kiss. It was too good, too sure of itself, and once again, Gwyn tried to tell herself that had to be the magic because surely a man named Llewellyn didn't kiss like this without some kind of magical intervention.

His hand was on her face again, that gorgeous hand she'd been watching earlier, thumb moving along her jaw and raising shivery sparks everywhere it touched. When that touch moved higher, brushing a spot just beneath her ear, Gwyn was pretty sure she actually whimpered.

That was a first.

Wells met that sound with a noise low in his throat, and she felt that growl everywhere, her knees actually going a little weak.

Without breaking the kiss, she turned so that his back was against the shelf, pushing him up against it hard enough to rattle something above their heads, but honestly, the entire thing could've come down on both of them, and Gwyn wasn't sure she would've noticed.

Not when his hand was on the back of her neck, the silver of his signet ring cool against her heated skin, not when his tongue was sliding against hers, his mouth tasting like citrus and sugar from the tea he'd been drinking. Not when she could feel him through the fabric of his trousers, hard for her.

Wanting her.

Because of a spell.

Finally, that voice started to cut through some of the haze.

A spell.

A stupid love spell that had rained down on them because they'd been arguing, which is all they *ever* did, so it was clearly the most powerful love spell in existence, and Rhiannon's *tits,* she was climbing all over a man she didn't even *like* because of a shower of cotton candy *sex dust.*

Head clearing, Gwyn broke the kiss, stepping back so quickly that she bumped into the shelf just behind her. This time, something from the top did fall, a little votive-candle holder, and the glass shattering at their feet seemed to bring both of them fully back to themselves.

Wells was still breathing hard, his face streaked with the pink dust, his eyes wide and his hair a wreck.

I did that, Gwyn thought almost wonderingly, and then she shook her head, pulling at the hem of her dress to straighten it.

"This," she panted, reaching up to push her hair back from her face.

She didn't even have to finish the sentence. Wells was already standing up straight again, jerking at the lapels of his waistcoat. "Too right," he agreed to something she hadn't said.

"And that," she added, pointing up at the box still teetering on the shelf.

"Burning it," he replied. "Salting the earth."

Gwyn gave a brisk nod, then spun on her heel, hoping her legs weren't too shaky to carry her back up the stairs.

She didn't look back.

CHAPTER 13

The cold night air was a relief as Gwyn stepped back out onto the street. She was still overheated, still felt like she was burning up from the inside out, a fire a thousand cold showers couldn't put out.

Her truck was parked in its usual spot in front of Something Wicked, but Gwyn bypassed it, heading instead for the small alley beside the store, her fingers still trembling as she did a quick spell on the side door that led up to Vivi's apartment.

When her cousin opened the door, Gwyn knew she must look as completely bonkers as she currently felt because Vivi, who had really seen some shit when it came to Gwyn, muttered a term in Welsh Gwyn had never heard her use before, her eyes wide.

"Good lord, what provoked *that* reac—oh."

Rhys appeared over his wife's shoulder, and Gwyn pointed at him. "Out," she said. "Vivi and I have . . . coven business."

"Usually code for the two of you wanting to drink wine and talk about things you don't want me to hear, and given the state of you right now, Gwynnevere, that seems fair."

Pressing a quick kiss to Vivi's temple, Rhys reached for his jacket where it hung by the door, squeezing past Gwyn with another quizzical look, but, mercifully, no questions.

As his footsteps faded down the stairs, Vivi ushered Gwyn inside. "What is all over you?" she asked, closing the door behind her.

Oh. Right.

Gwyn had been so busy focusing on the effects of the love spell that she'd almost forgotten she was still literally wearing it.

"Spell," she said, her voice still dazed as she sat heavily on Vivi's sofa. The apartment was Gwyn's home away from home, and she reached for her favorite throw now, the soft purple one she'd bought for Vivi years ago and that always had a place of honor on the back of the couch.

"What kind of spell?" Vivi asked, her brow wrinkled, and Gwyn looked up at her, blinking.

"Love spell."

Vivi stood very still for a long moment, then without a word, disappeared into the kitchen. When she returned, she was carrying her two biggest wineglasses and a full bottle of Pinot Grigio.

Vivi really had always been Gwyn's favorite person in the whole world.

She gratefully accepted a glass now, taking a long sip.

Okay, a gulp.

She could still taste Wells's kiss, her lips tingling and raw from the scrape of his beard, and she shivered a little as she set her wineglass back on the table.

Vivi, patient as always, was curled up in the armchair opposite her, her feet clad in black socks covered in bright green spooky eyes. It was easier to look at those eyes than it was to look into Vivi's as Gwyn told her cousin what had happened that night. About the crystal, about going over to Wells's for some well-earned gloating, about wanting to see what else he might have in storage, and then, finally—*humiliatingly*—about the part where a shower of pink glitter that smelled like a cupcake made her put her entire face on Wells's entire face and kiss him like kissing was in danger of going extinct.

By the time she'd finished, her glass was empty and Vivi's mouth was hanging open, neither of which made Gwyn feel that great about her life choices tonight.

"Wells," Vivi finally said. "You kissed . . . Wells. Because of a love spell."

It sounded so innocent put like that. Just a kiss between two adults thanks to a little light magic, no big deal!

But that didn't get across just how *devastating* the kiss had been, how it seemed to have rattled everything inside Gwyn.

"It wasn't just a kiss," she said now, rubbing her face and grimacing when her hand came away still streaked with glitter. "It was a *magicked* kiss. Love spell magic, Vivi! Just hanging out in some box in Wells's store. Anyone could've bought that and then ended up making out with someone they hate."

That's what she needed to do—turn this around to how irresponsible this was, how dangerous that Wells had come to town and opened a magic store and didn't even know what he was doing.

She opened her mouth to say just that, but Vivi was frowning, leaning forward slightly, her thinky face very much in evidence.

"Love spells don't work that way," she said, and Gwyn blinked. "What?"

Getting up from her chair, Vivi went to one of the many bookshelves lining her walls, her fingers dancing along the spines until she found what she was looking for. "Magic can't make people act against their basic will," she said, paging through the book as Gwyn's stomach began a slow descent to somewhere south of her knees. "It violates the . . . the basic tenets of magic. You can do *bad* spells on people, obviously, and those *can* do harm, but you can't make a person do something they don't want to do. Our spirits are inherently too strong to be bent, even with magic. Right, here it is!" She planted her finger on a page and began to read.

"'While the idea of a love spell has loomed large in popular culture, such magic is nearly impossible to pull off unless both subjects feel a mutual pull toward one another.'"

Did Gwyn just think Vivi was her favorite person in the entire world? That couldn't possibly be right. Her favorite person in the entire world would not be a *lying liar*.

"Let me see that."

Gwyn got up from the sofa, trailing the purple blanket as she took the book from Vivi, her eyes skating over the page and, to her horror, reading the exact thing Vivi had just read.

Slamming the book shut, Gwyn pushed it back toward Vivi. "This is obviously a stupid book. A stupid book of extreme wrongness that I can't believe you have on your shelf. It must be one of Rhys's books."

Vivi only laughed, shaking her head as she slid the book back into its space on the bookcase.

"Sorry, girl. The books don't lie, and the spell didn't make you do anything. You kissed Wells Penhallow because you *wanted* to kiss Wells Penhallow."

WHEN WELLS HEARD footsteps on the stairs leading down to the basement, his heart gave a quick leap in his chest.

She's back.

But the tread was too heavy to be Gwyn's, the shoes not clacking the way her boots always seemed to, and after a moment, Rhys came into view, hands in his pockets as he sauntered down the stairs.

Wells told himself he was only disappointed because he was *always* disappointed to see Rhys. It had nothing to do with the feel of Gwyn's mouth lingering on his lips or the way his hands were practically aching to be back on her body.

Not the time nor place for those kinds of thoughts, but luckily, his younger brother's voice was better than any cold shower.

"You down here?" he called, and Wells, who had not moved from the spot where Gwyn had left him, who was, in fact, not sure he would ever be capable of moving again, managed a rather feeble, "Yes."

Rhys appeared around the corner, a bobbing ball of light

hovering just above his left shoulder. "Thought I'd—" he started, but then he froze, his eyes going slightly wide as he took Wells in.

Wells scowled, then glanced down at himself. The spell was still shimmering all over him, streaking his dark clothing pink, and he rolled his eyes, ready for whatever quip his brother undoubtedly had to deliver.

But Rhys didn't say a word, only stood there stock-still, his face going a rather alarming shade of red before he burst into laughter.

Not just any laughter, either, but the full-throated cackle of a younger brother getting to make fun of the eldest, and that, finally, gave Wells the strength he needed to stop standing around like a fucking numpty.

"All right, yes," he said, attempting to dust himself off. "I look as though I just raided a thirteen-year-old girl's makeup, but that's really no reason to get quite this amused, Rhys."

But Rhys only shook his head, leaning against the nearest shelf as he wiped tears of mirth from his eyes. "Oh, mate," he said, and then he collapsed into laughter all over again.

Scowling, Wells folded his arms over his chest and did his best to look as foreboding as a man covered in pink glitter could. "It may look silly, but this is actually rather serious. Someone sent a box with actual magical artifacts in it. This"—he gestured at the glitter—"is a spell. A love spell, Rhys. Which could've been a disaster in the wrong hands."

"Looks like it already *was* a disaster," Rhys replied, still grinning. Then he jerked his head in the direction of the stairs. "Especially since Gwyn Jones is currently sitting on my sofa covered in that same shite."

Bollocks.

So that's what Rhys had found so amusing. Wells had hoped to get out of this without his brother ever, *ever* knowing what had transpired in this room, but this was, he was quickly learning, the issue with small towns and families *in* said small towns—secrets didn't really exist.

"Yes, well," he said, sniffing and tugging at the ends of his waistcoat. "It's all over now and a lesson learned. Now, help me clean this up, and let's figure out just *why* I had this spell in the first fucking place, hmm?"

To his relief, Rhys gave an easy roll of his shoulders and moved farther into the cellar. "I want you to put it in writing later. How you needed my help."

"Fine," Wells gritted out, and Rhys grinned before crouching down and picking up the little bag that had held the love spell.

"Careful!" Wells warned. "That's strong magic. No idea where it came from."

Rhys studied the bag for a moment before turning back to Wells, his expression carefully schooled.

That wasn't a good sign.

"The spell. It was in this?"

Wells nodded, and knew immediately by the absolutely unholy grin that spread across Rhys's face that something was very, very wrong.

Rhys rose to his feet and pointed to the torn box still on the upper shelf. "And it came out of this?"

"Oh, for fuck's sake," Wells muttered, crossing back to the shelf. "Why don't you just tell me what you're thinking rather than playing Poirot, hmm?" he asked, already reaching up for the box. "You make such a bloody production out of everything, I swear to Saint Bugi."

The box came down easily, and Wells set it on one of the low shelves, tearing open the flaps. "Whatever else is in here will need to be disposed of safely," he said. "There's no telling how many other dangerous spells might be—"

Wells blinked at the contents of the box as Rhys stepped closer, peering over his shoulder.

"I don't know, Wells," he said with a shrug. "Some of that stuff looks a bit *adventurous,* maybe, but nothing *dangerous* per se."

Reaching into the box, Wells pulled out a pair of purple fuzzy handcuffs, still trying to make sense of what he was seeing even as Rhys's grin grew wider.

"Looks like there was some kind of mix-up," Rhys said, tapping the side of the box where, for the first time, Wells noticed a rather grubby and torn shipping label. "And I have to say, I wonder what the . . . "

He leaned closer, trying to make out the name on the label. "The Pleasure Palace is going to do with all the witch shite they undoubtedly now have."

"This isn't . . . " Wells said, digging through the box, wondering why so much of his life here in Graves Glen seemed to involve plastic phalluses. "I don't understand."

That was possibly the biggest understatement he'd ever made in his life. He didn't understand how he'd ended up with this box, he didn't understand how this box had somehow still contained a love spell, and he certainly didn't understand why he was suddenly so completely, painfully attracted to a woman who clearly spent most of her waking moments thinking up new ways to make his life as annoying as possible.

Because he'd been thinking about kissing her long before that spell had descended on them.

Rhys was still holding the velvet pouch, and he reached inside it now, a small piece of paper trapped between his fingers. "I think this might explain some things," he said, thumping the paper against Wells's chest before turning and heading back toward the stairs.

Wells looked at the words printed in pink curling script, his eyes already searching out the word "spell."

But there was nothing about spells or magic written there, only . . .

"Oh, fucking hell," Wells whispered.

Or possibly whimpered.

From the stairs, Rhys only laughed.

CHAPTER 14

G wyn could not believe she was lying in her bed, staring up at the ceiling and thinking about kissing Llewellyn Freaking Penhallow.

And yet.

Outside, the sun had just come up, filling her bedroom with a cozy warm light. It was one of her favorite times of day, sunrise. The world always seemed so quiet, which meant her mind got to be a little quiet, too.

But this morning, it was a full-on marching band of noise in her head.

A marching band that comprised howler monkeys and toddlers and banshees and—

Groaning, Gwyn covered her face with her hands. Great, now the bastard had even taken *this* from her, the one peaceful part of her day, all because he had the nerve to be that good at kissing despite . . . despite . . . well, everything about him.

Vivi had to be wrong was the thing. That *book* had to be

wrong, and once she was done at the store this evening, Gwyn was going to prove it to herself. She'd make the strongest cup of tea known to man, maybe find a pair of her mom's reading glasses just to make sure the universe knew she was really serious right now, and devote some serious time to researching love spells. And then she'd prove that that kiss had been the result of magic and nothing more.

She gave a firm nod. "Right," she said out loud to her empty bedroom.

But the problem was, as soon as she started thinking about how to prove the kiss was a magical fluke, she started thinking about the *kiss itself* again, and that's how she lost another ten minutes to glowering at the ceiling while thinking about how she'd made out with a man who probably wore *sweater vests*.

"Kiss?"

Startling, Gwyn glanced down at the bed where Sir Purrcival had just managed to rouse himself, lazily making his way up to her. "Kiss?" he said again, bumping against her.

Gwyn sat up, pressing a quick kiss to the top of his head even as she gave him a dark look.

"You're not funny," she told him, but he only blinked his eyes slowly before yawning and curling up in the warm spot in the bed Gwyn had just vacated.

Her clothes from last night were still draped on the over-stuffed velvet chair near the window, the pink shimmery stuff sparkling in the sunlight, and with a grimace, Gwyn picked up the bundle and tossed it into her hamper and then, after a beat, went ahead and shoved the clothes to the very bottom of the pile.

Out of sight, out of mind.

If only it would be that easy to get rid of Wells Penhallow.

THE ONLY WAY out is through, Gwyn told herself grimly as she opened the door of the Coffee Cauldron an hour later.

The familiar and comforting smell of roasting coffee wafted over her as she made her way to the counter. It was crowded this morning, as it always was around this time. That was fine, though. The longer she could put off the inevitable, the better.

But the Coffee Cauldron worked with just the littlest bit of magic running through it—every employee was a witch at the college—which meant that before she knew it, Gwyn was at the register, facing a smiling Sam.

"The usual?" Sam asked, and Gwyn nodded before leaning in and lowering her voice to ask, "Does Wells Penhallow come in very often?"

"Um, our archenemy? Sometimes?"

"Do you by any chance know what he usually orders?"

Sam looked baffled, glancing around her. "Okay, are you gonna like . . . put some kind of spell in his coffee, Glinda? Because that seems very uncool, I gotta say."

"No!" Gwyn said, maybe just a little too loudly given that Sam actually flinched.

Shaking her hair back off her shoulders, Gwyn made herself smile and say, "I just need a peace offering."

Sam, thank the Goddess, didn't question that. She just shrugged and said, "He usually gets a plain black coffee."

"Of course he does," Gwyn muttered, then sighed and handed over her debit card. "One of those, then, and my usual."

Gwyn didn't actually have a usual, she just liked saying that, and Sam liked making up various concoctions she thought *could* be Gwyn's usual. Today's was some kind of lavender tea situation with vanilla and cardamom, and Gwyn took a restorative sip of it as she headed out of the Coffee Cauldron and made her way to Penhallow's.

It was still fairly early, the streets quiet, the sky that perfect shade of blue she associated with this time of year. There was just the barest chill in the air—by the afternoon, she knew she'd have to ditch the black cardigan she'd thrown on over her *Crystals&Cats&Wands&Brooms* T-shirt—but fall was officially here, and Gwyn took a deep breath, psyching herself up as she stepped into Penhallow's.

Wells was behind the counter as usual, looking over some kind of ledger similar to the one he'd shown her last night, and when he looked up and saw her standing there, she could swear his ears went a little red.

That made her feel better. If he was as embarrassed as she was, the playing field was level at least.

Clearing his throat, Wells came around the counter. He was

wearing a navy button-down today with dark-wash jeans and, Gwyn was very relieved to see, an actual sweater vest.

That sweater vest was better than any cold shower. She was going to buy him extra ones. Maybe something in polka dots.

Standing up a little straighter, Gwyn thrust the paper cup of coffee at him. "I got this for you," she said.

He didn't take it. "Is it poisoned?"

"Yes, I finally decided the only way to handle a mild retail feud was with some murder. Well done, Esquire."

The tiniest hint of a smile flickered at the corner of Wells's mouth as he reached out and took his drink.

"I asked them for the most boring thing they had, and it turns out that was your usual," Gwyn told him as he took a sip.

"Nothing boring about a well-made black coffee," he said, then nodded at her cup.

"I suppose yours is filled with glitter and the tears of unicorns."

"They were out of unicorn tears this morning. Had to use Splenda instead."

That made him smile outright, and Gwyn was forced to admit that he actually had a very nice smile. It probably hurt his face given that all those muscles had to be way more accustomed to scowling, but still.

"So why are you bringing me an unpoisoned cup of boring coffee this morning?" Wells asked, and Gwyn took a deep breath.

"Peace offering," she replied, and his eyebrows rose.

"Hmm."

Thunking her cup down on the counter beside her, Gwyn folded her arms over her chest and gave herself a mental shake.

You are Gwynnevere Fucking Jones, she reminded herself. *You are a grown-ass woman who is not going to be embarrassed that she kissed a guy,* come on.

"Look," she said to Wells. "Last night was a momentary lapse of sanity brought on by a stupid love spell that had no business being in this store."

Wells frowned over his cup, but he didn't interrupt her, so Gwyn barreled on.

"But the thing is, we wouldn't have gotten caught up in the stupid love spell had we not also been in this stupid fight over the stores. So I am proposing a truce."

Wells put his own cup down and faced her, mimicking her pose. And if that stretched his stupid, completely unsexy vest over the surprisingly broad chest Gwyn was now unfortunately much more familiar with, she only let her eyes drop from his face for a teensy moment.

"I am . . . amenable to this," he said. "What are the terms?"

"One." Gwyn lifted a finger. "You never say 'amenable' again, and maybe start practicing phrases from the twenty-first century, like 'that sounds good!' or something similar. Two." Another finger. "You stay on your side of the street and I stay on mine. I will run my business, you run yours, and—"

"Never the twain shall meet, understood."

"You really did not listen to point one at all, did you?"

Ignoring that, Wells quirked an eyebrow at her. "Is there a

point three, or have we exhausted this already exhausting conversation?"

"That's pretty much it," Gwyn said, then held out her hand. "Agreed?"

Wells looked down at her hand, and Gwyn suddenly realized that shaking hands was touching, and given all the touching she and Wells had done last night, maybe even something as safe as a handshake was not the best of ideas.

Maybe he was thinking something similar because he cleared his throat again, and when Gwyn glanced up at him, she realized he was . . . well, not blushing, exactly. But there was a definite flush climbing up his throat, and she had a very visceral memory of wanting to put her mouth there last night, right at the hollow between his collarbones, and—

His palm pressed against hers, her fingers automatically closing around it, and then, thank the Goddess, the moment was over and her hand was safe.

"So are we friends now?" Wells asked, flexing his fingers against his side. "Colleagues? Compatriots?"

"We're . . . neighbors," she decided. "Congenial business owners sharing a space."

Wells nodded at that. "Works for me."

"And," Gwyn added, pointing at him, "as your neighbor and fellow business owner, I need to know that you got rid of that box of spells."

The strangest expression flickered across Wells's face for a second, and Gwyn frowned.

"You got rid of it, right?"

"Of course," he answered, then paused again, like there was something more he wanted to say. Whatever it was, he clearly decided against it because he shook his head and said, "All taken care of, never to be an issue again. Witch's oath."

That wasn't an actual thing, but Gwyn would take it.

"Good. So. I'll . . . see you when I see you, Esquire."

He gave her a funny little salute in return that made her roll her eyes even as she chuckled, relief sweeping through her.

This was over, then. A weird magical blip, something she could brush off and forget. By this time next week, she probably wouldn't even remember that kiss.

CHAPTER 15

I t was, Wells reflected as he placed a new display of amulets on the counter of Penhallow's, much more peaceful when he wasn't feuding with Gwyn Jones.

It had been a week since the . . . incident in the cellar, and after Gwyn's offer of coffee and a truce, he'd barely seen her. Occasionally they were opening up or closing down at the same time, and when that happened, they'd give each other a cordial wave. No arguments, no attempts at outdoing one another. Just two local business owners with an appropriate Business Relationship, all very civilized.

So yes, much more peaceful.

And also, he had to admit, much duller.

He caught himself glancing at the front window again, something he was doing more and more frequently lately. Wells always told himself it was because he was keeping an eye out for any potential customers, but the truth was, he was hoping to see a glimpse of red hair, and that was so pathetic he could hardly stand it. This was what came of living a fairly celibate life for too many years, clearly. One kiss, and he was practically pining. He'd be doodling "Mr. Llewellyn Penhallow-Jones" in a notebook next.

And Gwyn had made it very clear that she was not doing the same.

You should have told her about the "spell," you numpty, a voice in his head reminded him, and Wells sighed, sliding the display case closed.

"To what end?" he muttered out loud just as the bell over the shop door rang.

Another stupid leap of his heart, hoping it might be her—although if she heard him say "to what end?" he was in for a pretty thorough mocking, he knew—but as he looked over, he saw it wasn't Gwyn but another woman, slightly shorter, dressed all in black. Her hair was black, too, so dark it had an almost blue sheen in the lamplight.

Her skin was pale, her lips a deep crimson, and the magic radiating off her was so strong that Wells nearly took a step back. He hadn't felt power like that . . . well, ever, really. And his family was full of very powerful witches.

"Good morning," he called down, stepping around the counter, and she turned toward him, those bright red lips curving into a smile.

"Llewellyn," she said, and he paused, his eyes searching her face, looking for anything familiar. Surely, he'd remember her.

Not just because she was beautiful—although she was certainly that—but for this sensation, like electricity was coming off her. He half expected to find his hair standing on end.

"I'm sorry, have we met?" he asked, and she laughed, waving one elegant hand.

"Oh, not really," she said, a faint Southern accent rounding her vowels. "We were at Penhaven at the same time, but I don't think we ever actually spoke."

Ah. That would explain it. He'd had his nose pressed against the proverbial grindstone so hard in that brief time at Penhaven, it was a wonder he had any nose left at all.

"I'm Morgan. Morgan Howell," she said now, offering her hand for Wells to shake. He was reminded of the other morning, that brief press of his palm to Gwyn's, how he'd been intensely aware of her skin and the warmth of it, how such a simple gesture had had him flexing his hand for the rest of the day, like he could still feel her touch there.

There was no such spark with Morgan, which was both a relief—he hadn't developed some kind of handshaking fetish—and also an annoyance since it was just another tick in the column reading, "Wells Is a Stupid Git With a Wildly Inappropriate Crush."

"Your store is lovely," Morgan said, gesturing around, and Wells slid his hands into his pockets, rocking back on his heels a little. It was a new feeling, this pride in his establishment, and he was rather enjoying it, if he was honest.

"Thank you. I've only been open for a couple of weeks, but so far, it's done well."

"I can see why," Morgan said as her gaze took in his neat shelves, the dull glimmer of the various amulets, the crackling fire against one wall.

Then her dark eyes moved to him, and Wells had the sense he was getting the same level of assessment she'd given the shop. "But nothing in here is . . . real," she added.

"Oh, it's all very *real*, I assure you," Wells replied, knocking on the shelf that held the grimoires. "It's just that none of it is magic."

Grinning, Morgan reached out with one hand, swatting at him. "Obviously, that's what I meant," she said, and Wells didn't miss the way she ducked her head just the littlest bit or the dimple that appeared in one cheek.

She was *flirting* with him.

And if he had any fucking sense, he'd flirt right back. This was a beautiful woman who was also a powerful witch, and she was clearly interested in more than just his wares. Women like this were not exactly thick on the ground.

But then he once again felt his eyes wander to the front window.

Morgan followed that look. "Gwyn Jones still runs Something Wicked, right?" she asked, and Wells snapped back to attention.

"Indeed she does," he replied. "It's got, as I believe she'd say, 'a different vibe,' but it's a lovely store in its own way."

"Gwyn was always a firecracker," Morgan mused, still looking out the front window, and Wells couldn't help but smile.

"That has not changed, I assure you."

Morgan turned back to him then, her gaze assessing. "Are the two of you . . . " she asked, trailing off suggestively, and Wells could actually feel himself about to launch into some sort of terrifyingly prudish bumbling speech, all stammers and formal words like he was in some dire romantic comedy.

Instead, he stepped back from the window, giving what he hoped was a carefree-sounding laugh. "Oh, no," he said, even as visions of his hands in Gwyn's hair, her lips parting under his, laid siege to his brain. "Merely fellow local business owners. And . . . family, I suppose. Her cousin is married to my brother."

Morgan nodded. "I heard all about that. And it's the Jones family's magic currently running the town now, yes?"

Wells nodded even as he waited for the irritation he normally felt at that reminder to bubble up. But there was nothing there this time. Maybe it was because he'd been in Graves Glen long enough now to see how smoothly things seemed to be running. How happy his brother was.

Maybe, though he'd never say it out loud, his father had actually been . . . wrong.

No lightning bolt crackled out of the sky to singe him for such a disloyal thought, so Wells added, "Doing a bang-up job of it, too."

Morgan smiled again, reaching up to tuck a strand of dark hair behind her ear. "That's actually why I'm here," she said. "After Penhaven, I went back to Charleston and joined a coven there.

It's been wonderful, don't get me wrong, but Rhiannon knows Charleston has plenty of witches, which means hundreds of covens, and I was starting to feel a little lost in the shuffle. I thought it might be nice to settle somewhere smaller, closer to a direct source of power. And when I heard that that power was now being channeled through Gwyn and her family, I knew this was the right time to come back."

Reaching into her coat, she pulled out a cream-colored envelope, his name written elegantly across the front, a purple wax seal affixed to the back.

"I've got a place just outside of town, near the college, and I'm having a little housewarming party Friday night. Local witches only." She said that with another one of those sharp smiles. "I hope you'll drop by."

The invitation was heavy in his hand, the paper thick and expensive, and Wells had to admit he was a little impressed even as something about Morgan's story . . . well, it didn't *bother* him exactly, but something about it didn't quite add up for him, either. Wells may not have had that many customers at The Raven and Crown, but you didn't run a pub for years without learning how to read people.

And right now, Morgan was trying slightly too hard.

He thought again about what Bowen had said, about how shifts in magical power could draw all sorts of bad people.

Was that why Morgan was here?

This, Wells reminded himself, was why he'd come here. To be of use to the town his ancestor had founded and keep it safe.

So he smiled back at Morgan, tapping the invitation against his palm. "Wouldn't miss it."

"**HAVE I MENTIONED** how much I'm gonna miss you?"

Gwyn was sitting cross-legged on Vivi and Rhys's bed, watching as her cousin did some last-minute packing. Or Vivi's version of it, at least. She'd been packed for weeks as far as Gwyn knew, but she always ended up doing this, taking everything out and doing a thorough *re*packing in case she'd forgotten something.

Now, as Vivi folded up one of her skirts and laid it in the open suitcase by Gwyn's hip, she shook her head slightly, blond hair falling over her shoulders. "We'll be back before you know it. The weeks leading up to Samhain are always nuts, anyway, so you'll be too busy to actually miss me."

Gwyn gave a dramatic sigh and fell backward on the bed. "You're right, I know you're right." Propping herself up on one elbow, she narrowed her eyes at Vivi. "Ooh, and with you *and* Mom gone, this makes me the head of the family."

Vivi laughed at that, and encouraged, Gwyn sat up. "The matriarch," she continued. "Head Witch in Charge. *Queen* Witch. I'll be drunk with power by the time you come home. Just full-on Galadriel, beautiful and terrible."

Flicking Gwyn with one of the sweaters she was about to fold, Vivi grinned. "Okay, now I think you're trying to convince me to stay home."

"Oh, there will be none of that," Rhys announced, coming into the room. He was holding a beer, his dark hair tousled, and

Gwyn swore Vivi actually *swooned*. Who swooned for their own husband?

Then Gwyn glanced behind Rhys and spotted Wells standing there. She'd heard Rhys open the door to him earlier, assumed he was also dropping in to say good-bye since Rhys and Vivi were due to leave at a truly illegal time of morning tomorrow.

Wells also had a beer, and if his hair was a little neater that Rhys's, he definitely looked more casual than he usually did, dressed in jeans and a V-neck sweater.

Whatever that little swoop in her belly was, it was definitely *not* a swoon.

Sitting up, Gwyn tucked one leg underneath the other, fluffing her hair a bit as she did. "I was just reminding your wife that with her gone, I'll be the most important witch in town and was therefore planning my tyrannical and power-hungry reign."

"And the town shudders," Rhys replied, stepping close to Vivi and sliding an arm around her waist. She lifted her face to his, and as Rhys kissed her, Gwyn saw Wells grimace slightly.

"They do this all the time," she told him. "It's the worst."

"Indeed," he muttered against the lip of his beer bottle. As he took a sip, Wells glanced over at her, and when their eyes met, Gwyn could swear there was a slightly conspiratorial twinkle there.

"The two of *you* are the worst, and I will not be shamed for kissing my gorgeous wife in my own home," Rhys said, pointing at Wells and then Gwyn, and Gwyn lifted her hands in surrender.

"Fine, I'll admit, your own apartment is the correct space for that kind of thing."

"Oh, come on," Rhys replied. "Every space is the 'correct' space for a bit of snogging. Apartments. Cars. Libraries." One side of his mouth kicked up. "Cellars . . ."

Vivi elbowed him in the side, and he gave an exaggerated wince even as Wells shot him a dark look. Gwyn, for her part, willed herself not to blush. They were all adults here, for fuck's sake. She could take a little light teasing about one freaking kiss.

"You know, Rhys," she told him, "when I'm Queen Witch, I could have you executed for that kind of thing."

"And while I will actively lead a resistance against the dark sovereignty of the Witch Queen Gwyn, I will support her in this one thing," Wells said, tipping his beer bottle in Rhys's direction.

Rhys frowned, looking back and forth between them. "Wait. Wait, no, I hate this. Go back to being mean to each other, please."

Vivi laughed. "Serves you right," she said, and Gwyn caught Wells's eye again. He was smiling a little, looser and more relaxed than she was used to, and she had to admit, this was kind of . . . nice. Having another person to share these little looks with when Rhys and Vivi were being Peak Them. Maybe it wouldn't be so bad having Wells around more after all, especially if he could be *this* Wells.

Except that this Wells also made her fingers itch to touch his sweater and see if it was as soft as it looked. To slide her hands underneath it and feel his skin, warm and solid beneath her palms. To—

Gwyn looked away so fast she was pretty sure her eyes made an audible snapping sound.

"I still don't like it," Rhys continued. "Me finished packing before you, Gwyn and Wells teaming up, Wells getting a date—the whole world is off its axis."

Gwyn looked over at Wells again, eyebrows raised.

He was allowed to have dates, of course. He *should* have dates. Wells having dates would be a very good thing for all kinds of reasons she was sure she would think of any second now, but there was still just the tiniest little bit of relief that spilled through her when Wells rolled his eyes and said, "For the last bloody time, it's not a date."

"Are you sure?" Gwyn asked him. "I realize whoever this woman is, she probably didn't ask your father's permission to court you, but it might still be a date to those of us who aren't time travelers from 1823."

Wells threw her a scowl even as Rhys hooted with laughter.

"I assure you, it's not a date," he said again, but since he didn't offer any additional information, Gwyn wondered.

Not that it was any of her business.

Getting off the bed, she nodded at Vivi's suitcase. "I think you've achieved Packing Utopia, Viv. Just one more thing."

Gwyn reached for her bag, tossed carelessly to the side of the bed when she'd come in, and pulled out a piece of amethyst, wiggling it between her thumb and forefinger.

"Never leave home without it!"

Leaning over, she placed the crystal on Vivi's things and laid a hand on top of it, the cool stone pressed against her palm. It was a spell she'd done a thousand times, a completely simple protection ward that would ensure Vivi's luggage wouldn't get lost.

Given that Rhys's particular magic talents dealt with luck, especially when it came to travel, there wasn't much chance of that anyway, but Gwyn still wanted to send a little piece of home off with Vivi.

A little piece of her.

She thought the words of the spell and waited for that warm feeling to spread up from her toes, down her arm, into the hand now resting against the amethyst.

Nothing happened.

Her eyes shot up, her brow wrinkling as she looked at her hand.

"Gwyn?" Vivi asked, and Gwyn looked up at her cousin, giving her a smile even as the faintest alarm bells started ringing in her head.

"It's nothing," she said. "Just wasn't concentrating hard enough."

This time, she didn't just whisper the words in her mind. She shouted them, as loud as she could, her eyes squeezed shut, tiny drops of sweat popping out on her brow.

Immediately, she felt magic surge through her, the crystal glowing warm, and she laughed, a little breathless.

"There," Gwyn said, straightening up, then opening and closing her hand a few times, shaking it like she was trying to wake it up. "That was weird."

Vivi wasn't smiling, though, and even Rhys looked serious.

Wells was behind her, so she couldn't see his face, but Gwyn could still feel his gaze on her.

"What?" she said, looking around. "It's fine! I was just lazy, and the magic was, like, 'Nope, not the vibe, girl,' so I put my back into it a little more, and voilà!"

Gwyn knew that could happen. Magic was a wild thing, after all. Sometimes it might not cooperate.

It's just that it had never happened to her before.

She wiggled her fingers again, sending little showers of golden sparkles into the air, then, just for good measure, called up a quick light spell, a glowing orb hovering just over her shoulder.

Trying not to look as relieved as she felt, Gwyn shrugged. "Right as rain."

"Future as Witch Queen secured, then," Rhys said, and Vivi's shoulders relaxed.

"Sorry," she said, a little sheepish. "I guess after everything last year with the curse and Rhys's magic, I'm a little paranoid."

"Understandable," Gwyn acknowledged, "but there's nothing to worry about. You two go on your big honeymoon, and don't think about this place for a second. I will have everything absolutely under control."

"And you'll have Wells," Rhys said, gesturing at his brother, a slightly evil gleam in his eye. "The two of you will hold down the fort admirably. Like a team."

Gwyn glanced over her shoulder, and saw Wells seemed every bit as horrified by that idea as she felt.

Still, she made herself smile. "Sure. A team."

CHAPTER 16

I feel like I maybe fucked something up."

Those were never words you wanted to hear from a witch, and Gwyn frowned as she looked up from behind the counter at Something Wicked.

It was a gray and drizzly afternoon, the kind of weather that tended to keep people inside and out of shops, so Gwyn had agreed to let Sam, Cait, and Parker work on their spellcraft in the storage room.

Clearly not one of her best ideas given the look on Parker's face right now as they peeped out from behind the curtain.

Sighing, Gwyn walked around the counter. "Vivi only left this morning," she said, "and if y'all have created some magical disaster in the less than twelve hours she's been gone, I'm going to be very disappointed in you."

"They're being dramatic!" Cait called from the storage room, and when Gwyn pulled back the curtain, she saw the other two witches sitting on the floor, surrounded by pieces of parchment, some bags of loose herbs, and a heap of wax pieces. In the center, there was a small cauldron perched over a pinkish flame, the milky contents inside bubbling.

"Okay, when I said you could work back here, I didn't know you were doing candles," Gwyn said, crossing her arms over her chest as Sam and Cait flashed each other slightly guilty looks.

"Well," Sam said, "we thought if we told you, you'd say no. And this is the *best* place to work on witchy stuff!"

Gwyn couldn't disagree with her there. She'd always loved the back room of Something Wicked. They might call it "storage," but it was actually a magical space, cozy and lush with velvet curtains and flickering sconces on the wall, thick carpets underfoot. A light enchantment kept customers from ever wandering back into it, and Vivi, Gwyn, and Elaine all took turns magically redecorating it to their tastes. Right now, it was still in Vivi mode, but Gwyn had added a few touches of her own. A hanging plant in one corner, a window just to the left where it always appeared to be raining.

So she couldn't blame the Baby Witches for wanting to hang out in here. *And* as someone who had lived most of her life asking forgiveness rather than permission, Gwyn figured this was karma.

"What exactly seems fucked up?" she asked, sitting down in their circle.

Parker handed her a candle, the wax still lumpy and a little warm in her hand. "It just feels wrong," they said, flicking their dark hair out of their eyes. "I was trying to give it a calming enchantment, you know. So when it's lit, you feel all Zen. But I'm not feeling it."

Gwyn wasn't, either, and she closed her eyes, trying to get a sense of what was going on with the candle.

When she'd gotten back from Vivi's last night, she'd damn near exhausted herself trying out her magic. She'd used it to brew a pot of tea, she'd flicked her fingers and turned all the lights in the cabin on, then off again. She'd even given Sir Purrcival bright purple claws and a pretty striped bow perched between his ears. (He was still wearing it. When she'd tried to magick it away, he'd howled, "Pretty! Preeeetttty!" at her until the bow was restored.)

Whatever that little blip had been with the crystal, it was clearly just that—a fluke, a weird little moment—but there was still a little flicker of worry in the back of her mind as she summoned up her magic.

But it was working now, that familiar warmth spreading through her, and after a second, she smiled.

Opening her eyes, Gwyn handed the candle back to Parker. "Nothing wrong with the actual enchantment. It's there."

Parker breathed a sigh of relief, then frowned at the candle in their hand. "Then why—"

"It's just ugly," she told them. "That's what you're feeling. Your spellwork is good, your actual candle crafting is shit."

Cait hooted at that. "Tell 'em, Glinda!"

Parker scowled, flipping Cait off. "Okay, I'm sorry that I didn't excel in arts and crafts at summer camp or whatever, but you heard Gwyn. The *spell* was good, and that's all that matters."

"Not exactly," Gwyn said, rising to her feet. "It's all the parts of a spell working together. Yes, the magic part was well done, but if no one wants to buy that candle, or they think it *kind* of looks like a melting penis, then the spell can't really do its job."

Parker still looked unhappy, but after a second, they nodded. "Okay. That makes sense."

"You should totally be teaching at the college, Gwyn," Sam said, her eyes practically shining behind her glasses. "You're way better at this stuff than our *actual* Ritual Candle Making teacher."

"Is it still Professor McNeil?" Gwyn asked. She remembered that class and the frankly terrifying woman who had taught it. She'd passed, of course, but by the skin of her teeth.

The three witches all gave the same glum nods, and Gwyn laughed, patting Sam's shoulder. "You'll survive, promise. And Penhaven already claimed one of the Jones witches. It can't have another one."

"Still," Cait said, picking up another handful of wax chunks and tossing them into the cauldron. "Thank you, Glinda."

Gwyn smiled back at her, and okay, maybe she did feel a little warm and fuzzy at the thought of teaching these kids. Didn't mean she wanted to work at the college, but she had to admit, it was nice, sharing her knowledge, seeing the admiration in their faces.

She should have them come by and work on their spells more often.

The wax roiled in the cauldron, a fat bubble bursting on the surface and splattering onto the carpet with a faint sizzle that made Cait shriek as Parker scooted back, and Sam leaned away, upsetting a bowl of herbs, little bits of green flying everywhere.

Okay, so maybe they needed to find a new place to practice magic.

From out front, Gwyn heard the raven over the door caw and turned back to the witches with a pointed finger. "If you burn my store down while I'm out there, I will turn you all into newts."

"That's not really a thing," Parker said, and Gwyn narrowed her eyes at them.

"Do you want to test that theory?"

"We don't," all three said in unison, and Gwyn gave a firm nod. "Good."

It really was hard work being a matriarch.

Swishing back the curtain, Gwyn stepped out into the store.

"Gwyn!"

Gwyn hadn't seen Morgan Howell in ten years, but she recognized her instantly. Her hair was shorter, cut in a sleek bob, and she was wearing an outfit that *looked* simple but probably cost more than the mortgage on the cabin.

She also had maybe the best red lipstick Gwyn had ever seen, which automatically raised her even more points in Gwyn's eyes.

"Morgan!" she said, stepping forward and into the other woman's hug. "What brings you back to Graves Glen?"

It wasn't unusual, seeing witches who once went to the college.

Not many stayed in Graves Glen, but they usually made their way back at some point if only to visit.

Gwyn assumed that's what Morgan was doing, so she was surprised when Morgan replied, "It was time for a change of pace."

She pulled back, still holding Gwyn's shoulders. "I heard you were still running this store, and I had to come pick something up for myself."

Gwyn laughed, nodding at the shelf Morgan was standing next to.

"You did not strike me as a glow-in-the-dark-stickers-on-the-ceiling kind of gal, but I *do* love being surprised."

Glancing over, Morgan picked up one of the packets. Her nails were the same deep red as her lips, and on her finger a cabochon emerald ring set in antique gold caught the light.

"Are these big sellers?" she asked, and Gwyn nodded.

"Trust me, cheap plastic stuff keeps the lights on every year. Stars, pumpkins, little cauldrons . . . "

Morgan watched her for a moment, her dark eyes thoughtful. "And this is all that's in the store? These kinds of . . . trinkets?"

Gwyn wasn't nuts about that word or the way Morgan said it, but defending a blinking pumpkin that had *BOO!* written on it was not exactly the hill she wanted to die on.

"Yup," she replied, keeping her tone cheerful. "Too dangerous to sell the real stuff. We get too many tourists, and there's already such strong magic in the town. Not worth the risk."

Morgan raised her eyebrows, a corner of her mouth kicking up. "I don't know. The best magic is always a little risky, right?"

Now Gwyn's eyebrows went up. Was Morgan flirting with her? Because that was the kind of sexy-but-dangerous line someone usually delivered before moving in a little closer, eyes dropping to lips and all that.

But Morgan was staring straight into her eyes, and Gwyn made herself laugh as she said, "Why does that sound like the opening pitch for some kind of magic-based multilevel marketing scheme?"

Morgan smiled, but her eyes never left Gwyn's. "I'm serious!" she said. "Don't you ever do anything a little heavier than this? I remember you being wildly talented. That leaf in Dr. Arbuthnot's class! It took me ten years before I could do a transformation spell like that, and even then, it wasn't nearly as impressive as yours."

Gwyn liked flattery as much as the next gal, but there was something a little avid in Morgan's gaze she didn't like, something that made her uneasy.

"What can I say, I peaked early," she said, then gestured to the street outside. "Now I use my talents on things like town planning committees."

Morgan took in the fluttering banner proclaiming the Graves Glen Gathering, coming soon, and drummed her nails on the shelf in front of her. "I forgot about all of the festivals and parties and things the town does."

She turned back to Gwyn and flashed a bright smile. "Maybe I can help."

"Sure," Gwyn said, wondering yet again why these faint alarm bells seemed to be ringing in her head. "I know Jane—that's our mayor—can always use extra hands."

Morgan nodded at that and then, after a second, picked up several packs of the stars. "And you know what, maybe I *am* a glow-in-the-dark-stickers-on-the-ceiling kind of gal," she said. "Only one way to find out."

"Solid choice. I'd suggest seeing if you're also a papier-mâché-witch's-hat kind of gal, but baby steps."

They made their way over to the register, and as Gwyn rang up Morgan's purchases, Morgan leaned on the counter, her sandalwood perfume filling the air. "I actually had an ulterior motive for coming in here today," she said, then reached into her bag, pulling out an envelope.

Gwyn's name was written in curling letters across the front, and as she took it, Morgan's fingers brushed hers briefly. "I'm throwing a little get-together at my house this Friday. A sort of housewarming thing. I'd love it if you could come."

Gwyn studied the envelope, her eyebrows shooting up at the heavy wax seal on the back. "I take it this is a wine and fancy dresses kind of party rather than a backyard barbecue," she said, and Morgan laughed.

"It's over the top, I know, but *c'est moi.*"

"No, it's great," Gwyn said. "I'd love to come."

"Excellent!" Morgan replied, taking her bag of stick-on stars from Gwyn. "Then I'll see you Friday."

She paused for a moment, her brow wrinkling as she sniffed the air. "Is . . . someone's hair on fire?"

"*ThankyoufortheinviteenjoyyourstickersseeyouFriday!*" Gwyn all but shouted as she dashed out from behind the counter and threw open the storage room curtain.

Sam, Cait, and Parker were all standing right there near the doorway, looking sheepish, and Cait was holding the end of her braid. Smoke still coiled about the candle Parker was clutching, and Sam whispered, "I don't even know what a newt is. It's a lizard, right? I really don't want to be a lizard."

Glaring at the three of them, Gwyn hissed, "What did I say about not burning things?"

"We're sorry!" Cait said. "But . . . ohmigod, did *Morgan Howell* just invite you to *her house?*"

All three of them were watching her with expectant faces, and Gwyn wrinkled her nose. "Why did you say her name like that? Like she's a movie star or one of those people that makes the little videos you keep sending me?"

"Morgan Howell is better than any movie star *or* influencer," Parker said. "She's, like . . . the coolest witch ever."

"The other day," Sam rushed in, "she came into the Coffee Cauldron, and I asked her what lipstick she wears, and it's not even a brand you can buy. Someone makes it *just for her.*"

"A friend of mine said that he heard that when she was living in London, her coven actually got kicked out of the country because they were doing magic that was way too hard-core," Cait said, her eyes bright. "We're talking necromancy, curse work, love spells . . . "

"I knew they were real," Gwyn muttered, and when Cait just blinked at her, she shook her head.

"I knew Morgan in college, and she was a good witch, but she wasn't *that* good. And honestly, none of that stuff is anything you should be admiring. It's dangerous."

Sam, Cait, and Parker all tried to look properly chastised, but Gwyn wasn't fooled.

"I'm serious," she added. "All three of you were around last year when that curse Vivi and I did went so haywire. We're lucky we were able to fix it, and it took every bit of magic we had. The three of you are just dazzled by admittedly *excellent* makeup and a very cool wardrobe."

Gwyn didn't add that she was maybe just the *teeniest* bit jealous of how starstruck her Baby Witches seemed over Morgan. Hadn't they just been giving *her* the glowy faces and hero worship eyes a few minutes ago?

"Are you gonna go to her party?" Sam asked, and Gwyn looked back over her shoulder toward the store, thinking of that heavy invitation sitting on the counter. She'd always liked Morgan, but she had to admit, there was something weird about her suddenly showing up. Why come back to Graves Glen now?

And with Vivi and Elaine out of town, if there was Witchy Fuckery afoot, it was up to her to get to the bottom of it.

"Oh, yeah," she told the witches. "I'm going."

CHAPTER 17

F riday night arrived quicker than Gwyn would've thought. The store had been busy, plus Sam, Cait, and Parker had had a test on moon phases in their Natural Magic class, and Gwyn had agreed to help them study for that. Then Sir Purrcival had a vet appointment for his annual checkup, Elaine had wanted to have a Skype chat, Vivi had called to check in . . .

It was honestly a wonder she'd remembered the party at all, but now here it was, Friday evening, and she was in her truck, following the directions on Morgan's fancy invitation.

The mountains and hills were a hazy blue against the last of the sunset, houses—any kind of building, really—getting sparser until Gwyn was driving down into a valley she had a vague memory of driving through before.

There hadn't been a house there, though, and Gwyn picked up the invitation again, checking that the directions were right. There was no address listed, just a vague bit at the bottom about "You'll see the house," and Gwyn peered out the windshield as the road narrowed, the rocky hills on either side of her blocking a view of anything else.

Then the road turned, widened, and Gwyn's mouth dropped open.

She saw the house, all right.

Apparently, whatever Morgan had been doing for the past decade had served her well because this wasn't just a *house*. It was like something out of a movie, the classier, less terrifying version of the Penhallow house.

Turrets pierced the violet sky, narrow windows spilling golden rectangles of light onto the lawn. Gwyn spotted a balcony over the alcove leading to a massive front door, and just behind the building, she could see a greenhouse, misted with condensation.

Cars were parked in neat rows in the field just beyond the house, and Gwyn slotted her red truck in next to a Mercedes. There were a lot of Mercedes, she noticed, as well as a couple of Audis and even a Rolls-Royce.

Rhiannon's tits, who all had Morgan invited to this thing?

The sharp heels of her boots pierced the grass as Gwyn stepped out of the truck and made her way to the house. As she approached the front steps, she heard a car door close behind her and turned.

It was already dusk, the light a soft purple, but she'd recognize that ramrod-straight posture anywhere, and when Wells stepped into the light spilling from the windows, she hated the way her heart gave an extra kick in her chest.

He was wearing a white button-down and dark pants, no vest

tonight, but back in that really, *really* good coat he'd had on the night he'd arrived in town, and she wondered if she had some heretofore-undiscovered kink for outerwear because honestly, this was getting ridiculous.

"Gwyn," he said, coming up short, and she didn't miss the way his eyes skated over her. It was subtle and, since it was Esquire, fairly respectful, but it was definitely there.

And she was suddenly glad she'd decided to wear the dress Vivi always referred to as "the sexy sorceress one." It was a blue so dark it was nearly black, and even though it had long sleeves and a skirt that would've brushed the ground if her boots hadn't had a slight heel, the front was cut low enough to show off a particularly pretty silver and sapphire pendant she'd picked up at a Beltane festival a few years ago.

She fought the urge to fiddle with that necklace now. Gwyn Jones was *not* a fidgeter, after all. She was the one who made *other* people fidget. So instead, she straightened her shoulders and gave him her best smile.

"Esquire," she replied, and a muscle ticked in his jaw.

"I see our truce doesn't extend to the nickname."

"Wasn't one of the terms."

He heaved a sigh, shoving his hands in the pockets of that damn coat, and walked closer, the gravel crunching underneath his shoes.

"I suppose I shouldn't be surprised to see you," he said. "It's clear this is a party exclusively for witches."

Gwyn didn't have to ask what he meant. She could feel it herself, the magic so heavy you could almost taste it. Everyone inside that house had power, and if she was judging it correctly, a *lot* of power at that.

Suddenly, a thought occurred to her, and her eyes widened. "Ohhh . . . this was your Not a Date Date," she said, and there was that muscle tic again.

"Now demonstrably proven to be Not a Date," Wells replied, gesturing at the house, and Gwyn shrugged, shifting the chain of her evening bag on her shoulder.

"For all we know, they're doing witchy speed dating in there." Wells visibly shuddered. "Christ, what a ghastly concept."

Gwyn was inclined to agree, not that she was going to let him know that. "Only one way to find out!"

He followed her up the steps, his tread heavy. "Did you know Morgan?" Wells asked. "Back at Penhaven?"

Surprised, Gwyn glanced back at him. "What, you didn't?"

Wells shook his head. "I assume I got an invite because of my last name."

"Well, that and she had a massive crush on you," Gwyn replied, and was gratified to see Wells look slightly surprised.

"What?"

"I know, I found it very hard to believe, too, but there truly is no accounting for taste!"

She'd expected one of the patented Wells Penhallow Scowls at that, but instead, he just shrugged. "I suppose she was a bit flirty when she came into the store."

That little nugget of information should not have bothered Gwyn in the slightest, so it was very annoying to feel her stomach do just the tiniest drop at thinking of Morgan—beautiful, mysterious Morgan—and Wells *flirting*. Did Wells even know how to flirt?

He sure as hell knew how to kiss.

Not a helpful thought right now.

From inside, Gwyn could hear the low sounds of people talking and distant music, and at her side, she sensed Wells steeling himself.

Clearly not a party person, Esquire, so why had he accepted the invitation?

She was just about to ask him when he turned to her, offering his arm. "Well," he said on a sigh. "Shall we?"

GWYN WAS STARING at his elbow like she'd never seen that particular bit of anatomy before, and Wells wondered if he should just drop it and knock on the door.

But after a beat, she laid her hand almost gingerly on his arm, fingers curling into his sleeve.

He could tell himself he was offering his arm just to be gentlemanly, but he wasn't that deluded. From the second he'd seen her standing there in that dress, the urge to touch her had been almost overwhelming. She looked like something out of legend, a siren, a sorceress, the kind of woman men happily went to their dooms for.

It was distracting as hell when he was meant to be here getting a better sense of what Morgan might want in Graves Glen, but then Gwyn Jones had been distracting and unsettling him from the moment he'd walked into this town.

He wondered if he should share with her his suspicions about Morgan, but Gwyn and Morgan were clearly old friends. She'd probably just roll her eyes at him again and tell him he was being an idiot. And it was very possible that he was, but an ounce of prevention was worth a pound of cure.

Wells frowned and made a mental note never to actually say that out loud in front of her.

Raising one hand, he went to knock on the door, but as he did, it eased open on its own, revealing a front hall lit up beneath a sparkling chandelier.

The music and talking were louder now, and Wells moved inside cautiously, Gwyn's hand in the crook of his elbow.

That feeling he'd had outside of an almost overwhelming amount of magic was even stronger now, and at his side, Gwyn took a deep breath, her head swiveling from one side to the other as she took in their surroundings.

The front hallway was massive, soaring up at least two stories. There was a staircase just ahead of them carpeted in deep red, almost the same shade of the lipstick Morgan had been wearing the other day, and the floor underfoot was a dark wood so shiny, Wells could practically see his reflection in it.

Rooms opened off the hallway, and Wells chose the one on their right, a drawing room with gilded furniture and gold silk wallpaper.

It had been a while since Wells had been to a party, and as he stepped into the room, he remembered why exactly that was.

There were just . . . so many people.

Groups of them, standing around holding champagne flutes or cocktail glasses, talking, draped over furniture, laughing. Over a dozen in this room, at least, and Wells had gotten a glimpse of another drawing room, similarly crowded.

He'd been worried about maybe being a little overdressed tonight, but as Wells glanced around, he saw that, for perhaps the first time in his life, he was actually the casual one. There were two men in tuxes chatting next to a piano, and several in the formal robes his father favored. Almost every woman was dressed similarly to Gwyn, in clinging gowns with low necks and subtly shimmering jewelry.

Next to him, Gwyn leaned in a little closer, her long hair brushing his sleeve. "Okay, if I didn't know for sure that vampires weren't real, I would *definitely* think these people were vampires."

Wells glanced down at her, screwing up his face in confusion. "Vampires are real."

Gwyn's head jerked up, her eyes going wide. "Wait, seriously?"

"How do you not know that?"

"Because I've never seen one!"

"And I've never seen the Loch Ness Monster, but I still know she exists," he said with a sniff, and Gwyn's eyes somehow, impossibly, got even bigger.

"Nessie's real, too?"

Wells held his pompous stance as long as he could, but the absolute shock in her voice had his lip twitching, and when her eyes narrowed at him, he couldn't help but smirk, and then that smirk actually became a laugh as she hip-checked him.

"Okay, you know what? Just for that, when these weirdos pick someone to ritually sacrifice tonight, I am absolutely volunteering you."

"No less than I deserve," he replied, and she smiled a little, shaking her head.

"I hate when you make me like you, Esquire."

"I'll endeavor to be more unlikable in the future," he promised, and Gwyn snorted.

"Sentences like that help."

A waiter passed by then, holding a tray of champagne flutes, and Wells and Gwyn each took one, Gwyn's hand finally dropping from his arm.

He felt the loss of that touch more than he wanted to admit, so to distract himself, Wells studied their fellow partygoers. He didn't expect to recognize anyone, so he was more than a little shocked when he spotted a familiar face. Bronwyn Davies was a member of one of Cardiff's most influential witch families, a pretty blonde Simon had once hoped Wells might be betrothed to. She'd decided not to marry anyone, as far as Wells knew, and he hadn't seen her in ages. What was she doing here?

And there, near the large bay window, he recognized Connell Thomas, another Welsh witch he'd known briefly at Penhaven.

"Is this supposed to be a reunion?" Gwyn murmured, and when he looked over at her, she gestured with her glass.

"These are Penhaven witches," she said. "From our year. And what would've been your year, I guess, if you'd stayed."

She'd barely finished her sentence before there was a squeal, and a tall brunette was crossing the room, arms spread wide. "Gwynnevere Jones!" she cried, and Gwyn smiled back, letting herself be pulled into the woman's embrace. "Hi, Rosa," she said, and as she pulled back, she nodded at Wells.

"You remember Llewellyn Penhallow. Or maybe you don't, I don't know. He isn't all that memorable, really."

Rosa laughed at that even as Wells shot Gwyn a look before offering his hand to Rosa.

"It's Wells, and it's lovely to meet you."

"Oh, I remember you," Rosa all but purred, her dark eyes bright as she smiled at him, and though he couldn't be certain, he thought Gwyn's shoulders might have stiffened just the tiniest bit.

Biting back an unattractive amount of smugness, Wells smiled back at Rosa. "I'm afraid I was something of an idiot during my brief time at Penhaven. That's the only excuse I can think of for not remembering you."

Rosa gave a pleased chuckle, and Wells was very sure Gwyn was now gritting her teeth.

"Well, we're all reunited now," Rosa said. Wells wasn't sure how exactly she made such innocuous words sound so . . . promising, but there you had it.

Slinging back the rest of her champagne, Gwyn turned to the two of them, smile fixed in place. "I will leave you two to get reacquainted while I go find Morgan and say hello."

Wells watched her retreating back—and the eyes of every other man and quite a few women in the room did the same.

"She was always something," Rosa said, then nodded in Gwyn's direction in case Wells had missed her meaning. "Gorgeous *and* smart *and* powerful. I couldn't believe it when I heard she stayed in this Podunk town, selling cheap tchotchkes to the humans. Such a waste."

Wells clenched his jaw, his fingers going tight around his champagne flute. "And yet," he said, the words clipped, "it's her magic currently fueling this town. And frankly, even if it weren't, the life Ms. Jones has built for herself here hardly seems wasteful to me. Her store is a lovely place that brings happiness to everyone who enters it. We should all be so lucky to provide such a thing. Now, if you'll excuse me."

He moved away from Rosa, her lips slightly parted in surprise, and plunged deeper into the party.

A waste.

If that term applied to anyone, it was him. Spending his time doing his father's bidding. No, what Gwyn had done was use her magic in a way that made her and those she cared about happy. That was downright bloody noble when you thought about it.

Pausing in front of a table set up with tiny plates of canapés, Wells sighed.

Making up excuses to touch her and now defending her honor in public. He truly was a hopeless case.

Glancing around now, he tried to spot Gwyn's red hair, but she was nowhere to be seen. Neither was Morgan, and Wells slipped out of the drawing room into another long hallway.

It was dim and deserted here, but that sense he'd had outside the house, like magic was lying in heavy waves all around, was stronger here.

And not just strong.

Wrong.

This had always been Wells's skill set, sussing out the tenor of magic, what kind of spell was being used, the intent behind it. Whatever was happening in this house wasn't dark or evil, exactly, but it wasn't good, either. It was like a discordant note in an otherwise beautiful symphony, and the farther he walked down the hall, the stronger it got.

He came to a door at the very end of the hall, right next to a rather lovely landscape painting of mountains and fields that reminded him of home.

From back in the drawing room, Wells could still hear the low murmur of conversation, and someone had started playing the piano.

Looking around him one more time, Wells curled his fingers around the doorknob, twisting it slowly.

The door opened soundlessly, and breathing a sigh of relief, Wells darted in, closing the door as quietly as he could behind him.

A light blazed on, nearly blinding him, and he threw up a hand against the glare even as his heart pounded hard in his ears.

He'd say he was looking for the loo. He'd say he took a wrong turn. He'd—

"Esquire?"

CHAPTER 18

W hat are you doing here?" Gwyn whispered from a staircase as she quickly extinguished her light spell, plunging them back into near darkness. There was a window somewhere at the top of those stairs letting in just enough moonlight to barely make him out there by the door. She'd nearly had a heart attack when that door had opened, already plotting excuses for why she was in here, so she was relieved it was Wells.

And also surprised.

And also kind of annoyed.

Apparently, mixed feelings were going to be the norm around him.

"What are *you* doing here?" Wells countered now, and Gwyn rolled her eyes, gesturing at the stairs in front of her.

"I was obviously about to go sneaking around because something about this place is—"

"Extremely off-putting and dubious in nature, yes," Wells replied, and Gwyn stepped back a little, the banister pressing into her hip.

"I was going to say 'super fucking creepy and sus,' but I guess that's technically the same thing, yeah."

They stood there for a moment, staring at each other while Gwyn attempted to come to grips with the fact that A) she and Esquire were agreeing on something, B) whatever was up with Morgan and this house, he felt it, too, and C) he just smelled . . . really, really good.

Telling herself that C very much did not matter right now, Gwyn turned her attention back to the stairs.

"Why did you come up here?" she asked Wells, keeping her voice low even though she could still hear the sounds of the party in the other room. "Like, why this door specifically?"

"I'm assuming the same reason you did," he said as he braced one hand on the stairwell wall. "Whatever it is that we're both picking up on, it seems to be emanating from this area."

Gwyn nodded even as she wrinkled her brow, looking up into the looming darkness ahead of them. "You know, I would've thought Morgan might be a little more original than this. If you're going to do some kind of dark magic, don't do it in the most obvious place in the whole house, right? 'Ooh, I know, I'll raise demons or whatever in a terrifying attic!'"

"I feel like you might be stalling a bit."

"I am most definitely stalling a bit," Gwyn replied on a sigh. Honestly, couldn't her witchery go back to mostly involving tea and paint? Did she *have* to keep risking spiderwebs in her hair?

She started to make her way up the stairs, but Wells stopped her with a hand on her arm, that signet ring of a weight she could feel even through the fabric of her dress. "I'll go first," he told her, and Gwyn raised her eyebrows.

"Esquire, I'm shocked! Isn't 'Ladies First' a sacred rule of etiquette?"

"Normally, yes," he said, not rising to the bait. "But it does seem like bad form to insist on it when said lady might be the *first* to walk directly into some kind of magical trap."

"Gallant," Gwyn allowed. "But unnecessary."

With that, she turned, making her way gingerly up the steps. They creaked underfoot as she rose higher and higher, Wells a solid presence at her back, and Gwyn told herself it was nerves making her mouth suddenly dry.

The stairs ended, opening onto a looming dark space, that one window providing a little bit of light but not nearly enough. Gwyn could make out a plank floor and several hulking shapes but nothing else, so lifting her fingers, she went to summon up a ball of light again.

Earlier, it had worked fine, but now, there was a sort of fizzle of sparks from the tips of her fingers, and that was it.

"Problem?" Wells asked, and she shook her head, wiggling her fingers again, waiting to feel the magic course through her. It was there, she could sense it, but . . . sluggish. Just like that night at Vivi's.

Maybe it's whatever magic Morgan has going on in here, she told herself, *maybe it's blocking me.*

But that thought didn't make her feel any better.

Once was a fluke.

Two times? That was the start of a pattern, and one she did not like at all.

"It's probably the magic in this house," Wells said, and she glanced back at him. He was watching her hand, brow slightly furrowed, but he wasn't attempting a light spell of his own. He was waiting on her to get it together.

That was . . . sweet. Respectful.

Ugh.

Pushing those disturbingly squishy feelings aside, Gwyn concentrated on her spell, and after a moment, there was a sort of sputtering noise, and the ball of light flared to life, hovering just beside her.

"Well done, Jones," Wells murmured, and Gwyn gave a satisfied—and relieved—nod.

"Figured we needed to see what we were doing," she said, but then she really looked around and kind of wished the light spell hadn't worked.

The rest of the house was elegant if a little—okay, a lot—over the top. But the attic?

The attic was downright spooky.

Paintings were stacked haphazardly against one wall, all of them, as far as Gwyn could tell, depicting some dark and horrible moments in witchcraft history. Burnings, drownings, eviscerations.

Heavy black trunks with rusted locks were clustered in a group toward the center of the room, and there was a pile of what appeared to be thumbscrews just beneath the window. Shelves with dusty bottles lined the back wall, and when Gwyn moved closer to those, a figure loomed out of the darkness, making her yelp and jump back before noticing that it wasn't a person, it was a . . .

"Is that an iron maiden?" she asked, staring in fascinated horror at the person-size metal form in front of her.

"Bloody fucking hell," Wells muttered, coming to stand next to her and examine the thing himself, his hands in his pockets as he rocked back on his heels.

"Strong words from Esquire," Gwyn replied, and he looked over at her, his expression wry.

"Warranted, wouldn't you say?"

"Oh, fuck yeah," she replied, and there was a brief flash of white teeth in that dark beard, a Genuine Esquire Smile, which made her want to say other things that might make him smile like that again.

But given that they'd apparently stepped into Hellraiser's lair, now probably wasn't the time for jokes.

Instead, Gwyn gestured around them and said, "Do you think we're just picking up on bad vibes from this stuff? Because the vibes in here are definitely bad. Vibe check thoroughly failed."

"I don't really know what that means," Wells said slowly, "but I think I get the gist, and yes, that's definitely possible."

Then he frowned. "But why have a collection like this at all?"

Wells turned more fully toward her, the light from her spell playing over his face, his gaze serious. "How well did you know Morgan at university?"

"We were friends," Gwyn said, "but not super close. It was . . . I don't know, a college friendship. We had a lot of the same classes, ate lunch together in the dining hall sometimes, had a slightly drunken make-out at an Ostara celebration." She shrugged. "You know. College."

Wells stared at her for a beat and then said, "Right. Okay. All of that is . . . right." Then he shook his head slightly, turning back to study the paintings against the wall. "Did she seem interested in this sort of thing back then?"

"She did not have ancient torture devices in her dorm room as far as I recall, no," Gwyn replied, shivering a little as she looked back over at the iron maiden. "But then, we weren't in that many classes together after sophomore year. I was majoring in Practical Magic, and she was doing . . . I don't remember. One of the weirder ones, like Ritual Witchcraft, I think. And then our senior year—"

Gwyn stopped, and Wells turned back to her. "Then what?"

She'd forgotten about it until just now, had never really thought about it, not even when Morgan had reappeared, but now, a memory resurfaced. "She left," Gwyn said, thinking. "In the middle of our last semester. Like I said, we weren't close, and by that point, I hardly ever saw her, but I remember one of my friends telling me a handful of students were asked to leave for some reason. She didn't know why, it was all kind of secretive, and I've gotta be honest, I wasn't too interested in it since it didn't seem all that scandalous. I mean, 'asked to leave' is not exactly *expelled,* right?"

Wells rubbed a hand over his chin, considering all that as

Gwyn racked her brain, trying to come up with any other details. But it had been a decade ago, and like she said, she hadn't paid all that much attention to it at the time.

She glanced around her again.

Clearly, she should have.

"I wonder if any of those other students are here tonight," Wells mused, and Gwyn looked back toward the stairs.

"I can't remember how many of them it was. Maybe five? But Rosa, she was definitely one of them."

"Hmm," was Wells's only response, and Gwyn turned back to him, hugging herself against the chill in the attic.

"What are you thinking with that thinky face?"

He dropped his hand, brows drawing together. "All right, is that an American saying, or is it just unique to this place?" he asked, and before she had time to ask what he meant, he shook his head, waving it off. "Never mind. Before I came here, I had a visit from my brother Bowen."

"Werewolf Brother," Gwyn said, nodding, and Wells narrowed his eyes at her slightly before conceding, "The beard is a lot. In any case, he told me that when a place like Graves Glen, somewhere with literal magic running through it, undergoes the kind of transformation that this town did last year, it can make it a kind of magnet for other witches who might not have the best intentions."

Well, nothing about that sounded good.

Still, Gwyn had to admit it made sense. Magic was unpredictable and volatile, and she could see where something as massive as a change in power would ping some kind of witchy radar.

"And you think that might be why Morgan has suddenly shown up?"

"I think we need to find out exactly why she was asked to leave Penhaven ten years ago," he replied, and Gwyn grinned at him.

"So we're going to be detectives, huh? *Magical* detectives."

"I wouldn't go quite that far," he replied dryly, then nodded in the direction of the stairs. "And we should probably get back to that party before someone notices we're gone."

Gwyn followed him down the stairs, twisting her fingers as she did, the light spell vanishing. "Jones and Esquire, Magical Detectives," she mused, and he threw her a dark look over his shoulder.

"Penhallow and Jones."

"Jones and Penhallow."

"Penhallow, full stop."

"Jones and Son."

Wells stopped just at the bottom of the stairs and turned to her, head tilted slightly to one side before his expression cleared. "Ah. The cat."

"Sir Purrcival would be an asset to any case."

He snorted at that and had just reached the bottom step, Gwyn coming to stand beside him, when they heard footsteps.

Voices.

Very, very close voices.

And now the footsteps had stopped outside the door, and yes, that was definitely Morgan saying, "I've actually been storing it up here."

There wasn't any time to think, but Gwyn had always preferred to be a woman of action.

Turning to face Wells, she grabbed the lapels of his jacket and yanked him close.

"What in—" he started, but before he could say anything else, she pressed her mouth to his.

CHAPTER 19

*R*hiannon's tits.

Wells had spent the past couple of weeks telling himself that kiss in the cellar had not been as good as he remembered it, that it had rattled him so much simply because he hadn't kissed a woman in ages before that.

But as Gwyn's lips parted underneath his, he understood that such thinking had been deeply, deeply stupid.

No, that kiss had been so bloody devastating because *she* was so bloody devastating, and he was in very serious trouble now.

Not that Wells gave a flying fuck.

His hands landed on her hips, the material of that dress—that *dress;* he'd nearly swallowed his tongue when he'd seen her outside the house this evening—just as soft as he'd thought it would be. Better, though, the warmth of her skin making the fabric even more touchable, even more irresistible, and Wells couldn't help the sound he made, low in his throat, as he pulled her closer.

The rational part of his brain, the part that remembered she was only kissing him so that they had plausible deniability for skulking around, was quickly being overwhelmed by that darker, more primal part of him that only she seemed to bring out.

And maybe he brought something out in her, too, because she was pushing closer to him, her arms twining around his neck, her breasts tight against his chest, and her tongue—

"Oh! Sorry about that!"

The attic stairs were suddenly illuminated by a bright rectangle of light as the door opened, a figure silhouetted there.

Gwyn pulled away and it took everything in Wells not to chase her mouth with his own, but then she pressed her palm against his chest, giving a breathless laugh as she turned to face Morgan.

"Oh god, *we're* sorry," she said, then looked back at Wells, tugging her lower lip between her teeth and giving the impression of someone who was genuinely a little sheepish. Performance of a lifetime, clearly, because he doubted Gwynnevere Jones had ever been sheepish in her life.

"We were just admiring your gorgeous house, and I think that *very* lovely wine you served must've gotten to us," Gwyn continued, letting her arm drape naturally around Wells's shoulders as he rested his palm on her hip, fighting the urge to curl his fingers tighter, to bring her right up against him.

Morgan looked at them, her dark eyes taking in everything, Wells was pretty sure, and even as she smiled, there was a brittleness to it. Was it simply because she—sensibly—was not a huge fan of people snogging each other's face off in the private areas of her home, or was it something more? Was it to do with what she had up here in the attic?

"It was appallingly rude of us, Morgan," Wells offered, maneuvering Gwyn down the last step and wondering if he could channel Rhys enough to charm his way out of this.

Morgan just waved a hand. "No, no, not at all! I'm just surprised."

She turned that dark gaze on Wells. "I did ask you if the two of you were together. Don't tell me you lied to me, Llewellyn Penhallow."

Lying seemed a far lesser sin than collecting dark magical artifacts, but what did he know?

"It's new," Gwyn offered now, her fingers tightening just the littlest bit on his shoulder as though she could sense what he wanted to say.

"Very, very new," Wells confirmed, patting her hip lightly. *Message received.*

Her grip loosened a bit, and she gestured toward the door. "And hi! You're . . . "

For the first time, Wells realized there was someone standing just behind Morgan, a man around the same age as all of them, blond hair scraped severely back from a rather narrow face.

"Harrison Phelps," he said, offering his hand to shake. "And we actually knew each other back at Penhaven. You're Gwyn Jones."

"Oh, right!" Gwyn said brightly, but Wells had a feeling she had no idea who this man was.

"And Llewellyn Penhallow," Harrison continued, shaking Wells's hand next. "We never met, but of course I knew you by reputation."

Whether Harrison meant his *family's* reputation or the brief bit of glory Wells had managed to bring on himself at Penhaven, he wasn't sure, but he nodded all the same, giving the man a tight smile.

"Quite the reunion you've put together, Morgan," Gwyn said, and Morgan smiled, her teeth very white against those red lips.

"I was feeling nostalgic, I guess," she said. "And it seemed like the right time to revisit old friends. Old haunts."

Wells was about to ask why that was when Morgan said, "Now, if the two of you will excuse us, I had something I wanted to show Harrison in the attic."

Looking between the two of them, her smile still fixed firmly in place, she asked, "Did the two of you head up there?"

Wells had to hand it to her—she did a decent job of keeping that question light, but there was something in her eyes he didn't like, something that made it clear she wanted, needed, perhaps, the answer to be no.

"Oh god, no," Gwyn said, laughing a little and raising one hand to her cheek. "To be honest, we're lucky we got the door closed behind us before we . . . well."

She smirked a little, cheeks still flushed, and Wells felt the tips of his ears go hot, which was ridiculous. He was a grown man, and they'd only been kissing, but she put so much suggestion into that "well" that he was half hard just from one bloody syllable.

Not just ridiculous, *pathetic.*

Wells stepped out of the stairwell, Gwyn just behind him, and gave Morgan a little nod as he said, "And on that note, I think we'll take our leave."

Until he figured out just what Morgan and her friends had been kicked out of Penhaven College for, it seemed safer to spend as little time in their company as possible, plus the magic in this place was starting to make his head ache, a tension building between his shoulder blades, a dull sort of weight behind his eyes. The quicker they got out of here, the better.

"Normally I'd be saying 'leaving so soon?' but in this case, I'll allow it," Morgan said with a wink, and Gwyn once again moved to Wells's side. It was a little alarming how much he enjoyed that and how natural it felt to once again slide an arm around her.

"Let's get together next week," she said to Morgan. "I'd love to catch up."

"Of course," Morgan practically trilled, but Wells didn't miss the way her eyes were going to the attic again or the nervous energy radiating off Harrison.

Yes, something was definitely afoot here.

GWYN WASN'T SURE she'd ever been so happy to leave a party, and given that she'd once had to go to a wedding reception where both the bride and the groom were her exes, that was saying something.

"Can you actually die from a case of the heebie-jeebies?" she asked Wells as they stepped out onto the front porch. She still had her hand loosely in his, part of their whole "We're a couple!" schtick, as they'd made their way out of the party, but there was no one around out here, so no reason, really, to keep holding hands.

But he wasn't letting go and neither was she and now, as they walked down the front steps, she let her gaze linger for just a second on his profile in the moonlight, that sharp nose and strong jaw, and why in the name of all that was holy had she kissed him again?

It was the best excuse for why y'all were being sneaky! And it worked!

But even as her brain offered up those very true and factual facts, Gwyn knew it wasn't quite that simple.

And now that she knew that kiss in the cellar, magic fueled or no, hadn't been some kind of Freak of Kissing Nature, she wasn't sure how she was supposed to spend time with him and *not* want to kiss him.

Which, given that they had Witchy Duties to fulfill together, was a pretty major issue.

For now, though, Gwyn let her hand casually drop from his, crossing the lawn to where her truck was parked.

That shiny BMW of his was just behind her, and they paused for a moment, Wells thrusting his hands into the pockets of his coat.

"So," he said, clearing his throat and shooting her a sideways glance briefly before looking somewhere in the middle distance. "First step, find out why Morgan and the others were asked to leave Penhaven. I can attempt that on my own, or *you* could, really, there's no reason for us to team up on this when you—"

"This doesn't have to be weird," Gwyn interrupted, leaning against the back of her truck, and he swung his head back around to face her again. "It's only weird if we *make* it weird."

Wells tilted his head. "I wasn't making it weird. I think you're making it weird by suggesting we not make it weird."

Then he frowned. "I really want to stop saying 'weird' now."

Gwyn laughed at that, tucking her hair behind her ear even as she watched him from the side of her eye. She really did laugh . . . kind of a lot with Wells. And that, weirdly, seemed somehow even more dangerous than a couple of good kisses.

But for now, she shook her hair back off her shoulders and said, "Look, it makes more sense to work on this together. Otherwise we'll spend all our time looking into the same stuff, then telling the other what we found out, and having to be, like, 'Yeah, I already knew that,' and by then, Morgan and her friends might have opened up a Hellmouth or something."

"You do have a way of getting to the heart of things, Jones," he said with a slight smile, and Gwyn grinned at him.

"It's my specialty. And yes, I get the kissing thing makes it a little awkward, but it's not like we *wanted* to kiss each other. First kiss?" She lifted up her thumb. "Magic spell. Second kiss?" She lifted her second finger. "A tactical strategy to get us out of a sticky spot."

Wiggling the rest of the fingers of that hand, Gwyn added, "The way I see it, unless we end up in some kind of weird situation where we have to kiss to save the world *or* one of us needs to give the other CPR, I think we can avoid each other's mouth while trying to protect Graves Glen."

Gwyn was proud of herself for how sensible she sounded, how completely unbothered.

Heck, she'd presented such a good case, *she* almost believed it.

Whether or not Wells did, she had no idea. His expression was neutral, and it was too dark to read his eyes.

"So we're agreed," Gwyn went on. "This is a joint effort."

Wells sighed and looked up at the sky for a moment before finally nodding. "Agreed. Penhallow and Jones it is."

"Jones and Esquire."

But she smiled as she said it, and when he did, too, she felt her pulse kick up. "Shall we shake on this as well?" he asked, leaning back against his own car. "Or, given that we'd informally agreed to work together in the attic, maybe that kiss was meant to seal the deal as it were?"

Gwyn wet her lips, not missing the way his eyes dropped to follow the movement. "That kiss," she said, trying not to sound as turned on as she felt, "was a distraction for Morgan and the creepy ventriloquist doll she's apparently magicked into a real live boy."

Wells chuckled, and even that low sound was enough to have her clenching her fingers in her skirt so that she wouldn't do something crazy like step forward and touch him.

But he straightened up, his stare not quite as intense now, the mood broken.

"Fair enough," he said, turning away and opening his car door.

Gwyn went around to the driver's side of her truck and was just unlocking it when Wells said, "Edible body glitter."

Gwyn's key scratched the red paint near the handle, missing the lock completely.

"Excuse me?"

Wells was still standing there, his car door open, his arm resting along the top of it as he watched her. "That's what was in that bag. The one that fell on us," he said, and Gwyn felt something unsettlingly swoopy in her stomach as she straightened up, keys still clutched in her hand.

"There was a mix-up," he went on, "and I got a box from some place called the Pleasure Palace."

Gwyn should have had a joke for that. That was the *perfect* setup for a joke, but all she could do was stare at Wells as he stared back.

"You're making that up," she finally said, and even though she couldn't make out his expression, she could practically *hear* his quirked eyebrow.

"Do you really think I'd make up 'the Pleasure Palace'?"

She had to admit that was unlikely, but her kissing Wells that night just because she'd *wanted to* went past unlikely and into inconceivable territory, so she had to press it.

"It still had to be a spell," she insisted. "Maybe . . . maybe one got in there accidentally, and—"

"Oh, I thought that, too, for a bit. Hoped, even. But I promise you, there is nothing magical at all about Pixie Licks. It's just—"

"Edible body glitter," she finished for him, and he nodded. "QED."

Another perfect time for a joke, but nothing was coming to her, nothing but a kind of whooshing noise in her brain, because it *had* to have been a spell that night. She'd been out of her mind with wanting him, and up until that very second, she hadn't given a single thought to Wells Freaking Penhallow in any kind of sexy sense.

Except . . .

That moment at The Cider Shack. And how he looked behind the counter at Penhallow's. And a hundred other little moments that were now flashing through her mind.

"So," Wells summed up, clearing his throat again. "While I can't disagree that tonight's kiss had an ulterior motive, I'm afraid that first one was in fact real."

She wished it weren't so dark, wished she could see his face more clearly because it suddenly seemed very important to know how he was looking at her.

Swallowing hard, Gwyn tightened her grip on her keys. "I'll . . . take that into account the next time I'm calculating Kiss Risks for Jones and Esquire," she offered weakly.

He made that sound he sometimes did, that sort of huff that wasn't quite a laugh but was close enough. "You do that," he told her. "Good night, Gwyn."

And then he drove off, leaving Gwyn standing there, still holding her keys.

CHAPTER 20

It was, Wells reflected the following Monday, somewhat distressing to have finally taken the crown of Family Jackass from Rhys.

His youngest brother had had such a good run, after all, but by telling Gwyn about the not-actually-a-spell love spell, Wells now had no doubt he was firmly in the lead. Bowen was going to have to accidentally blow up Snowdonia to have a chance.

Wells still couldn't say exactly why he'd done it except that there had been something about how dismissive she kept being about the whole thing that had rankled. He knew she'd been just as affected by those kisses as he had, had felt it in the way her body had molded against his, the boldness of her tongue, her lips. So maybe he'd wanted her to acknowledge that or, at the very least, deal with the same confusion and vague sense of alarm he'd felt ever since Rhys had handed him that blasted bag and laughed himself senseless.

In the cold light of day, however, Wells wasn't sure that had been the best idea. Surely it would have been better to let it lie, to let her believe that it was nothing more than a stupid bit of magic and move on. Gwyn might be attracted to him, but it seemed pretty clear to Wells she had no interest in actually pursuing that attraction, and besides, things were complicated enough. Her cousin—who might as well have been a sister—was married to his brother, they were all living in the same town, and they were all involved in the town's witchcraft in one way or another. None of those ties were easily broken.

What if they went on a few dates, and this . . . whatever it was between them fizzled out almost immediately? He'd be stuck seeing her every day, it would put Rhys and his Vivienne in an awkward position, and this rather nice new life Wells had built for himself would go up in smoke.

And if it *didn't* fizzle out . . .

Wells had no idea how his father would react to *two* of his sons being involved with the women he now considered the Penhallows' mortal enemies, and frankly shuddered to think of it.

Simon had called just the night before. Well, "called" meaning he'd shown up in the scrying mirror Wells had brought with him specifically for that purpose. It hadn't been the longest conversation, but Simon had managed to ask about "the Jones women" at least three times. Wells had reminded his father there was currently only one Jones woman in town, and then he'd lied and said he didn't see much of her.

To his surprise, his father hadn't liked that. "It makes sense to keep your enemies close, Llewellyn," he'd said, and Wells had barely refrained from rolling his eyes.

"She's not my enemy, Da," he'd said, and Simon had grumbled again about legacy and magic and "all the Penhallows have done for that town," which had given Wells a good opening to ask if his father had ever heard of any witches being kicked out of Penhaven College.

But Simon had waved that off. "The college is named after our home, but I've stayed out of its business ever since they introduced those ridiculous classes. Tea Leaves and the like." He'd snorted. "Rubbish."

Wells hadn't actually expected his father to be helpful, so he'd ended the call with a promise to "keep an eye on things," and didn't bother mentioning Morgan or his suspicions.

Next he'd tried the internet, and while he found some hints of Morgan's past—a review left on the website of a magical shop in Rome, her name on a list of donors to a secondary school in London—there wasn't much else. That didn't surprise him as most witches tried to stay under the radar.

He'd then spent some time flipping through various spellbooks in the house, wondering if there was any kind of clarity spell that might give him the answer even as he knew that would be tricky. Pulling out information someone didn't want you to know was definitely on the darker side of magic, so, as he'd suspected, a spell like that involved complicated ingredients that weren't easily on hand. The finger bone of a man hanged for treason, a bowl of water from a spring that had dried up one hundred and one days before, and, maybe most disturbingly, an eyeball.

Didn't specify whether it had to come from man or beast, but in either case, Wells decided magic wasn't going to be the way on this one.

Still, since things were slow at Penhallow's this afternoon, he was flipping through some other books he kept there in the shop, hoping he might come across another spell that would work and involve far less body parts.

He'd just landed on one that looked promising—although "piece of lace from a drowned bride's veil" was definitely going to present a challenge—when the bell over the door rang.

He hadn't seen Gwyn since Friday night, and it seemed pretty certain to him that she'd somehow spent the past two days getting even lovelier. Her hair fell around her face in long red waves, that pink streak faded a bit but still very much in evidence, and she was wearing some sort of long black sweater over leggings, another item of clothing that he knew would be unbearably soft underneath his hands.

Not that he was going to get to find out, of course.

But it was more than that. Her face was glowing, her smile bright, and that, *that* was what had him feeling a little light-headed, if he was honest.

"Baby Witches to the rescue!" she announced, and only now did Wells realize there were three people crowding in behind her, all of them looking equally excited.

"Come on," Gwyn told them, waving them toward the counter. "Tell him what you told me."

Sam, the girl with turquoise hair, spoke up first. "So Glinda was telling us how you're trying to find out about someone getting kicked out of Penhaven, and I was telling *her* that I dated this girl who works in the records department. Her name was Sara, and she was really nice, but she was also a Pisces, and *I'm* a Leo, so—"

"You can skip that bit," Gwyn told her, laying a hand on her arm, "much as it did enhance the original story."

"Right." Sam nodded. "Anyway, she told me that every student who ever went to Penhaven has a file. Like, a *literal* file. No computers, honest-to-god paper on every single student."

Wells straightened up, closing his book. "Interesting," he said slowly. It did seem like it might be easier to get their hands—or at least their eyes—on a piece of paper rather than hack into a computer.

"The files are in this cabinet in Dr. Arbuthnot's office," Sam went on. "Not just any cabinet, obviously, a magical one given that it's holding over a hundred years of students, but it *looks* normal."

Gwyn nodded, crossing her arms. "I saw it, like, a million times when I was at Penhaven. I basically lived in Dr. Arbuthnot's office."

Wells knew Dr. Arbuthnot was the current head of the witchery department at Penhaven, and he'd had her as a teacher for one class when he was there, but there was something else about that name ringing a very faint bell. Something that had him looking at Gwyn because . . . it felt like it might involve her somehow?

But then Sam was hurrying on. "Anyway, all of this is not the crazy part! Well, the cabinet is a little crazy, but—"

"Sam!" Cait said, grabbing her by the shoulders and shaking her a little. "Get to it!"

"There's no magic on the cabinet," Sam said in a rush. "Seriously. Zero protection spells at all. Sara said it had never been an issue because who wants to go through those files? It's only past students, not current ones. And no one has the balls to just waltz into Dr. Arbuthnot's office and try to take anything."

"And!" Parker added, holding up a finger. "Dr. Arbuthnot's office *is* protected with spells. You couldn't break in there if you wanted to."

"*But,*" Gwyn said now, throwing a look to Wells, "if someone were already in her office, someone could, conceivably, get in that cabinet and find Morgan's file. Especially if that someone was a respectable and valued member of the witch community who would be completely trusted alone in that office."

"Hmm," Wells said, because he'd learned over the years that was a good reaction when you had no fucking clue what to do or say.

Gwyn's grin widened. "We're both closing up early today, Esquire."

CHAPTER 21

T his is never going to work."

"It is absolutely going to work."

Gwyn and Wells had been having a version of this discussion at least half a dozen times since they'd locked up their respective stores. They'd had it when they'd both driven up the mountain to their homes to get ready ("I don't think it's going to be nearly as simple as you think it is." / "It is totally going to be that simple.").

They'd had it after Wells had emerged from his house, dressed in the most formal and severe outfit he owned that *wasn't* a set of robes ("It's ridiculous to think we'll just be able to waltz in there and do this." / "Well, start counting in three-quarter time, Esquire, because we're waltzing.").

They'd had it as they'd driven back toward the college in Gwyn's truck, Baby Witches crowded onto the bench seat in the back ("If we spent a little more time actually planning this, we might see any holes in said plan." / "There aren't any holes, plan is flawless.").

And now, as Gwyn parked on a side street about a block from campus, she turned to Wells in the passenger seat. "Just channel your dad. You know. Authoritative. Snobby. Kind of a dick."

Reaching over, she laid a hand on his shoulder. "Should be easy. That's just you cranked up a couple of degrees."

The Baby Witches chortled at that as Wells glared at her, but Gwyn just kept smiling, and finally, Wells rolled his eyes and she thought she might have seen the barest hint of a smirk.

"Fine. And you'll be how far behind me?"

"Ten minutes. Maybe fifteen. Depends on how quickly these guys can do their thing." She gestured to Sam, Cait, and Parker, all of whom were practically bouncing with excitement, and while Gwyn loved that for them, she was also maybe just the *teeniest* bit nervous and maybe *slightly* less confident in The Plan than she'd insisted.

But once she and the Baby Witches had come up with it, it had seemed imperative that they put it into place right away, right that second. After all, the sooner they found out what Morgan's big secret was, the sooner they could know if she posed a threat to Graves Glen.

And, okay, yes, maybe Gwyn had been thinking of a reason to go and talk to Wells ever since Friday night, and this had finally given her the perfect excuse, but she wasn't going to think too much about that right now.

Just like she *hadn't* been thinking about how that kiss had had nothing to do with magic and everything to do with the fact that she was very, very into Llewellyn Penhallow, Esquire, apparently.

So better to throw herself directly into this rather than look at any of that up close.

Wells reached up, adjusting his tie. He was all in black, his hair brushed back from his face, that signet ring on his finger the only bit of color besides his blue eyes.

It worked for him, this look. Stern, spare.

Sexy as hell.

Pushing that thought away with the force of a Mack truck, Gwyn checked her own reflection in the rearview mirror. She'd kept the leggings and boots she'd been wearing earlier but replaced her sweater with an oversize T-shirt that screamed *FLY, MY PRETTIES!* in violent green print, and over that, she'd thrown on a fuzzy cardigan in that same green, a pair of sparkly purple brooms dangling from her ears.

Even for Gwyn, it was a bit much, but like Wells, she had a role to play this afternoon.

"So I'll just take this file out of the cabinet and hope she never notices?" Wells asked now. "Shove it inside my jacket?"

"That's the plan," Gwyn replied, but Parker leaned up from the back seat, something in their hand.

"Actually," they said, "I made this."

It looked like a coin, slightly bigger than a silver dollar, and as Wells plucked it from Parker's hand, Gwyn caught a slight shimmer from it, like oil in water.

"Touch it to the pages, and it'll record the information," Parker said. "Then you just put it on another sheet of paper, and everything that was on the original paper will appear there."

"That is . . . quite clever," Wells said, holding the coin up to the light, and Parker beamed.

"Thanks! It's my own creation, and I think it'll make *bank* if I can make more and start . . . "

They trailed off as Gwyn and Wells both slowly turned around to look at them, and shrunk back into their seat. "Certainly *not* selling them around campus," they finished up, and Sam elbowed them hard in the side.

"Good to know," Wells said, then sighed and opened the truck's door.

"Ten minutes," he said to Gwyn, and she nodded.

"Ten minutes."

He turned then, heading in the direction of the college, and Gwyn waited a beat before throwing open her door.

"Esquire!" she called, jogging after him, and he stopped, waiting for her.

Leaves skittered down the street, the afternoon clear but turning chilly, especially here in the shade between buildings, and Gwyn tugged her cardigan closer around her, shivering a little. "I love my Baby Witches so much," she told Wells, "but I gotta be honest with you. There's . . . at least a thirty percent chance that thing catches fire or possibly explodes."

Wells studied the coin in his hand. "Thirty percent?"

"Conservative estimate."

He looked up, meeting her eyes, and now Gwyn felt shivery for a whole new reason.

"This will end in disaster," he said, but she didn't think he really meant it this time.

"It's gonna end in *triumph*," she retorted, and he sighed, slipping the coin into his pocket.

"I suppose we'll see, won't we?"

"GLOATING ISN'T ATTRACTIVE, Jones."

Gwyn laughed, thumping her hand on the steering wheel as the truck headed back toward downtown, afternoon sliding into evening.

"All I said was that I wanted you to admit that I was right, and also to take out an ad in the paper saying that I was right, and then to make yourself some kind of social media page and have your first post say, 'Gwyn Jones was right, and I, Llewellyn Penhallow, Esquire, was wrong.'"

She thought Wells might be trying to glare at her, but it was a struggle given that he was clearly just as pleased the plan had worked as she was.

If anything, it had worked even *better* than she'd hoped.

Wells had indeed been able to meet with Dr. Arbuthnot in her office, giving her some story about his family and wanting to be more involved in the college now that he was back in town.

When Gwyn had burst in ten—okay, nearly twenty—minutes later, with her frantic story about seeing some of the college witches practicing a spell that looked like it had gotten out of hand, she'd almost believed the haughty scowl Wells had thrown her way.

It had actually been kind of hot, especially the way his eyes had moved over her, clearly meaning to convey his disdain at her aggressive outfit but carrying enough warmth that Gwyn was glad Dr. Arbuthnot had been distracted.

Dr. Arbuthnot had, as hoped, followed Gwyn out of the room and to the quad, a space that was glamoured so that the regular students only ever saw what looked to be other kids, reading, studying, throwing a Frisbee.

The Baby Witches had done their job a little too well, but once the gaping crack in the ground was closed and the trees went back to normal, they'd gotten off with a fairly light punishment (two weeks of volunteering in the dining hall), and Gwyn had been left alone with Dr. Arbuthnot.

"Thank you," her former teacher had said before narrowing her eyes. "Why were you on campus anyway?"

"I was picking up something in Vivi's office," Gwyn said, holding up the Welsh history book she'd actually snagged from the cabin earlier. Some of Vivi's stuff was still up there, and Gwyn had known the perfect prop when she'd seen it. "She needed it for the research she's doing in Wales right now."

Dr. Arbuthnot would probably be suspicious of Gwyn until one or both of them died, but she liked and respected Vivi, so she'd bought that excuse, and within minutes, Gwyn was back in her truck, waiting for Wells.

She waited awhile.

It was almost half an hour later before he came hurrying up the street, and when he'd gotten in the truck and pulled the file folder out of his suit jacket (he'd clearly taken her advice about Parker's coin), Gwyn had officially begun The Gloating.

Now, as she turned to head back to Main Street, she nodded at the folder still sitting in Wells's lap. "Have you looked at it?"

"No, I was just happy to find it, honestly. Do you know how many Howells have gone to Penhaven through the years? Didn't want to risk her coming back and catching me with it, so I just shoved it in my jacket. And then I had to sit there and keep up the ruse after she was done with whatever it was those three did."

He glanced toward the back seat now. "Speaking of, where are they?"

"They stayed on campus to do some studying," she said, and he nodded, looking back at the file.

"So shall I open it now, or do you want to save it for when we can look at it properly?"

Shaking her head, Gwyn rolled up her window. "Go ahead and check it out."

Wells flipped the file open, his eyes scanning the page. "You were right about her major being Ritual Witchcraft. She was a good student, too. Almost all A's, commendations from her professors . . . "

Gwyn snorted. "I don't ever want to look at my file," she said. "Probably has 'HERE THERE BE DRAGONS' stamped on it and that's it."

Wells smiled at that, his eyes still on Morgan's record. "And mine no doubt says, 'FUCKED OFF,' so no real desire to look at that, either. Ah!" He tapped the page. "Here we go. 'Student advised to withdraw before graduation due to inappropriate and unseemly magical practices.'"

Wells looked up, a trio of wrinkles appearing between his brows. "And that's it."

"That could be anything," Gwyn said, and Wells sat back, thinking.

"Anything *bad,*" he said. "So at least we know that whatever it was, it wasn't good."

Gwyn nodded, but she couldn't help but feel a little disappointed. "This honestly feels like a waste of a very excellent plan," she told Wells, and he made that "Hmm" noise again, that thing he did when he didn't know what else to say.

And it bugged her, just a bit, that she was already starting to recognize his sounds. The faces he made. The way he rubbed his beard when he was thinking hard about something.

Now he reached up and loosened his tie, unbuttoning the top few buttons of his shirt, and Gwyn fought very hard to keep her eyes on the road. "So I'll drop you off at yours?"

He'd taken his car from the store earlier, but they'd left it back at his house before heading to the college. Twilight had fully fallen, and Gwyn didn't feel like opening the shop back up just for a couple of hours.

But she didn't really want to go home, either, the excitement and adrenaline still coursing through her, no matter what a letdown the actual file was.

She rolled down the window again, letting in the cool evening air, the smell of woodsmoke and leaves. Nights like this in Graves Glen were magical in every sense of that word, and as Gwyn's truck made its slow way down Main Street, the lights strung up along the sidewalks lit up, reflecting off the windshield.

Next to her, Wells rolled down his own window, leaning back in his seat. "What a gorgeous night," he said, his voice soft, and Gwyn suddenly knew exactly where she wanted to go.

CHAPTER 22

Darkness had fully fallen by the time Gwyn turned her truck down a familiar dirt road. It snaked between the hills, gnarled tree roots arching up from embankments around them. The windows were still open, and Gwyn could hear the faint trickle of water as it dripped from rocky outcrops overhead, the soft hoot of an owl, the rustle of the breeze through the trees.

"You aren't taking me out somewhere to murder me now that I've served my purpose in your plan, are you?" Wells asked, and Gwyn winked at him.

"Don't give me any ideas."

The road curved slightly as they headed uphill, and Gwyn nodded off to the left. "If you go that way, you'll end up at the Johnsons' apple orchard. Just a heads-up, they're nice people, but the war between the Apple People and the Spooky People is an ancient one in any town that goes hard for Halloween."

"Noted," Wells said with faux solemnity, and Gwyn smiled, shifting gears as the truck began to climb higher.

"Normally, we let them have pretty much all of September, but if they end up doing the Autumn Apple Hayride on Halloween night like they've been threatening, all bets are off."

The truck rose over one last rise, and Gwyn put it in reverse, maneuvering around until she was parked exactly where she wanted. She'd been up here enough times that she could practically do it with her eyes closed, but Wells was looking around, a little wary.

"I was joking about the murder earlier, but I truly have no idea where we are right now."

Turning the truck off, Gwyn opened her door. "Hold on to your waistcoat, Esquire."

"I'm not even wearing one," he grumbled as he got out, but then any other complaints died on his lips as he looked out at the view spread before them.

Gwyn had parked so that the bed of the truck faced a steep cliff, the land suddenly dropping away to reveal the valley below. Graves Glen was a collection of lights glimmering in the darkness, homey and warm but far away, shadowy hills rising all around it.

Just beyond the town, the moonlight picked up the silvery ribbon of a train chugging through the valley, and the sound of its horn carried across the air to them faintly.

Reaching into the back seat, Gwyn pulled out the quilt she always kept in the truck for whenever she wanted to come up here and tossed it into the bed, climbing up after it.

Wells was still standing beside the truck, taking in the view, and as Gwyn got the quilt situated, she said, "Vivi actually found this spot first. Back when we were teenagers. She liked to drive around in the mountains, and she said this was the prettiest view for miles."

"It's hard to imagine anything topping it, yes," Wells said, his voice soft, his eyes drinking it all in.

Settling herself on the quilt, Gwyn gestured for him to climb into the bed. "Come on, Esquire," she said. "If you're going to be a Georgia boy, you need some experience sitting around in the back of trucks."

"You're rather imperious, you know that?" he replied, but he hoisted himself up into the truck with surprising grace, sitting next to her with his long legs stretched out in front of him.

For a while, they were quiet, and if it occurred to Gwyn that she'd never brought anyone up here before, she didn't let herself overthink it.

Too much.

Instead, she tilted her head back, looking up. Stars twinkled through the trees overhead, and the moon was a perfect crescent just to the right of the tallest hill.

Next to her, Wells leaned back on his hands. "It's so clear here. The air, the sky."

Gwyn leaned back, too, her hand brushing his. She wanted to pretend she wasn't aware of it at all, that the warmth of his body didn't make her want to curl up against him, breathe him in.

But it was getting harder and harder to pretend that kind of thing when it came to Wells, so she let herself scoot closer to him, close enough that their hips touched as they looked at the stars.

"I'm pretty sure Wales does okay for itself in terms of natural beauty," she said, and he huffed out a soft laugh.

"More than okay, yes," he acknowledged, and Gwyn glanced

over at him even though it was so dark, he was little more than a shadow. "But it's different here. It's very . . . American," he finally said.

For once, he didn't say that like it was a bad word, and when he turned and looked at her, Gwyn thought there was something a little wistful in his expression. "Did you miss it?" she asked. "Graves Glen. When you went back to Wales."

Wells rubbed at his beard as he thought it over. "I didn't think I did, not at first. I'd only been here a few months, and most of that time was spent at school. But once I got back, I found myself thinking about it at the strangest times. I'd be walking down the sidewalk in Dweniniaid and remember the way the leaves blew across campus, how pretty all that green grass looked with the red brick. Or—and mind you, this was fairly rare—a group of blokes would come into the pub who were clearly mates from their uni days, and I'd wonder about the people I might have met had I stayed longer. The people who might have still been in my life."

Shaking his head, he gave a self-conscious laugh. "I suppose that makes me sound like quite the sad bastard."

"I already thought that about you, so no harm, no foul," she replied, but her hand was still next to his, and he only smiled at the words.

"Anyway, yes, I did miss it. Or rather, regretted all I'd missed out on by leaving so soon."

Wells's gaze slid back to her, lingering for a moment before he turned his attention back to the view. "For example, I had no idea drunken Ostara party hookups were on offer."

Gwyn laughed, drawing her knees up and wrapping her arms around them. "It was a make-out, not a hookup," she corrected him. "Very different things."

Bumping her shoulder with his, she added, "And I'm sure you had at least one drunken hookup *or* make-out of your own. Girls at Penhaven were practically putting pictures of you up on their walls."

Another one of those huffed laughs as Wells reached up to scrub a hand over his hair. "As we've established, I was something of a git back then, so no, I never seemed to make time for any of that while I was here."

"Seriously? Not once?"

He was still looking at the view, his profile in shadow, and Gwyn thought back to that arrogant boy coming into Dr. Arbuthnot's classroom, how she'd been so annoyed with him, how she'd assumed everything must be so easy for him because of his last name.

And that whole time, he'd actually just been . . . lonely.

"Not once," he confirmed, then flashed her one of those wry smiles. "If it's any consolation, I did have *very* good grades."

There were a million jokes she could make right now. Probably a million and five.

But Gwyn really didn't want to make any of them.

Instead, she turned to face Wells, coming up on her knees as she did and laying her hands on either side of his face.

His beard was soft against her palms, and when she swung a leg over his, coming to settle in his lap, he sucked in a quick breath even as his hands came up, resting just there below her waist.

For a second, Gwyn wondered if he was going to stop her, or list all the reasons this was a bad idea, or maybe launch into a soliloquy about it.

But he only pulled her closer.

Gwyn felt a slow smile curve her lips as she lowered her face to his, their mouths just a breath apart. "Feel like making up for lost time, Esquire?" she murmured.

"We're not drunk, so I'm not sure this counts," he replied, but his hands were still on her, and he tilted his head just the littlest bit, skimming his nose along her jaw in a way that had Gwyn's eyes fluttering shut.

"Oh," Gwyn promised, rolling her hips and hearing his breath catch again, "trust me. It's going to count."

There was no pretense when she kissed him this time. No spell, no one to fool. No one out here at all except for the two of them in the darkness, Graves Glen glittering in the distance, but a million miles away in her mind.

In a way, it felt like a first kiss, and that made something in Gwyn's chest tighten even as she opened her mouth against his, her hand fisted in the front of his shirt, his fingers digging into her hip.

When she pulled back, his lips went to her neck, his beard abrading the skin there in a way she knew she'd wince at in the morning, but for now, it just felt good. Everything felt good. His mouth, his hands, the softness of his hair as it brushed against her cheek, the slow and steady ache building between her legs as she moved restlessly against his lap.

Despite the coolness of the night, she reached up to peel off her cardigan just as Wells lifted his head to kiss her again, and then she was distracted, kissing him back even as her sweater pinned her arms to her sides.

And when his tongue did a particularly lovely thing against hers, she gave a needy whimper, moving to clutch at his shoulders only to be brought up short by her traitorous cardigan.

Chuckling against her mouth, Wells raised his hands, helping her to push the rest of the offending garment off, and with a frustrated sound, he broke the kiss just long enough to fling the cardigan over the side of the truck and into the night.

"You are a beautiful woman, but that was a hideous piece of clothing," Wells said, breathless as she kissed his jaw. "So I can't regret its sacrifice tonight."

"It was my favorite," she lied, "and I'm going to make you buy me another one."

He laughed again, and Gwyn chased that sound with her mouth, the night air cold against her flushed skin. Wells had one palm resting against her ribs, a heavy, warm weight through her thin T-shirt, and she wondered if he could feel just how fast her heart was beating.

She could feel him, hard underneath her despite the layers of fabric between them, and she pressed even closer, her hips rocking, the friction sending shivery sparks through her veins, her thighs clenching, and the kiss suddenly got wilder.

One of Wells's hands, those beautiful, elegant hands she'd been having dirty thoughts about for way longer than she wanted to admit, was on the back of her head, tangled in her hair. The other rested just above her ass, holding her tight against him as she moved, their bodies locked together, and Gwyn wondered how something as simple as kissing while fully clothed could feel this filthy.

The man was still wearing a *suit*, for fuck's sake.

But maybe that was part of it. Serious, formal Wells Penhallow in his black suit, kissing her in the back of a pickup truck like they really were a pair of horny college students who'd sneaked away from campus.

For just a moment, something like longing pierced through her, a wish to go back in time so that they could be that Wells, that Gwyn, without all the other stuff, all these other complications.

"You know," Gwyn panted, lifting her lips from his, "you're awfully good at this for someone who claimed never to do this kind of thing."

"I claimed never to do this kind of thing *here*," Wells corrected her, his hand brushing her hair back from her face, finger briefly tugging at that stripe of faded pink laying against her cheek even as the hand on her backside urged her to keep moving. "I wasn't a monk, Jones."

"Ah, so there are Welsh girls you seduced in the back of trucks. Sorry, *lorries*."

"I believe you were the one who got into *my* lap," he reminded her, moving in to press another hot, biting kiss against her neck.

Gwyn's brain was feeling decidedly scrambled, her eyes closing as she managed to say, "I may have made the first move, but you're the one who really ran with this, Esquire. I'm beginning to think your whole Waistcoat Guy thing is an act."

His hand falling from her ass, Wells leaned back a little, studying her even as his chest still heaved up and down. "Do you always talk this much during sex?"

Gwyn licked her lips, taking a few deep breaths of her own. "Is that what we're doing?" she asked. "Having sex?"

Wells reached up with one hand, ruffling his hair before leaning back on both hands, Gwyn still perched in his lap. "It certainly felt like the prelude to it."

"Is that what you want?" Gwyn asked, suddenly a little cold now that his body wasn't tight up against hers.

That was good, though.

She needed the space, needed the breather, because what had started out as something fun, something she'd felt very in control of, had started to feel like something bigger than that, and that was frankly terrifying.

"We can," Gwyn went on. "Have sex. Or we can just keep doing this, maybe take it up a few notches. I mean, you haven't even felt me up yet, and *multiple* sources would tell you my tits are not to be missed. So." Gwyn shrugged. "Whatever you want."

Wells was so quiet for so long that Gwyn wondered if maybe he actually *was* an android and she'd just short-circuited his system. Or maybe all the blood suddenly having to return to his brain took time.

The wind was still blowing through the trees, a soft rustle

overhead, and the truck creaked slightly on its wheels as Wells slowly sat back up, his chest against hers, one of his hands coming up to cup her cheek.

There was enough moonlight for Gwyn to make out his expression as he looked into her eyes, and if she'd hoped to put a little distance between them, that mix of warmth, annoyance, and lust shot any chance of *that* straight to hell.

"What I want," Wells said, his voice low, "you infuriating."

His lips brushed hers, the barest hint of a kiss, and Gwyn shivered.

"Completely terrifying."

Another brush, slightly firmer this time.

"Bloody gorgeous madwoman, is to watch you come."

A real kiss now, quick, over too soon, but dirty enough that when he pulled back, Gwyn's hands were once again clutching his shirt, and he was breathing hard again, his gaze hot on her face.

"Oh," was all Gwyn managed to say, her mouth dry, but every other part of her was liquid and on fire all at once.

One corner of Wells's mouth kicked up as he once again brushed her hair back from her face, his touch gentle enough to raise goose bumps. "If that means you want me to fuck you, then I will," he went on, his thumb skating over her lower lip, a light touch she felt everywhere. "But I'm just as happy to touch you. Or taste you."

Gwyn blew out a shaky breath. All of her was shaking, she realized, and she wanted him to keep talking like this forever, his voice warm and low, rough, but sliding over her like something silken and smooth; wanted him to keep filling her mind with images of the two of them, of the things he could do to her, the things he'd do *with* her.

"If you want us to keep on every item of clothing we're currently wearing and grind against my cock until you come, I'd enjoy nothing more. If you want to touch yourself while I watch, I . . . well."

Wells shifted underneath her, hands holding her hips and pressing her down into his lap just in case Gwyn wasn't sure how much that particular idea appealed to him, and she swallowed hard, her hands resting on his shoulders, digging into his suit jacket.

"So that's what I want, Gwynnevere Jones," he said. "You. Coming for me. In whichever manner you choose."

Gwyn stared almost wonderingly down into his face. "Who are you, and what have you done with Llewellyn Penhallow, Esquire?" she muttered, and Wells smiled, leaning forward to kiss the hollow of her throat.

"But if what *you* want is for us to stop this here and go back down the mountain and pretend this never happened, I'm amenable to that as well," he murmured against her skin.

"Ah, there he is," Gwyn said, and Wells gave a rumbling chuckle that she felt rather than heard.

He looked up at her again, lifting her hand from his shoulder and pressing a kiss into her palm. "So what do you choose, Jones?"

CHAPTER 23

I t was freeing, completely losing one's fucking mind.

Because clearly that's what he'd done, and Wells was not sure he'd ever been happier.

Or maybe that's because he had Gwyn in his lap, her body warm and pliant against his, her face a mixture of want and need and a delicious kind of surprise that had him wanting to tell her every filthy thought he'd ever had about her, every delicious, debauched thing he desired.

It would take a while because Wells was pretty sure that where this woman was concerned, he wanted *everything*, but that was all right. Up here in this hidden space, far above the town below, far away from everything but her, Wells felt like they had all the time in the world.

Time seemed frozen now anyway as he waited for her to make up her mind, to tell him what it was she wanted. He knew the smartest thing was for them to go back to Graves Glen, to find some other reason to explain this moment of madness away, but Christ, he was tired of being smart.

And she must've felt the same because she leaned forward, kissing him again, sucking at his lower lip in a way that had him thinking he might come just from this, her mouth on his, her legs straddling his lap, her breasts a soft weight against his chest.

Then she pulled back, a dangerous smile playing on that lovely mouth.

Her hands slid down her body, crossing at the hem of her T-shirt, and as she slowly drew it up her body, Wells's eyes hungrily took in every inch of skin revealed to him. She was pale in the moonlight, her skin like marble, and Wells couldn't help but rest his hand there on her stomach, the tips of his fingers just brushing the edge of her bra as she tossed her shirt over the side of the truck with that awful sweater.

Wells leaned back, wanting to look at her, wishing there were more light, then reminding himself that he *was* a witch.

"May I?" he asked, taking his hand off her stomach, a faint spark already appearing between his fingers, and when she nodded, that spark grew to a soft glow, barely brighter than a candle, but enough to let him see her.

Her bra was sheer black, nearly transparent except over the nipples, where two black cats' faces grinned back at him, and Wells laughed even as his hand itched to cup the side of her breast, to skate his thumb over one of those stupid cat's embroidered whiskers.

"God, I should not be as turned on as I am right now," he said, and Gwyn grinned down at him.

"Does it make it better or worse to know that I'm going to start selling these at Something Wicked?" she asked, and he shook his head.

"I honestly cannot say."

Still smiling, Gwyn reached behind her, unclasping her bra. That, Wells noted, didn't get flung over the side, but placed next to his hip, and then he couldn't think of much of anything else at all because Gwyn was half naked in his lap, fingers combing through his hair, her nails scratching.

"Just so you know," she said in a husky voice, guiding his hand to her breast, "you can both look *and* touch."

Breathing hard, Wells brushed his knuckles over her nipple, then his thumb began making slow circles as she sighed, her hips rocking again.

"And if I wanted to do this?" he asked, ducking his head and letting his breath ghost along that puckered flesh, and with a sound suspiciously close to a whimper, Gwyn nodded, pressing herself closer as his lips closed around her nipple, sucking gently at first, then harder.

Wells had always thought she smelled amazing, carrying the scents of tea and herbs and candles with her, as much a part of her as her red hair and green eyes. But that was nothing compared to the taste of her skin, the slight salt of her sweat, and as he moved to her other breast, he wanted to chase that taste everywhere, wanted it imprinted on his tongue for the rest of his life.

He could tell himself all he wanted that she only did this to him because it had been so long since he'd been with any woman, but he was done with lying. This was her, and it was him, and it was whatever magic their bodies somehow kindled together, and there had never been anything like it for him before, and he knew down to his bones that there would never be anything like it for him again.

"You're wearing too many clothes," Gwyn said, her voice shaky even as she tried to laugh, and Wells reluctantly released her nipple, shifting so that he could take off his suit jacket. Gwyn helped, then her hands went to the buttons of his shirt, and Wells shucked that off as fast as he could, shivering as her nails made a slow track through the hair on his chest, lower, grazing his stomach and tapping against his belt buckle.

She was shivering, too, he realized, and maybe not just from his touch. The night had grown cooler around them, almost cold now, and without thinking, Wells raised his hand again. He quickly mumbled a few words, and the air around them warmed by a few degrees, chasing back the chill. It had been a useful spell in Wales, and not one he'd ever expected to have much need for in Georgia, but then, he hadn't thought he'd be getting naked in the back of a truck in the middle of the woods.

Gwyn smiled against his mouth as she kissed him again, and then she slid off his lap, coming to her feet in a surprisingly elegant motion.

The truck rocked slightly as she reached down, taking off one boot and then the other, and Wells lay sprawled there at her feet, propped up on his elbows as he watched her slide her leggings down until she was standing naked over him, looking like some sort of ancient goddess, framed against the night sky, long red hair blowing in the breeze.

Oh, I am so fucked.

Wells hadn't realized he'd said the words out loud until she laughed, going back down on her knees on the quilt, a woman again, but still the most gorgeous thing he'd ever seen.

"You will be eventually," she promised. "But I seem to remember something about lady's choice when it came to how *I* come tonight."

Surprised he could still form words, much less quip, Wells managed to say, "That was the agreement, yes. Witch's oath."

"Still not a thing," she said, and then her hand slid along his jaw, eyes on his mouth.

"Never had someone with a beard go down on me before," she said, and every drop of blood that had been anywhere else in Wells's body was now clearly in his cock because he had never been this hard in his life.

"Always happy to provide new experiences," he managed to croak out, and one corner of Gwyn's mouth lifted.

"*Upscale* experiences, even."

"That's the Penhallow brand."

They both seemed to reach for each other at the same time, meeting in the middle, and Wells carried her down with him until he was lying on his back, the top of his head nearly brushing the end of the truck bed, Gwyn on top of him, his hands moving over her back, her thighs, her arse, any part of her he could touch as he kissed her, until she sat up, legs on either side of him.

Her eyes moved to the space on the quilt beside them, and her body had already started turning that way when Wells clutched her hips tighter, holding her in place.

Gwyn looked down at him, eyebrows raised, skin flushed in the soft light from his spell.

"You said it yourself," he reminded her as he slid down in the truck bed, raising his knees even as he urged her to slide up his chest. "Upscale experiences, Jones."

Gwyn's mouth dropped open just the slightest bit even as she obeyed the tugging of his hands. "Well, aren't you just full of surprises?" she murmured, and Wells allowed himself the smuggest of grins.

"You have no fucking idea," he replied, and then he pulled hard, and her knees were there at his shoulders, her thighs open before him, and his mouth was on her.

Wells heard a dull thud as Gwyn gasped and leaned forward, her hands hitting the back window of the truck, arms braced as her hips moved against his mouth, and she was wet and hot and perfect, heady, and he felt drunk off her as she cried out, as she panted his name, as she chased her pleasure with the same kind of ruthlessness that had made him want her in the first place.

And when she finally shook and fell apart above him, when he looked up her body and saw her eyes close, her lips part, her red hair bright against the dark sky, he knew that he was nowhere close to having had enough of her.

CHAPTER 24

"So how are things going with Wells?"

FaceTime was such a cursed invention, Gwyn decided as she looked at Vivi's happy, glowing face on her laptop, propped on the counter at Something Wicked.

Why couldn't people just talk on the phone? Why did they have to *see* each other?

Over the phone, no one could see that you weren't wearing makeup, or that you were still in your pajamas at noon. No one could see that your brief experiment with bangs had ended in tragedy.

And no one could see you blush.

Vivi frowned now, leaning in close. "You look guilty. Please tell me you haven't blown up his store. Or turned him into some kind of amphibian."

"I haven't!" Gwyn insisted. "Promise!"

I just rode his face in the back of my pickup truck at your favorite overlook, that's all, and it was the best sexual experience of my life, and I have no idea how to deal with any of that, so maybe I should turn him into an amphibian because at least then I could be sure I'd never do that again, except the thing is, I really, really want to do that again.

For a second, Gwyn imagined actually saying all that to Vivi, but since she really liked Vivi's head as it was as opposed to all exploded, she decided just to add, "We actually hung out yesterday and were perfectly civil."

Not *exactly* a lie.

Last night had definitely been . . . friendly.

Vivi was clearly unconvinced, but she let it go, glancing back over her shoulder. She was in some kind of lovely stone cottage, and while Gwyn couldn't see Rhys, she could hear him cheerfully humming in the background, which probably meant he was cooking. She'd been around him long enough to pick up on that habit.

"Go on," she said to Vivi now. "Go see what annoyingly amazing thing your husband is making you for dinner, and sleep well knowing that me and Wells are not at each other's throat."

Vivi looked back at her, tucking her hair behind one ear. "You're sure everything is fine there? I know the Graves Glen Gathering is just a few days away, and then it's Fall Festival, and we won't be back for that, either, but—"

"All is well in the town of Graves Glen," Gwyn told her, another technical truth. She knew she should tell Vivi about Morgan coming to town, about all that weirdness at her house, but Vivi and Rhys had gone through enough last year, and they deserved a worry-free honeymoon. If something major happened, maybe then she'd fill Vivi in on Everything Morgan, but for now, Gwyn was happy to keep Vivi firmly out of the loop.

"Okay," Vivi said now, then waved at the camera. "Tell Sir Purrcival I said hi, and I'll talk to you soon."

"Will do!"

Laptop closed, Gwyn glanced across the shop to Cait and Parker, who were helping rearrange the crystal display. Sam was at work at the Coffee Cauldron, but she'd stopped by earlier, and all three Baby Witches had been a little glum to learn Morgan's file didn't have much information.

Gwyn wasn't exactly thrilled about that, either, but she was still trying to work out what the next step should be. She could always call Morgan, invite her to lunch, and see if Morgan might spill any information, but if Morgan *was* up to something, Gwyn didn't want to show her hand so soon.

She was still contemplating what to do—and trying very hard not to look out her front window toward Penhallow's every five seconds—when the raven over the door cawed.

"Welcome to Something Wicked!" she called out before turning to see Jane standing there.

"Oh," she said, then dusted her hands on the back of her skirt. "Well, you need no welcome, you're pretty familiar with this place."

Offering a weak smile, Gwyn crossed the store to stand in front of her ex. Jane was clearly in Full Mayor Mode today, sensible black suit, sky-high heels, two cell phones clutched in one hand, an iPad peeking out from the bag on her shoulder, and a pen behind one ear.

"Don't tell me you're here for a plastic pumpkin," Gwyn teased, and Jane smiled a little, shaking her head.

"Much as I enjoy them, no. I was actually going to ask you some questions about the stuff Vivi found at Penhaven for the Graves Glen Gathering. Do you want to . . . " Jane gestured back behind her. "Grab a tea or something and chat?"

Gwyn could think of few things more awkward, but she still nodded, calling out to Cait and Parker to watch the counter for a bit, and then she and Jane were walking down Graves Glen's picturesque main street to the Coffee Cauldron.

Gwyn ordered a dirty chai, waiting for Jane to order her usual, a coffee the size of her head, filled with enough caffeine to kill a herd of rhinos.

So when Jane ordered the peppermint tea with lemon and honey, Gwyn wondered if she'd actually heard right.

But no, Sam was definitely handing Jane a tea, and, bemused, Gwyn followed her to a back booth, sliding in across from her.

"You seem . . . calm," Gwyn noted, looking closely at Jane. She'd really liked the mayor, but there was no getting away from the fact that the woman was a whirling dervish of stress and Red Bull most of the time.

But apparently not anymore. Jane looked as chill as Gwyn had ever seen her.

And now she was blushing a little, ducking her head as she

smiled. "Lorna convinced me to switch to herbal tea instead of coffee, and she got me this app on my phone that's supposed to make me more mindful or something." Jane shook her head even as she held up the cell phone that was permanently attached to her hand.

"It's silly, but it's actually working."

"You must really be in love to give up your beloved Americanos," Gwyn joked, but there was nothing funny in the way Jane's whole face seemed to go soft.

"I am, yeah," she said, and Gwyn waited to feel a little sad, maybe even a little jealous, but there was none of that. She was just happy for Jane.

"This is a little weird," Gwyn said as she stirred her tea, and Jane shrugged, sipping her own drink.

"What? Have you never been friends with an ex before?"

"No," Gwyn said honestly, and Jane laughed, shaking her head.

"Have you ever tried?"

"No," Gwyn said again. "I figured they were all too busy cursing my name or writing really bad short stories about redheads named Brynn who ruined their lives forever."

Jane's eyebrows disappeared underneath her bangs. "Do you think you ruined my life?"

"No one could ruin your life," Gwyn admitted. "You're a force of nature, it wouldn't be allowed."

That made Jane smile, and Gwyn was reminded that Jane had really nice smiles.

"Gwyn, we just didn't work out," Jane said, reaching across the table to squeeze Gwyn's hand. "I didn't hate you, and you didn't break my heart. To be honest, I was mostly sad you didn't seem to want to hang out anymore. I liked hanging out with you."

"I liked it, too."

"And I don't see why we can't keep hanging out as friends," Jane went on. "Especially now that we're both in other relationships."

Gwyn almost choked on her tea. "What?"

Jane tilted her head, confused. "I just . . . I thought you and Llewellyn Penhallow were dating. Morgan Howell mentioned it to me the other day."

Right.

She hadn't really thought that part through when she'd thrown herself at Wells's face in the stairwell, that news might spread, that people would think they were a thing because, you know, they'd *said* they were a thing.

And last night . . .

Nope, nope, nope, not thinking about that right now.

Instead, she turned her paper cup in her hands, tapping her dark green nails on the sides as she asked, "So you've met Morgan?"

Nodding, Jane glanced at her phone, tapping something in. "She came by the office the other day to introduce herself. She's really interested in getting involved with everything. The Gathering, Fall Festival, Halloween . . . said if we needed anything, just let her know."

Jane looked up, brown eyes bright. "*And* she went ahead and made a sizable donation toward all those things, so she's my new favorite citizen, sorry."

Making herself smile, Gwyn waved that off even as her mind whirred. "Anyone can write a check, Jane," she teased. "When it comes to Halloween, you know who the real MVP is."

Morgan had said she'd wanted to help out with stuff. Maybe that was simply because she was determined to put down roots here in Halloween Town. Maybe she really *was* just an involved citizen.

But Gwyn couldn't stop thinking about all those things in Morgan's attic, the dark magic hanging all over the place, the weird timing of her showing up *now*, the first Samhain after the town's power had shifted hands.

Luckily, Jane didn't seem to notice Gwyn's distraction, and the two of them spent the next half hour planning out fun things for the Gathering, including a possible appearance by Sir Purrcival.

By the time Gwyn left the Coffee Cauldron, it was dark. She stopped back by the store to lock up, and as she did, she noticed the lights were still on at Penhallow's.

Fighting the urge to go across the street, Gwyn instead got in her truck and headed back up the mountain for home.

Her cabin looked warm and cozy as she parked in front of it, and she was thinking about taking a long hot bath and putting on her comfiest nightgown, the one Vivi said made her look like a girl on the front of a Gothic novel, when she noticed that the front door was slightly ajar.

Standing there on the front steps, she held her breath for a moment, trying to remember this morning. It had been windy today, a storm brewing, and the cabin was old. Doors didn't always close as firmly as they should, but she always locked the front door.

Had she today?

Of course she had, she thought, making herself walk up the steps. There was no feeling of magic in the air, no sense that another person was in there, but she still walked slowly, her heart thudding steadily against her ribs.

The door creaked as she pushed against it, and she reached inside, flipping on the lights, her eyes scanning the entrance.

No one there.

"Sir Purrcival?" she called. If someone had been in the house, he'd tell her.

That made her feel a little bit better until she realized the house was very quiet, no patter of paws, no howling for treats.

Sir Purrcival always met her at the door howling for treats.

Okay, now she was scared, and Gwyn took a deep breath, fingers moving at her side, pulling up a blast of magic even as she kept calling Sir Purrcival's name.

She was so focused on looking for her cat that it took her a minute to realize her hand felt almost dead at her side, no power flowing through it at all.

Breathing hard now, she looked down, moved her fingers, and there was . . . nothing.

"Sir Purrcival?" she called again, thumping up the stairs, checking her room, Vivi's old room, under beds, in closets, behind chairs, all his favorite spots, and all the while, she was trying to access her magic, her heart racing, her breathing starting to sound suspiciously like sobs.

Her magic wasn't working and her cat was missing, and as she made her way out onto the front porch, the woods, *her* woods on *her* mountain, suddenly felt like they were closing in on her, like anything could be hiding in them. She was alone, and she was powerless, and she was Purrcival-less.

Overhead, clouds were scuttering across the night sky, the wind picking up, and far off in the distance, Gwyn saw a flash of lightning against the heavy clouds. Rain was coming, and up here on the mountain, storms could get intense.

And Sir Purrcival was somewhere out there.

Wrapping her arms around herself, Gwyn took deep, steadying breaths, closing her eyes for a second.

And when she opened them, bright lights appeared in the trees, heading right for her.

CHAPTER 25

W ells had been thinking about Gwyn on a fairly constant loop for the past twenty-four hours, so when he drove past her cabin on his way home and saw her standing on the porch, he was almost sure that all that obsessing was resulting in visions now.

But then he saw her face, pale and worried in the porch lights, and slammed on his brakes so hard that the back of his car slid slightly on the dirt and gravel road.

He barely managed to get it in park before he was flinging open the car door and hurrying over to her.

"Gwyn?"

"Wells!" she cried, and that's when he knew that whatever was wrong, it was serious.

He made his way up the porch steps just as she started coming down, and now he saw that there were tears in her eyes, and by St. Bugi's heart, he was going to *kill* whoever had made Gwynnevere Jones cry.

Magic was already crackling in his veins, his hands clenched tight at his sides as he asked, "What is it? What's happened?"

"I can't find Sir Purrcival," she said, her voice small and scared and so very Un-Gwyn. "When I got home, the door was open. I thought someone might have broken in, but I think I just forgot to lock up this morning, and we had all that wind today, and it must've blown open and he got out."

As though she'd summoned it with her words, the wind picked up then, leaves raining down, the air heavy with the smell of rain and ozone.

She looked up at Wells, mouth trembling. "He's so little," she said, and Wells felt like something in his chest had cracked open. In that second, he would've given anything in the world to hand her that cat, to make her never look or sound like this again.

"We'll find him," Wells said immediately. *If I have to comb through every corner of this entire bloody mountain.*

"I tried," she said, her voice wavering. "I was going to do a location spell, but my magic is on the fritz or something. Nothing was happening."

Wells frowned. That was three times now Gwyn's magic had not worked as it was meant to, or at least three times that he knew about.

But they could worry about that later. Right now, he needed to get this cat back for her.

"You were probably too upset," Wells reasoned, "so let me try, hmm?"

She nodded, swiping at her eyes and taking a shuddery breath, and Wells grasped her shoulders briefly, squeezing.

Then he turned away, scanning the woods in front of him, trying to calm his own racing heart and focus. He'd only seen the cat a handful of times, but he pictured him as best he could, raising his hands as magic crackled along his fingers. He could feel a kind of tugging in his mind, and to that image of Sir Purrcival, he added Gwyn's tear-streaked face, the weight in his stomach when he'd realized she was crying, the fierce desire he had to fix this for her.

Light zipped from his hands, spilling out onto the ground, a twisting band of light that snaked out in front of him and through the trees.

Gwyn was already running, following the light as it zigged and zagged, and Wells was right behind her, careful not to trip over roots or stray rocks as they moved deeper into the forest.

The path of light ended at a hollow tree, and Gwyn stopped, panting as she called out, "Sir Purrcival?"

And there he was, the little bastard, sauntering out of the hole in the tree stump, his big green eyes blinking as he looked at Gwyn.

"Treats?" he asked, and she burst into tears then, big noisy ones, as she leaned down and scooped him up.

Relief surged through Wells. Relief and pride, and a fierce gladness, and then there it was again, that feeling in his chest, a tightness and a warmth all at once as Gwyn covered the cat in kisses.

"You don't deserve any," she told him. "But yes. All the treats you want. All the treats in the whole wide world."

"Treats," Sir Purrcival confirmed happily, settling in for more snuggles.

Wells never thought he'd be so envious of a cat.

Gwyn turned to him then, her face red and wet, Sir Purrcival tucked under her chin.

"Thank you," she said. "Seriously. I was panicking, and I don't know what I would've done if you hadn't shown up."

"You would've figured it out," he said, and she gave another one of those shuddery breaths as she scratched Sir Purrcival's belly.

"Still," Gwyn insisted. "I appreciate it. And so does Sir Purrcival, don't you?"

Sir Purrcival studied Wells for a moment and then gave a sleepy-sounding "Not Dickbag."

"Beg pardon?" Wells asked, eyebrows raised, and Gwyn waved him off.

"He calls Rhys Dickbag, so trust me, this is his version of a compliment."

"Ah. Well, in that Sir Purrcival and I are aligned," Wells said, and Gwyn shook her head at him as she started heading back to the house.

"We've talked about the Austen-speak, Esquire," she said, sounding more like herself now. "You clearly need to watch some bad reality TV or something, start picking up how we humans talk."

"Or maybe I'll just spend more time with Sir Purrcival here. He clearly has a vast knowledge of fun and exciting slang terms for me to learn."

Gwyn snorted at that, and Wells trailed her back to her front porch, pausing there at the foot of the steps as she made her way to the front door.

When she realized he wasn't following her, she stopped, turning to look down at him.

"I should head back to mine before the rain gets here," he said, gesturing toward his car. "Let you and Sir Purrcival settle in."

It had been easy not to think of last night when he was too worried about her being upset, but now that the crisis had passed, memories were sliding back in, lying heavily between them, and Wells felt . . . well, *shy* was perhaps not the word, but unsure. Did it mean something, those long, heated moments in her truck, far above Graves Glen?

Or had it just been a one-off, a fun way to pass an evening?

He knew which he preferred, but he didn't get to decide that himself, and it might be for the best to keep his distance for a while.

Self-preservation and all that.

But then she shook her head, rolling her eyes with what he thought—hoped—was fondness.

"You saved my cat, Esquire. At least let me make you a drink."

She pushed the door all the way open with one hip, then threw a look over her shoulder at him. "You coming?"

Self-preservation was, Wells decided as he all but ran up the front steps, truly overrated.

IT'S JUST A *drink*.

Standing in the kitchen, muddling black cherries and an orange peel, Gwyn repeated that like a mantra.

Sir Purrcival was happily napping in his bed on the kitchen table, purring away, and as Gwyn glanced over at him, there was a rumble of thunder, a pattering of rain against the windows. The storm that had been threatening all day had finally blown in, and Gwyn felt her throat go tight all over again. Sir Purrcival had been deeper in the woods than she ever would've guessed. What if he'd still been out there when it started storming? What if Wells hadn't come along when he did?

But he did. And that's why you're making him a drink, and then he'll drink it and go, and it doesn't have to be anything more than that.

It already seemed like more than that, though.

She'd *cried* in front of him. That was way more personal to Gwyn than coming in front of someone, and she'd done both in the past twenty-four hours with Wells. That had to be some kind of Emotional Vulnerability Record for her, and given that she was still feeling a little shaky, it would've been smarter to agree that he should go on up to his house.

Instead, she'd invited him in, and now, as she walked out of the kitchen, drinks in hand, her heart stuttered in her chest.

He was standing in the living room, his back to her, which let her admire his broad shoulders, his narrow waist, the way his hair curled against his collar, the things those dark jeans he was wearing did for his ass and thighs.

Should've made him get naked, too, she thought a little wistfully, then shook herself. She was supposed to be handing him his "thanks for rescuing my cat" drink and sending him on his way, not ogling him.

"Made you an old-fashioned. Felt appropriate," she said, and he turned slightly, accepting the cocktail from her, his fingers brushing hers. That simple touch sent a rush of heat through her, and she didn't meet his eyes as they clinked glasses.

"To Sir Purrcival and his continued safety," Wells said, and outside, there was another boom of thunder.

Wells glanced toward the front door, a crease between his brows. "I never hear that sound without thinking my father is somewhere nearby and in a bad mood."

"Is your father Zeus?" she asked. "Odin, maybe?"

That made him chuckle, and he shrugged as he took another sip. "Sometimes he feels like it. But no, his magic is tied to weather, which means anytime he's annoyed, it rains. And it rains a lot."

Gwyn had met Simon Penhallow once and not been impressed. Rhys had always insisted Wells was basically a younger version of his father, but Gwyn wasn't so sure. Yes, he could be as haughty as a Roman emperor, but Wells was also kind and thoughtful. Sweet in his way.

And apparently *very* generous in bed.

Those were Danger Zone Thoughts, though, so Gwyn turned

her attention to the shelf Wells had been studying when she came in.

"What were you looking at so intently?" she asked, and he reached out, tapping a tarot card lying there.

"This," he said. "It's beautiful."

It was the Ten of Swords, a rough card, one that usually showed someone on the ground, skewered there by all those blades. But while this one had those elements—a redheaded woman on the ground, her body surrounded by swords—it wasn't nearly as grim. For one thing, the swords weren't piercing her flesh, just the fabric of the long dress she wore, and while her eyes were closed, she didn't appear to be dead or hurt, just resting, the smallest smile tilting her lips. And in the distance, past a row of dark and forbidding trees, the sun was coming up, bathing the top part of the card in a soft pinkish light.

"Usually such a dark card," Wells went on, "but this one is lovely, and it seems to understand the real point of the card. That yes, the worst has come, but look." He tapped the sunrise in the background. "A new day is coming. And the wounds the swords have dealt aren't fatal, just binding for now."

Wells took a sip of his drink, and Gwyn watched his throat move above the collar of his white shirt, her own throat suddenly tight.

"I'll have to see who makes this deck, get it into Penhallow's," he went on, and Gwyn shook her head, placing her drink on the mantel just to her left.

"You can't," she told him, and when he looked over at her, she crossed her arms over her chest, tilting her head.

"That deck is a Something Wicked exclusive."

Wells raised an eyebrow. "Oh? Why is that?"

"Because I painted it."

Outside, the rain was pounding down now, the wind howling, and the lights actually flickered for a second before Wells said, "You really are a bloody wonder, Gwyn Jones."

She was wearing ripped jeans and a long-sleeved T-shirt that said, *IF I WERE A WITCH GIRL*. Her face was still red and probably a little puffy from crying, and whatever makeup she'd put on that morning was long gone. She felt tired and raw and worried about her magic, and Wells was looking at her like she was the most amazing thing he'd ever seen, a world wonder he could not believe he was in the presence of.

"That is so deeply unfair," Gwyn said on a sigh, and then took one last swig of her drink and stepped into his arms.

CHAPTER 26

H is mouth tasted dark and sweet, like the cherries and bourbon on her own tongue, and when he groaned, his hand coming up to cup her face, Gwyn deepened the kiss, pressing herself shamelessly against him, her hands clutching his waist.

Another crack of thunder shook the house, and the lights flickered again before going out, plunging them into darkness.

Lifting his face from hers, Wells looked around them, his hand still there at her jaw, thumb absentmindedly stroking.

"Don't tell me you're afraid of the dark, Esquire," Gwyn said, her voice husky, and his eyes moved back to hers, lips quirking.

"Actually, I was just thinking that one of these days, we're going to do this sort of thing in broad fucking daylight where I can see every inch of you," he replied, and she laughed, her hand sliding around to the back of his head, tugging his hair.

"Who said you were going to get to see anything tonight?" she teased. "This is just a kiss, after all. Not a guarantee of nudity."

Wells's expression sobered. "Of course," he said. "And you've had a rough night, so I wouldn't want to feel like I was—"

"'Taking advantage,'" she finished for him, then gave his hair another tug. "I know. Which is very sweet of you, but trust me, if anything, it's the other way around."

Leaning forward, she nipped at his lower lip, and he grunted, his hand flexing against her cheek, his eyes going dark.

"And," Gwyn added, tapping her nails against the buttons of his shirt, "the plans I have for you tonight actually involve gratuitous amounts of nudity."

"Do they indeed," he muttered, looking down at her, and Gwyn nodded, letting her hand slip lower. Even through his jeans, she could feel how hard he was against her palm, and she gave a slow smile, pressing gently against him, hoping he'd make that sound again.

"Executive levels of nakedness," she continued, and yup, there was that grunt again, and she was going to need to get to those nakedness levels as soon as possible because the ache between her legs was almost painful now, her nipples hard against the lace of her bra.

But when she stepped back and reached for the hem of her T-shirt, Wells placed a hand on her arm, stopping her.

"Much as I enjoyed last night, and as awkward as it is that I will now find pickup trucks to be highly erotic locations, if it's all right with you, I thought we might try a bed tonight."

The thought of Wells in her bed made Gwyn's knees a little weak and her stomach a little swoopy, because hooking up in her truck or on her living room floor was one thing, but letting him into her bedroom?

That made it real for her.

And, Gwyn found as she stepped closer to him, winding her arms around his neck, she wanted that.

"Okay," she said, "but just so you know, there's a flight of stairs now between you and seeing my—"

Gwyn broke off with a shriek, her hands clutching at his shoulders as Wells bent slightly at the knees, his hands grabbing her backside and hauling her up off her feet.

Giggling, Gwyn clung to him as he carried her toward the stairs, her thighs around his hips. "I never would have guessed that sex brings out this side of you," she told him, kissing his neck as he navigated the stairs.

"*You* bring out this side of me," he replied, gruff, and if that made her face suddenly break into a goofy grin, at least he couldn't see it.

"This one," she said as he approached her bedroom door, and Wells carried her inside, his mouth finding hers again before he lowered her to her feet.

It was even darker in here, her room a minefield of clothes, discarded shoes, books, a shoebox of painting supplies, and they tripped and stumbled and laughed against each other's mouth all while peeling off clothes, tossing them aside to join the rest of the mess.

Her bed, at least, was thankfully free of debris, and Gwyn tossed back the quilt, climbing in just as there was a slight hum and the lights surged back on.

She'd only left a small bedside lamp on, but that was plenty of light to see Wells standing at the edge of her bed, naked and gorgeous and perfect, and her eyes drank him in even as his gaze roamed over her.

"Oh, I have never been so thankful for electricity as I am right now," Wells murmured, and Gwyn smirked, reaching out, her hand closing around his cock as he sucked in a quick breath, stomach muscles tensing.

"Definitely a big fan, too," she replied, watching his face as she stroked him, loving the way his mouth fell open, his eyes unfocused and wild, his chest heaving.

She could have watched him forever, could have *touched* him forever, but then he was gently pulling her hand away.

"If you keep doing that while you're *looking* at me like that," he said, pressing a kiss into her palm before gently teasing the fleshy pad at the base of her thumb with his teeth, "I'll come before I have a chance to be inside you."

His eyes met hers then, pupils wide, the blue a thin ring around the black. "Provided you want me inside you."

"I do," she said, nodding quickly. "I really, really do."

He smiled at that, that slow, sexy smile which she somehow knew was hers and hers alone, and Gwyn licked her lips, scooting back on the bed as he followed, his arms braced on either side of her body as he stared down at her.

The sheets were soft underneath her, her colorful quilt a tangled mess at one corner of the bed, and he looked so right here in her bedroom, he *felt* so right, that she waited for that surge of panic to swell up, but there was only heat and desire, and something that felt suspiciously like happiness.

Tilting her face up, Gwyn brushed her lips over his, his beard tickling. "There's a bag somewhere on this floor with condoms in it," she told him, and he kissed her back, muttering something against her mouth as he lifted one hand, sparks dancing on his fingertips.

The bag rose up off the floor, floating over to the bed. It made her laugh, but as Wells fumbled inside, it was also a reminder that her magic had deserted her yet again tonight.

That thought caused a chill to shiver up her spine, and the only thing for it was to pull Wells closer, to kiss him until she forgot anything but the feel of him, the taste of him, the gentle sting of his beard on her neck, her breasts, the soft skin of her stomach.

He made to move lower, but Gwyn wanted him with her when she came this time, and so she tugged at his shoulders, pulling him up her body, opening herself to him.

She wanted him like this, on top of her, as much of his skin touching hers as she could get, and when he slid inside of her and she clenched around him, they both moaned.

His face was close to hers, and Gwyn found herself fascinated with every flicker of emotion there as he began to move, the way he tensed almost like he was in pain, and then, when he opened his eyes, the heat and focus he fixed on her.

It was almost too much. It *was* too much, and Gwyn tore her gaze from his, her hips rising to meet his thrusts, pleasure and tension curling low in her stomach until she finally slid a hand between them, touching herself.

Wells's movements stuttered, his breath sawing in and out of his lungs, and he muttered something in Welsh that almost sounded like a prayer.

Everything was a blur after that, a hot, sweaty blur of his lips on hers and her fingers rubbing faster, and his thrusts harder, deeper, her brass bed creaking and the storm still raging outside, and then she was coming, her forehead pressed to his shoulder, her arms clasped around him.

Wells followed her just a few moments later, her name somewhere in there among all the Welsh, and this time, when their eyes met, Gwyn didn't look away.

CHAPTER 27

I like it here," Wells said drowsily, studying the ceiling over Gwyn's bed. He had no idea what time it was, and outside, the rain had softened to a gentle patter against the roof. In here, though, it was warm and dry, and Gwyn was a soft weight at his side.

She laughed now, lifting her head from his shoulder to look at him. Her skin was still flushed pink, lips slightly swollen, and Wells knew that no matter what happened from here on out, he'd always think of this moment and how lovely she was.

"Do you mean being in bed with me or in Graves Glen in general?"

"Delighted about the first, obviously," he said, rolling onto his side and skimming a hand over her hip. "But yes, it was the second I was thinking about."

"Any particular reason why?"

He sighed, still stroking her hip as she arched into him like a cat. "It'll sound daft," he warned, not sure he could explain it properly, "but it was the weather tonight. The storm. I used to lie in my bed in Dweniniaid, hearing it rain, and thinking how I'd get up the next morning and it would still be raining, and no one would come into the pub, and how all those rainy days seemed to string together. Every day some mild variation on the same thing."

"And now?" Gwyn asked softly, stacking her hands beneath her cheek.

"Now," he told her, "I was thinking how I was spending a rainy night in bed with this glorious woman, and tomorrow I'll open up my shop, where actual customers will come in and be happy to be there. And I have no idea what else the day may bring, and that feels pretty fucking spectacular."

She smiled at that, her bare foot nudging his. "Oh, so now you like surprises. But when it was me throwing a bachelorette party in your house, *that* was another issue."

"That," he said, putting an arm around her waist and pulling her closer, not missing the way her gaze went a little hazy, "was me being exhausted and confused and unprepared to find a house full of people."

"There were, like, six of us."

"Ah, but you count for at least five women all on your own, my Gwynnevere," he said, and she rolled her eyes but kissed him all the same, pushing him onto his back as she leaned over him.

"I *am* sorry your first night back in Graves Glen involved penis headbands," she told him now, and Wells chuckled, lifting his head to nuzzle her jaw before flopping back on the pillow, his hand coming up to tug gently at the pink streak in her hair.

Eyes flicking toward the side, Gwyn smirked. "You realize you do that a lot, don't you? Does pink hair really do it for you or something?"

"Hmm," Wells hummed, then let the strands of hair fall back against her neck and shoulders as her eyes widened.

"Wait, does it?" she asked, and he actually felt himself blushing a little as he looked up at her, which was completely insane given that he was currently naked and hard and pressed against her equally naked body.

"I realize it's bad form to discuss other women while in bed with someone," he started, and now Gwyn's eyebrows went up as she rested her hands on his chest, propping her chin on top of them.

"Okay, now I have to hear this."

Wells smiled at her, even as the tips of his ears went hot. "Fine. When I was at Penhaven, I occasionally saw this girl."

"'Saw' in the biblical sense?"

Reaching down, Wells pinched her bottom and she gave an exaggerated yelp.

"'Saw' as in 'saw romantically and piningly in the distance,' thank you very much," he informed her, turning his gaze back to the ceiling as he remembered.

"Anyway, she had the prettiest purple hair. Violet, really, and I'd catch sight of her out of the corner of my eye and think I should go talk to her. But, as we've previously established, I was an absolute wanker back then. And then, of course, I embarrassed myself horribly in front of her in a classroom by acting like a complete show-off, so it was yet another smashing romantic success from Wells Pen—why are you looking at me like that?"

He'd dropped his eyes back to her face to see her watching him with the strangest expression, one he couldn't even begin to interpret, and for a second, Wells wondered if he'd made a mistake in telling her about the girl with the purple hair.

"I'm not still pining for her," he told her, frowning. "In case you're worried that this return to Graves Glen was some sort of lost-love thing. I just really liked her hair, and yes, had several explicit fantasies about it, but—"

She cut off his babbling with another kiss, and then there was absolutely no woman in his mind except Gwyn herself as she threw her leg over his lap and rose up above him.

Later—much later—Gwyn sighed in his arms and said, "I've put off worrying about my magic for as long as I can, I think."

Wells was curled around her, her back against his chest, and he kissed her shoulder, tasting the slight salt of her sweat there. "You were upset," he reminded her. "And magic doesn't always play by the rules."

Lifting one hand, she moved her fingers.

Nothing happened.

Another sigh, and she lowered her arm, scooting closer to him. "It's more than that," she said. "Something's wrong. And it's been wrong ever since Morgan came back."

Twisting in his arms, Gwyn looked up at him. "Maybe it's time for the direct approach."

GWYN WASN'T SURE what the appropriate outfit was for confronting an evil witch about stealing your magic, but she sensed one couldn't go wrong all in black. So after her shower that next morning (which she had very graciously and magnanimously shared with Wells before sending him back to his house for a change of clothes), she'd pulled out her blackest jeans, an inky sweater, and a pair of black boots.

Problem was, when Wells returned from his house, he'd apparently decided black was a solid choice as well, and now, as they sped down the mountain in Gwyn's truck, she glanced over at him.

"I can't decide if we look intimidating or like we're forming a Goth band," she said, and he sniffed, tugging at his lapels.

"And here I was thinking we looked like a pair of undertakers."

That made Gwyn smile, something of a feat given how freaked out—and pissed off—she was, and seeing it, Wells reached over, squeezing her hand. "We'll get this sorted, Gwyn," he promised, and she squeezed back.

It was probably residual sex hormones, but it felt good, having Wells by her side. Scarier than that, it felt *right,* the same way having him in her bedroom had felt right last night.

Maybe, just maybe, it was time to get used to the idea that Wells felt right . . . in general.

And she would.

But first, she was getting her damn magic back.

As she turned past Main Street, Wells twisted in his seat a little, watching the street recede behind them. "I should've put some kind of sign on Penhallow's this morning, saying we're closed," he said, and Gwyn shook her head.

"No worries, Esquire. Parker is opening up Something Wicked, and I sent Cait over there to open up shop for you. Did you know the locking spell you have on that place is weak as fuck? Cait broke it in, like, three seconds."

Gwyn could feel Wells's eyes on the side of her face.

"You . . . sent your Baby Witches into my shop."

"Yes, you're welcome."

She hadn't gotten a Llewellyn Penhallow Patented Scowl in a while, but oh, it was in evidence now, and honestly, it was kind of a relief.

"Should I call my insurance company?" he asked. "Make sure my fire policy is sound?"

"Cait is under very strict instructions not to do any magic in there or even *touch* your fireplace," Gwyn assured him, and she thought Wells actually went a little gray.

"I forgot about the fireplace," he murmured to himself, and then he fumbled in his pocket for his cell phone.

"Rhiannon's tits," he bit out, glancing over at her as he pulled up an app, "how can I be this annoyed with you and still think your hair looks beautiful in the sunlight right now?"

Gwyn shook her head. "Something tells me that's a feeling we're both going to need some time getting used to."

Wells snorted, his fingers flying over the screen, that dark jewel in his signet ring winking.

"Are you thinking *my* hair looks beautiful in the sunlight, Gwynnevere?" he asked without looking at her.

"I was actually thinking that as soon as we make Morgan reverse whatever spell she's done on me, we should go back to your store, kick Cait out, lock the door, and fuck in front of that fireplace you're so proud of."

The slightly choked sound Wells made to that was so very gratifying, and now she could feel his eyes on her face again, but this time, the intent behind that look was very, very different.

"Amenable?" she asked brightly, looking over at him, and oh, yes, that was a *very* different look indeed.

"Terribly," he managed to reply, and Gwyn turned off on the road leading to Morgan's house.

Clearing his throat, Wells reached up and unbuttoned the top button of his collar, tugging at the fabric. "You're so sure it's Morgan, then? And that this will be easily undone?"

"First one yes, second one not as much," she admitted. It had been on her mind all morning, if she was being honest. Did she really believe it was Morgan causing this, or did she just *want* to because that was the easiest answer?

She didn't know, but Gwyn had always found it best to approach things with almost lethal amounts of confidence, and this time was no exception.

Morgan's house came into view, every bit as big and odd as it had been that night, and Gwyn thought she saw a curtain flick open then closed on one of the upper floors.

Good.

Taking a deep breath, she opened the truck door and climbed out. The grass was still damp underfoot despite the perfect autumn day, and Gwyn shivered as she stared up at the house.

Then she felt Wells's hand, warm and strong, in hers. "Let's get this over with, shall we?" he said, and nodded.

"Oh, we fucking shall."

CHAPTER 28

I n another life, Gwyn probably would've made a good general, Wells thought as he followed her up to Morgan's house. Possibly a cult leader.

Because he could think of a thousand reasons why bearding a potentially dangerous witch in her den seemed ill-advised at best, disastrous at worst, especially given that Gwyn no longer had access to magic, and yet, when she'd announced her intention to do just that this morning, he hadn't questioned it.

Part of it was that he wanted to believe she was right. That confronting Morgan would put an end to all of this, give Gwyn back her power, and restore the status quo.

And part of it was probably the fact that he was, he suspected, falling quite desperately in love with her and would do whatever she wanted him to.

An alarming thought given that he had only known her for a few weeks now, but he knew what he'd felt when he'd woken up beside her this morning. It wasn't a feeling he was terribly familiar with, really only had one serious brush with it years ago, but he recognized it all the same.

It wasn't lust—all right, it wasn't *only* lust—but something deeper.

Something stronger.

Something he'd decided to keep a very tight lid on for the time being given that he was fairly certain she didn't feel the same.

Yet.

But there was time, wasn't there?

That oppressive magic still clung to Morgan's house, making his teeth itch and setting off a dull headache at the back of his skull the closer they got, and when Gwyn climbed the front steps, he followed a little slowly.

Knocking on the door, she turned to look back at him and whispered, "We didn't decide who was going to be the Good Cop and who'd be the Bad Cop."

"What?" he whispered back, but then the door opened and Morgan was standing there, smiling, but clearly surprised to see them.

"Gwyn! Wells! What brings y'all all the way out here?"

"We need to talk to you about some things, Morgan," Gwyn said, and without waiting for an invitation, made her way inside, forcing Morgan to move out of the way.

Wells followed, and if he'd hoped the house might be slightly less awful in the daylight, he was sorely disappointed. Everything about it still pulsed with that feeling he could only describe as *wrong,* the heavy drapes and dark furniture seeming to absorb all the light in the place.

Gwyn's boots clicked on the hardwood floors as she made her way into the sitting room, and Morgan trailed behind, her brow furrowed. Like Gwyn and Wells, she, too, was all in black, a drapey kind of gown that really didn't do much to change the impression she was some sort of evil witch.

"As you know, Morgan," Gwyn said, folding her arms over her chest, "Wells and I are responsible for overseeing the magic in Graves Glen and making sure that it's used responsibly and safely."

Morgan's eyes flicked back and forth between them. "I knew your magic now controlled this town, Gwyn," she said slowly, and Gwyn nodded, her expression stern.

Did that make her the Bad Cop? Was he supposed to be Good Cop now?

Clearing his throat, Wells added, "There have been some . . . abnormalities, magically speaking, since you came to town that have Gwyn and I both concerned."

Now Morgan looked genuinely confused, her bracelets clinking together as she placed a hand on one narrow hip. "What do you mean?"

Coming to stand next to Gwyn, Wells mimicked her pose, then thought better of it lest they looked like they were posing for an album cover.

Instead, he clasped his hands behind his back and said, "We know you were asked to leave Penhaven College ten years ago."

Something in Morgan's expression went hard at that, her red lips pressing tightly together.

"And," he went on, "we know you have a collection of . . . well, let us say *questionable* artifacts in your attic."

"I knew the two of you weren't just making out in there," she said, trying to smile again, but it looked more like she was baring her teeth.

"Thirdly," Wells continued, "there is some sort of magic in this house that frankly sets my teeth on edge and has no rational explanation. One of these things would be cause for concern, Morgan, but all of them together?"

"Graves Glen has been cursed before, and we pulled it back from the brink," Gwyn said now, stepping forward as Morgan actually shrank back a little. "So we're a little protective of our town, and I take it *especially* personally when someone starts fucking with my magic."

Morgan had seemed nervous before, but now she slid right back into confused. "What?"

"My magic," Gwyn said. "It's not working, and that started right around the same time *you* came to town. So whatever it is you've done, I suggest you *un*do it. Now."

Yes, clearly Gwyn was Bad Cop because Wells thought he might be a little frightened of her right now.

And possibly more than a little turned on.

"I, I haven't done anything to your magic, Gwyn," Morgan said, and Wells studied her, the corners of his mouth turning down.

Maybe she was a remarkably good actress, but he thought she might be telling the truth.

Gwyn seemed less convinced, her eyes narrowing, and Morgan sighed, waving one hand, her sleeve making a dramatic arc.

"I was asked to leave Penhaven because Rosa, Harrison, and I, along with Merry Murphy and Grace Li, were doing forbidden magic. Glamours on humans, making plain pieces of paper look like money, changing our appearances, that sort of thing. It was . . . well, it wasn't harmless, I know that now, but we were kids, and we thought we were having fun."

She sucked her lower lip between her teeth, two bright spots of color high on her cheeks. "But it was embarrassing. Everyone knowing we'd been kicked out even if they never called it something that crass. So when I came back, I wanted . . . I don't know, to make a splash, I guess. To show everyone how far I'd come up in the world."

Her hand moved, fingers drifting through the air, and the walls around them seemed to blur and sway, making Wells blink and pinch the bridge of his nose.

He could still see the silk wallpaper, the gilded portraits, the heavy velvet drapes, but they wobbled, grew transparent. Behind them, he could make out plain pieces of lumber, cotton curtains.

Gwyn turned in a slow circle.

"The whole place is a glamour," she said, and Morgan nodded.

"I know. Clearly, I didn't learn my lesson there, but I promise, no one was hurt by this. I wanted to come back to town a success, and I tried to magick up an entire house, but, *Goddess,* that was hard, so it seemed easier to do this. I really was going to work on making it all real eventually, but I wanted to throw a party before the Samhain season kicked off."

The walls stopped moving, seeming to pop back into place, and Wells blinked again, trying to make himself see straight. That would explain what he was feeling, though. A glamour that big, that heavy, was bound to mess with his perception of magic.

"What about the things in the attic?" he asked, putting his hands in his pockets. "Are those glamours, too?"

"No, unfortunately those are very real. I bought another witch's estate sight unseen, and when I opened the trunks, I was as horrified as you were. But I didn't want to sell anything to the wrong sort of witch, so I just put it all up there."

Turning back to Gwyn, Morgan said, "That's what I was going to show Harrison. He was thinking about buying all of it and finding a way to safely dispose of it all."

Dropping her head, she sighed. "So there you have it. Stupid, I know, all vaguely mortifying, and I realize I have fucked up any kind of good impression I was hoping to make, but I promise, Gwyn."

Crossing the room, she took Gwyn's hands in hers. "I have not done anything to your magic. I never would. I came back here once I heard about you and your family taking over because we'd always been friends, and I . . . I thought maybe Graves Glen could be home again. I'm so sorry."

"No, I'm sorry," Gwyn said with a sigh, and Wells hated the way her shoulders slumped. "I shouldn't have accused you of anything. And I'm glad you're back, genuinely." She gave Morgan's hands a little shake, smiling. "We are friends, and you're welcome in Graves Glen. Just maybe find a new, less creepy house and get rid of Satan's yard sale up there?"

Morgan laughed, nodding. "That's a deal," she said, wrapping her arms around Gwyn in a quick hug.

When she pulled back, she gave Gwyn another sympathetic pat. "And seriously, I'll help with this magic issue if you want. I've heard of this kind of thing happening before, and I'm sure there's a solution."

Wells could see Gwyn willing herself to believe the same, gathering up that confidence she wore like armor. "That would be great, Morgan, thank you," she said, and then she nodded at Wells.

"We should head back to town."

After making plans to talk about something called the Gathering with Morgan later, Gwyn left, Wells just behind her, and they were silent as they made their way back to her truck.

The silence stretched nearly to Main Street before Gwyn sighed and said, "I'm glad Morgan's not evil, but I gotta be honest, Esquire. I'm really disappointed Morgan's not evil."

Wells smiled, picking up her hand off her lap and kissing the back of it. "Merely a minor setback on the path to triumph," he assured her, and she sniffed, one corner of her mouth kicking up.

"Just this once, I'm gonna allow that kind of talk."

Penhallow's was miraculously still in one piece, and Wells spent the rest of the day there while Gwyn and her Baby Witches ran Something Wicked.

As night fell, he was just about to start closing up when he saw her headed across the street, and for a moment, he wondered if her promise about the fireplace was about to be fulfilled.

But then he saw the three witches trailing behind her and understood this wasn't that type of call.

More's the pity.

Several minutes later, he found himself sitting in one of the armchairs in front of the crackling fire, Gwyn in the one next to him, Parker and Cait both shoved into the chair just to their right, and Sam stretched out on the carpet, paging through one of Wells's spellbooks.

"There has to be a reason Glinda's magic has gone tits up," she said. "If it's not Morgan, maybe it's some other witch?"

"Maybe it's a curse," Cait offered. "Like what you and your cousin did to her husband."

"That was an accident," Gwyn said. "And it turned out to be a lot more complicated than that."

"Still worth looking into," Cait insisted.

Gwyn shrugged, and Wells was struck by how tired she looked there in the firelight, how slightly wilted, her face pale against the deep red velvet of the chair.

Without thinking he reached across the space between them, lifting her hand from the arm of her chair and tangling their fingers together, palms touching.

Gwyn's head swung around, and her lips curved into a fond smile, some life sparking in those lovely eyes, and Wells smiled back.

"*Whaaaaaat* the fuck?"

Ah, yes.

They had an audience.

Sam was watching them with her mouth open, and Cait had her hands stuffed against her lips, her eyes wide. Parker was grinning so hard their face seemed to be in danger of splitting, and Wells rolled his eyes, his ears red.

"All right, all right," he muttered, dropping Gwyn's hand as the three finally exploded into a cacophony of giggles and questions.

"How long?! How long have you two been keeping an illicit love affair from us?!"

"Oooh, I thought the other day, when we were going to do The Plan, you guys were giving each other horny looks, and then I was, like, 'No, they hate each other,' but I guess hate sometimes *is* horny because now you're holding hands? Like?"

"Are you allowed to do sex with your cousin's husband's brother? Have you even *thought* of the family tree issue?"

Laughing, Gwyn kicked one foot at Sam as Wells pointed imperiously toward the door. "Out. Out, you heathens."

"Whatever, you're not my real dad," Parker said, getting out of the chair, and that set off another round of laughter as they pulled Cait out of the chair, Sam gathering up her book and her jacket.

Wells followed them to the front door, ignoring their continued teasing, finally locking the door behind them as they spilled out onto the street, still hooting and talking over one another, Cait leaping on Parker's back as the three of them made their way toward the Coffee Cauldron.

Shaking his head, smiling in spite of himself, Wells flipped the sign to *Closed,* then turned around, hands in his pockets as he made his way around the shelves and back to the fireplace.

"Far be it from me to speak ill of your mentoring skills, Jones, but those three are a menace and should—"

His words died in his throat as he took in Gwyn, standing naked in the firelight.

"I did warn you," she told him, and Wells, mouth gone dry, nodded.

"You did. But I thought after everything, that plan might be on hold."

She walked forward, slipping into his arms, and his hands smoothed over her skin, warm from the fire. "I'm disappointed," she acknowledged, stretching up to kiss him. "I wish it had been Morgan. And I really, really want my magic back."

Wells made a distressed sound at that, but she only kissed him again, lips curving against his mouth.

"And I'm going to get it back," she promised him as she began walking him backward toward his chair.

"I've got this big gorgeous brain of mine plus all the witchy resources I could want. I've got my family, I've got the Baby Witches—don't give me that look—and I've got you."

The backs of his knees bumped the seat of his chair, and Wells sat down heavily, pulling her with him.

"You have me," he agreed, and it sounded like a promise.

A vow.

And it was.

CHAPTER 29

Gwyn had known when she agreed to serve on the Graves Glen Halloween Season Planning Committee, it wasn't going to be a great time, but she was still somehow surprised by the amount of paperwork involved.

"Everyone has their folder, right?" Jane asked, standing at the head of the table in the tiny town hall where they had these meetings, and Gwyn glanced around at the other committee members, all of whom, like Gwyn, had a folder that looked like it had to contain at least fifty thousand sheets of paper. There were vendor forms for the Fall Festival, and sign-up sheets for what stores would be doing which Halloween events, plus a bunch of waivers, and, Gwyn thought, maybe the entire town charter.

Gwyn had been to a handful of these meetings over the past few months, but she'd mostly let Vivi be the Jones Family Representative at these things. She probably should've realized that this, the last meeting before the Graves Glen Gathering, aka their first big Halloween season event, was going to take Jane to her highest and most intense Jane Level.

Across the table, Morgan was sitting up straight, her hands folded, nails a deep maroon, and when she caught Gwyn looking at her, she offered a quick smile, her eyes briefly flicking to Jane and then back to Gwyn, widening slightly in a *So this is a lot* kind of look.

The kind of look Gwyn usually gave Vivi at these things, if she was honest.

Gwyn smiled back, but there was still a little bit of queasy guilt in her stomach over her big scene at Morgan's the other day.

Or maybe that was just the terrible coffee they served in the town hall.

Or, she reflected as Jane began to talk about the new artisanal popcorn truck that would be at the Gathering this year, it was because worry about her magic and what had happened was starting to gnaw at her.

Over the past few days, Gwyn hadn't thought of much else, and researching ways to fix whatever was broken had started taking up all of her free time.

She and Wells had tried a ritual meant to strengthen magic, hoping hers was maybe just tired. That had to be a thing, right?

But that hadn't worked.

The Baby Witches found a spell that would dampen someone's power ("Like a Wi-Fi blocker," Parker had offered) but that was easy to undo. Drink springwater collected under a full moon, take a bath with quartz and salt, *boom,* dampener removed.

Gwyn had done all those things, and still no magic.

It was getting harder and harder to put off telling Vivi and

Elaine, but Vivi was due home just before Halloween, and Elaine was hard to reach out there in the desert. Besides, it wasn't the kind of thing she really wanted to tell them over the phone, and, secretly, she was hoping she could just fix it on her own without ever having to worry them.

There had to be a solution, after all. Look at what had happened to Rhys. It hadn't been easy, but that situation had been a lot more dire, and they'd totally fixed it! Made things better, even.

So there was an answer somewhere—she just had to find it.

"And that's good with you, Gwyn?"

Shit.

Glancing up, Gwyn saw Jane looking at her with those big brown eyes of hers, and wondered what exactly she was supposed to be good with, and how to get out of this without Jane realizing she'd tuned out the last five minutes or so.

"I think Gwyn has so much on her plate with Something Wicked that maybe someone else should worry about the glow sticks." Morgan stepped in smoothly, flipping open her folder and making a note with a purple pen. "I can handle that, no problem."

Jane sagged with relief like the future of every citizen's survival depended on having glow sticks. "Thanks, Morgan. That will be perfect."

The meeting broke up soon after that, and as Gwyn made her way outside, Morgan fell into step beside her.

"So this is behind the curtain," she said, gesturing back toward the meeting room. "I have to say, when I was a student here, I had no idea how much effort the humans were putting into Halloween."

Shifting her bag to her other shoulder, Gwyn took a deep breath of the crisp night air. "Trust me, it wasn't always this intense. We did Founder's Day, and of course Halloween was big, but Jane added the Fall Festival, and now that Founder's Day is the Graves Glen Gathering, she's going even harder. Next year, none of us will be able to sleep from September first to Samhain, probably."

Morgan laughed softly at that, her heels clicking on the sidewalk. "It's fun, though. Seeing this time of year through their eyes."

The night was cool, and Gwyn tugged her leather jacket more tightly around her as leaves skittered down the street. "When you put it like that, it does sound kind of fun," Gwyn acknowledged, and glanced over at Morgan.

"I think you actually enjoy the planning committee. Massive folders and all."

"The massive folders are a big part of the appeal, yes."

"Not to gild the lily, but if you stay friendly with Jane, she might even give you a label maker at some point."

"Ooooh, now *that* is the dream."

They both laughed then, and Gwyn stopped, turning to look at Morgan, the night wind blowing her hair back from her face.

"Still feeling really bad about basically thinking you were evil," she said, and Morgan dismissed that with a wave of her hand.

"It's fine," Morgan said, kicking at a stray leaf with the toe of one elegant high heel. "I mean, I would've been suspicious, too. I come back to town all of a sudden, I have this weird house and all this crazy magic stuff in the attic."

She gave Gwyn a slightly chagrined smile. "And I have always been a little try-hard, I know. You just always seemed so cool to me back at college, and now you're basically running this place with your magic, and I . . . I wanted you to like me."

"I do," Gwyn said, reaching out and giving Morgan's arm a little squeeze. "Seriously. And I like you even more now that you've saved me from tracking down ten thousand glow sticks."

Groaning, Morgan tipped her head back. "Don't remind me. At least she wants those for Halloween, not the Gathering. I've still got time."

Then she looked back down at Gwyn, frowning. "Do you think I can maybe just make those? With magic?"

"It might be worth a shot," Gwyn said, smiling even as her stomach sank a little. "And I'd help you, but . . . "

She trailed off, and now it was Morgan's turn to touch her arm. "Still no magic?"

"No," Gwyn said, sighing, then tried to give her most confident hair toss. "But we're on it."

"If you need any help, I'm here for you," Morgan said. "And I can look through all that stuff I have up in the attic. Not," she added, holding up one hand, "the really scary-looking stuff. But there are some old books and things up there, might be worth it to try? Why don't you come by next week?"

Gwyn nodded even as the thought of spending any more time in that attic made her shudder. "I just might do that," she said, and the scary thing was, she actually meant it. If she and Wells couldn't figure this thing out soon, even a terrifying attic full of ancient torture devices didn't sound so bad.

She and Morgan said good night, and Gwyn walked the rest of the block to where her truck was parked.

Wells was supposed to be waiting for her back at her cabin so they could work on more solutions for restoring her magic, but when Gwyn opened the door, it was clear an entirely different kind of sorcery was brewing.

Following the mouthwatering scent filling the house, Gwyn walked into the kitchen to see Wells standing at her stove, her biggest soup pot bubbling away on the burner. He had a dishcloth tucked into his belt and was humming to himself as he stirred, and Gwyn leaned against the doorframe, happy to watch him without him knowing for a bit.

It wasn't just that there was something deeply appealing about a man who knew how to cook—although that could not be discounted—and it wasn't how good he looked there in her kitchen, his hair a little mussed, his sleeves rolled up. It was the feeling in her chest at how comfortable he seemed there in her kitchen, in her world, Sir Purrcival twining around his ankles, clearly hoping for a sample of whatever was in that pot.

Wells felt *right* here. In her space. With her and her cat, slipping right into things like there had always been a Wells-shaped hole in her life.

And the scariest part of that was it didn't scare her at all.

"Mama! Mama mama mama SOUP treats!"

Wells turned around then, and Gwyn pointed a finger at her cat, narrowing her eyes. "Snitch," she said, and Purrcival trotted over, coming up on his back legs as he pressed his front paws to her leg, stretching.

Bending down to pick up Purrcival, Gwyn nodded toward the stove. "Please tell me that's almost ready because I've never smelled anything so good in my entire life."

Clearly pleased with himself, Wells smiled, giving the pot another stir before lifting the wooden spoon and blowing over it, offering her a quick taste.

She leaned in, and yes, whatever it was he was cooking tasted just as divine as it smelled, and she widened her eyes at him. "Esquire, you never mentioned you were a Kitchen Witch."

He huffed out a laugh, reaching over and swiping a bit of the stew from her lower lip with his thumb, a simple touch that still had warmth spreading throughout her body.

"I'm not," he said, turning back to the pot. "I simply had a lot of time to practice my cooking skills whilst no one came into my pub."

Putting Sir Purrcival back down, Gwyn crossed to the sink to wash her hands before grabbing a couple of bowls and spoons. As Wells ladled out the soup, she asked, "So why were you there? In Wales running a pub no one went to? I mean, you're clearly a super-talented witch, why pour beers for a living."

"Excuse me, I was *pulling pints*," Wells corrected, carrying both soup bowls to the table. He'd lit candles, she saw, the nice bayberry ones her mom had made, and that made her bite back a smile as she took her seat.

"And," Wells continued, sitting across from her, "it was more than just a pub. It had once been an Anchor Point."

"What's that?" Gwyn asked, tearing off a hunk of bread from the plate Wells had placed in the center of the table.

"Old bit of magic," he said. "Not unlike the ley lines here, but not as strong. Basically, my family planted a spark of their magic in the center of what would become the village of Dweniniaid, sort of . . . staking a claim against other witches, I guess. Any other witch who came into the area would be able to sense there was already a coven there."

"So does that magic fuel you up or something?" Gwyn asked, intrigued, and Wells shook his head.

"No, nothing like that. It's more just a bit of our history, and it was important to Da that it be preserved. So I ran the pub and did the odd spell and rune work to keep that little bit of magic alive."

"And now that you're not there, it'll die?"

Wells shrugged, scooping up a spoonful of soup. "More like a candle going out. But honestly, it was time. We were just delaying the inevitable, and I think Da finally understood that."

Gwyn stirred her spoon through her soup. "So that's why you left school," she said. "To be the keeper of the flame as it were."

He nodded. "My uncle had been there for ages, but when he died, a Penhallow needed to take his place, so . . . "

He trailed off, and for a long moment, they were quiet, the only sound the scraping of their spoons and the wind rattling the trees just beyond the front porch.

"I met your dad," Gwyn finally said, and Wells looked up, his eyes very blue in the candlelight.

"Oh, I am aware," he said, and she laughed at that, pushing her hair back off her shoulders.

"We were not each other's biggest fan," she said, and Wells snorted, shaking his head as he looked back down at his bowl.

"He's all bark, not much bite," he said, but Gwyn remembered how Simon had sat at this very table, glowering at all of them, and wasn't sure that was actually true.

"I know he can come across as . . . well, I'm sure Rhys would have the appropriately colorful term for it, but he wasn't always like that. I think when my mother died, he found it easier to retreat into his magic and his family history, all of that. It gave him something to focus on instead of his pain."

Reaching across the table, Gwyn gave his hand a quick squeeze. "Rhys said your mom was pretty great."

Wells returned the squeeze with a tight smile before drawing his hand back. "He doesn't remember her. Not really. He was only four when she died. Bowen was just five. I don't think he has many memories of her, either, and certainly not of her and Da together."

"But you do," Gwyn said, and he nodded.

"She was a lot like Rhys, actually. Funny. Charming. She was good for Da, and without her, I think he was . . . lost, really. Magic gave him something to hold on to, something that made him feel connected to the world again."

Wells gave another one of those smiles that wasn't really a

smile at all. "It can certainly be a little much at times, his obsession with family legacy, but I'll take the grumpy old sod quizzing me about some Penhallow who died in 1432 over what he was those months after Mam died."

Gwyn nodded even as her heart broke just the littlest bit. It made sense now, Wells's dutifulness, his loyalty to his father. But if Rhys had been four, that meant Wells had only been seven. Seven years old, his mom gone, his brothers so little, and his father lost in grief.

"Christ, this is not the dinner conversation I'd expected us to have tonight," Wells said, turning back to his soup. "Just a few weeks in America, and look at me, talking about feelings."

Gwyn smiled and kicked his foot gently under the table. "It's a slippery slope from talking about your childhood to starting an Instagram that's nothing but sunset pictures and inspirational quotes, Esquire."

"Duly noted." He glanced back up at her. "What about you? I don't think I've ever heard you mention your father."

"Taliesin?" Gwyn shrugged. "He's great, but he's definitely a father only in the strictest, biological sense. Mom decided she was ready to have a baby but didn't want all the hang-ups that came along with marriage or co-parenting and all that. So she very sensibly picked the cutest, nicest guy at the Ren Faire in Tennessee, *et voilà*." Gwyn gestured to herself. "*Moi*. He sends me a card on my birthday—I mean, in the general *vicinity* of my birthday, he's sweet but kind of a flake—and we're friends on social media, but that's about as far as it goes. Which works for me. Mom was all I needed."

Gwyn missed her mom, she realized, and wondered what Elaine would say about Wells. She hadn't liked Simon, either, but she adored Rhys. And it was easy to picture Elaine at this table with them, Wells a part of things.

Part of the family.

More thoughts she shouldn't be thinking, and yet . . .

"So, what do you think your dad would feel about all this?" Gwyn asked, gesturing between the two of them with her spoon.

Wells placed his own spoon beside his bowl and laced his fingers together, studying her. "The two of us eating soup together?" he asked. "Or the two of us working together to restore your magic?"

"The two of us banging," she replied, and he gave that huffed laugh again, sitting back slightly, his hair falling over his forehead.

"Well, as I'm not in the business of talking about my personal life with my father, I can safely say that is a bridge we need not cross anytime soon."

But we will have to cross it, Gwyn thought. *If we keep doing this.*

And she was pretty sure they were going to keep doing this.

As if to illustrate the point, Sir Purrcival sauntered over, and rather than trying to jump up in the middle of the table, curled up peacefully on the floor next to Wells's chair, tilting his head to look up at him.

"*Esquire,*" he said, his little voice sleepy and fond, and Wells chuckled, leaning down to pet him.

And suddenly Gwyn knew she was in very, very deep trouble.

CHAPTER 30

The morning of the Graves Glen Gathering was gray and gloomy, the first real chill of autumn sweeping through the valley.

It was, in other words, completely perfect.

Or it would have been if Gwyn wasn't still worried about her magic.

After dinner two nights before, she and Wells had dug back into their research, coming up with a spell for a charmed crystal that was supposed to "restore what is lost," but the only effect it had had was that Gwyn finally found a pair of green Converse sneakers she'd thought were gone forever.

A win, but not exactly what she'd been hoping for.

Wells had assured her they would keep trying, and she clung to that even as she knew it was finally time to let Vivi and Elaine know what was going on with her.

But first, she needed to get Wells through his first big Graves Glen holiday.

She'd tried to warn him the night before that the Holiday

Formerly Known as Founder's Day was huge, kicking off the Halloween season and sending the first big influx of tourists into the town.

He'd smiled that infuriatingly smug Esquire Smile and said something like, "Prithee, Gwynnevere, do not fret for I am *well* prepared for any abundant onslaught of various and sundry travelers to our fair town."

Okay, that was maybe a slight exaggeration, but that's what she'd *heard*.

Now, as she situated herself behind the counter of Something Wicked, she saw a line already gathering outside Penhallow's and smiled to herself.

Hope you brewed a lot of tea, Esquire.

The next few hours passed quickly, customers pouring into the store, Gwyn nearly run ragged getting extra boxes from the back, ringing people up, answering questions about crystals, and by ten, she was frowning at the clock.

Sam would be at the Coffee Cauldron today, but where the heck were Parker and Cait? It wasn't like them to miss work, although there was so much going on during the Gathering that maybe they'd gotten distracted.

Gwyn didn't have time to worry about it, though, because there were more people coming in the door, and then a kid bumped into her display of plastic pumpkins, sending them crashing to the ground.

Around noon, she was finally able to take a little break, throwing up a sign saying she'd be back in fifteen minutes.

The streets were full, the air scented with popcorn and caramel and apple, and Gwyn snagged a popcorn ball before making her way into Penhallow's.

"Yes, welcome to—oh, thank the Goddess, it's you."

Gwyn had seen Wells irritated and she'd seen him worried and she'd seen him amused and she'd seen him consumed with lust, but this was the first time she'd ever seen him look *harried,* and it was, she had to admit, kind of great.

"I warned you," she said, sauntering up behind the counter where he had several teacups lined up in saucers, teapot in hand as he filled each one. Next to him, there was a stack of crystals waiting to be wrapped as well as boxes of tea.

"Yes, yes, everyone loves a round of I Told You So," Wells snapped, and Gwyn smirked, peeling off a part of the popcorn ball and popping it into his mouth.

He made a pleased sound as he chewed, and then, glancing around, ducked his head to press the briefest of kisses behind her ear before resuming his Tea Duties. "If you'll wrap those crystals up for me, I will make it *well* worth your while later."

"Oooh, erotic bribery, my favorite."

Finishing the popcorn ball, Gwyn dusted her hands off and did as he asked, ringing up several customers afterward, then making sure he had enough bags near the register.

"Above and beyond," Wells commented, taking in her handiwork before quirking an eyebrow at her, and she patted his shoulder, winking.

"I'd hydrate if I were you," she said, and he huffed with

amusement, sending her on her way with a look that promised he would more than fulfill his part of their bargain.

Stepping back out onto the street, Gwyn thought what it might be like, having this every day. Not the Gathering—her bank account would love that, her sanity would not—but working with Wells. The two of them dropping into each other's store, helping out.

A team.

The thought warmed her more than she'd expected, and she was so high on that feeling she almost didn't see the Baby Witches, huddled by her locked door.

"Where have you two been?" she demanded of Cait and Parker. "And Sam, why aren't you at the Coffee Cauldron?"

Looking more closely at them, Gwyn wrinkled her nose. "Are y'all okay? You look—"

"We've been awake for twenty hours and we've each had way more Red Bull than any doctor would think wise," Sam said. "But we think we're onto something, Glinda. With your magic."

Blinking, Gwyn unlocked the door, and they hurried into the store. They all had bags, she saw now, bulging with what looked like heavy books, and they were jittery with excitement and caffeine. "What exactly have you found?" she asked, even as people began drifting into the store again.

Sam shook her head. "We don't want to say just yet, but we're close. Really close. Can we use your storage room?"

Looking around, Gwyn sighed. She needed help in the store, but these three were clearly in no shape to provide it, so she nodded, flicking a hand toward the curtain. "Go on. But no fire!"

They hurried across the store, disappearing into the back, and Gwyn steeled herself for the onslaught.

Roughly twenty thousand plastic pumpkins later, Something Wicked was officially closed for the day, and Gwyn was pretty sure she'd never been so tired in all her life. Usually she had Vivi helping out, and she'd also done the odd tea charm to keep her going throughout such a long day. No help and no magic really wore a girl out.

When she heard the raven over the door, she wished her magic were working if only to send whoever that was spinning back out onto the street.

But it was only Wells, looking as beat as she felt, and she walked over to him, practically collapsing against him with an exhausted moan.

His arms came around her even as he pretended to sag to the ground, and Gwyn laughed, holding on tighter.

"Remember how I said I enjoyed being a shopkeeper?" he asked. "That was a different me. A foolish me. Ever so much younger then."

"Welcome to life in a tourist town during tourist season," she replied, and he kissed her temple, beard tickling.

"I can see I have much to learn."

"At least you have a week to prepare for Fall Festival," Gwyn reminded him, and Wells groaned, looking up at the ceiling.

"St. Bugi's balls, how many festivals can one town have? That's the one with the booths, right? Where we sell our wares in a field?"

"Mmm-hmm. And the caramel apple pies, which make it worth it, I promise. Plus we get to wear costumes."

Wells tilted his head back down, eyes narrowing. "Is that a trick? Are you going to show up in normal clothes while I look like a git in sorcerer's robes?"

"I bet you look very nice in sorcerer's robes," Gwyn countered, lifting her face to ghost a kiss over his jawline, which had his hands tightening on her hips.

"I bet you look very nice *out* of sorcerer's robes," he said, and she smiled at him, reaching up to twine her arms around his neck.

"That is the cheesiest thing you've ever said, especially given that you are *very* familiar with what I look like underneath all kinds of clothes."

He grinned at her. "Still turned you on, didn't it?"

"Little bit," she admitted, and his own smile widened as he ducked his head to kiss her.

Before he could, there was a sudden whiff of air from behind the curtain leading to the storage room, the scent of smoke curling through the store.

Turning away from Wells, Gwyn sighed, tugging at his hand as she pulled him across the store.

"I told you guys no fire," she said, opening the curtain, Wells beside her as they stepped into the dim space.

Sam, Cait, and Parker were all sitting in a circle, runes drawn on the floor in front of them in chalk, candles guttering, and as she and Wells walked in, they all turned, almost as one, and glared at her.

Gwyn made a surprised sound. "What—" she started, but then she realized they weren't looking at her like that.

They were looking at Wells.

CHAPTER 31

Wells looked into the three hostile faces currently sending daggers his way and blinked, confused. The last time he'd seen these three, they'd been laughing and joking with him.

Now they all looked like they could happily see his insides on the outside, and he wasn't sure what it was he'd done to effect that change.

"What is it?" Gwyn asked, stepping forward, her hand falling from his.

"Yes, did I commit some kind of holiday faux pas here?" he asked, hands in his pockets. "Because if I did—"

"It's you, dude," Sam said, standing, arms crossed over her chest. "You're the reason Gwyn's lost her powers."

It was such an unexpected reply—such an *absurd* one—that Wells actually laughed in disbelief. "What?"

No one else was laughing, though, and for all that he had teased Gwyn about her coven of Baby Witches, in this moment, each and every one of them seemed very grown-up. Very serious.

And very pissed off at him.

"What are you talking about?" Gwyn asked them, her face thankfully looking as confused as Wells felt. But she wasn't standing as close to him anymore, and when Sam bent down and picked up a heavy leather book, she took it with eager hands.

"It's an old spell and really hard to do. I mean, it would take years to find all the stuff you need," Sam said, tapping a page as Gwyn read it, her eyes narrowed. "We didn't even look at it at first because who could do this kind of magic? And then Parker saw the reference to the ring and remembered another spell."

Now Parker stood up, their face solemn in the candlelight as they held out another book. "That's why this has been so hard to find. It's *two* spells combined. So I looked up the one about using a ring, and that's when I saw this."

They pointed to something on the page, and Wells saw Gwyn stiffen, her throat working.

She looked up at him, and her face might as well have been a mask.

"Your ring," she said, and Wells looked down at his hand, where his father's signet ring rested. The jewel looked black in the candlelight, but there was nothing more sinister about it, no sense of power clinging to it.

"This?" he said, holding up the offending hand. "This . . . it's a family heirloom, not a spell. Been in the family for generations. Surely if it could take power from a witch, it would have done so before now."

Wordlessly, Gwyn handed him the book.

Wells took it, and he realized his hands were shaking. With

anger, yes—ridiculous to think he'd have had anything to do with taking Gwyn's power. But with fear, too. He could admit that.

That distant look in her eyes . . .

The page was difficult to read, English and Welsh crammed together on narrow lines, but there, inset in the right corner, was a drawing of a ring.

A ring that looked very much like the one Wells currently wore.

"No, this . . . this isn't . . . I don't see how—"

"Who gave you the ring, Wells?" Gwyn asked. She stood there, flanked by Parker and Sam, Cait still sitting at her feet, her face just as stony as the others', and Wells began to feel something like real panic crawling up his throat.

"My father," he admitted.

"Right before he sent you here to steal Gwyn's magic," Sam said, and Wells shook his head, rubbing a hand over his hair.

"No. *No*. I volunteered to come. My father didn't want me in Graves Glen, to tell the truth. The, the ring was a gesture, nothing more."

"Give it to me."

Gwyn held out her hand, and Wells didn't hesitate, pulling the ring off his finger and placing it in her palm. This was all a mistake, after all. Gwyn's students were good kids, but they were still young witches, still prone to fuckups, and that's all this was. A monumental fuckup, same way they'd thought Morgan was to blame.

"Gwynnevere," he began, but she was already turning away.

"Is there a way we can find out for certain?" she asked, and Sam nodded, moving back to the circle.

"We can use our magic to fuel you, but just for a few seconds," she told Gwyn. "That should be long enough, though."

Gwyn nodded, and as the others sat back down, she moved into the middle of their circle.

Sam lit another candle, and Parker sketched another rune on the floor as Cait began murmuring words under her breath, the candles flickering.

Gwyn sat there, her eyes closed, his ring held out in front of her as the other three joined hands. It took a moment, but Wells felt it, then, a slow pulse of magic, rising from them, centering on Gwyn, and as he watched, her red hair blew back from her face, like someone had just slammed a door.

Then the ring started to glow.

First the silver itself, then the jewel in the center, pulsing with dark light, and Wells felt a sudden sharp stabbing pain in his hand, like he'd been burned.

He glanced down, and there, on the finger where his ring had sat, a small black band appeared.

It slithered over his skin as he watched in horrified fascination, and when he looked back up, Gwyn was watching him.

"I swear," he told her, his heart pounding, almost dizzy. "I swear on everything I am that I don't understand what's going on here."

"What's going on is that your father gave you a ring cursed

with ancient blood magic that slowly drains power away from another witch's bloodline," Parker told him, their eyes dark. "Probably because he was pissed off about Gwyn and her family replacing *your* family's magic in the town."

"No," Wells said, shaking his head. "My father is many things, I'll admit to that, but this . . . this is evil. He's proud and arrogant and not always the kindest man, but he's not *this*."

He thought back to that night in the pub when his father had seemed so broken. So sad but accepting when Wells had said he'd go to Graves Glen. He'd called him son and slipped that ring off, that ring Wells had seen him wear his whole life.

There had to be more to it, something he wasn't seeing.

"Gwyn," he said now, and she turned to him, but those lovely eyes of hers were blank, her arms wrapped around her body. "Please. You have to believe me."

"I believe that you didn't know," she said, her voice flat. "I believe that you would never do something like this. But yes, Wells, I believe your father would load you like a weapon and send you here to destroy my family."

"You don't know him," Wells insisted. "I'm telling you, this is . . . it's something else. We were wrong about Morgan, we're wrong about this."

"I don't think we are," she said, and he moved across the room, wanting to touch her, *needing* to touch her, to make her see that they could fix this together.

But she moved back, and his hands dropped to his sides, an ocean opening up between them.

"Is there a way to take the magic out of the ring? Put it back in Gwyn?" he asked Sam now, turning to look over his shoulder.

She shook her head, eyes bright, and Wells realized she was trying not to cry.

"No. The magic isn't in the ring. It's in whoever's blood created the spell in the first place. And pulling magic out of one person to put into another without some kind of cursed fucking object is pretty hard."

"Right."

Wells stood there, thinking, trying to ignore how he felt, like someone had just stabbed him in the chest, his blood seeping across the chalk runes on the floor.

This was his fault, so he had to be the one to fix it.

And there was only one place he could think of to start.

Reaching into the pocket of his waistcoat, his fingers curled around the Traveling Stone he kept there. "I'm going to make this right, Gwyn," he said. "I promise."

He focused on Wales, on home, on Simon.

And then Gwyn and her sad eyes vanished from view as everything went black.

CHAPTER 32

I t was the middle of the night in Wales, but luckily for Wells, his father had never kept the most regular hours.

When he suddenly appeared in Simon's library, his head spinning, his stomach lurching, Wells saw his father was at his usual spot, near the large map table under a huge window that faced the rocky hills of Dweniniaid.

It was dim, as it always was, and as Wells stumbled forward, his father's heavy brows drew together.

"Llewellyn?"

He came out from behind the table, robes swishing, and Wells remembered a hundred other moments in this room, a thousand. His father congratulating him on his first successful spell, telling him he was going to Penhaven, asking him to run the pub now that his uncle was dead.

This had been the scene of nearly every important meeting they'd ever had, so it felt right to be here now dealing with maybe the most important problem he'd ever faced.

"Da," Wells said. "Something's happened. In Graves—in Glynn Bedd."

"Slow down, boy, slow down," Simon said, reaching out to steady Wells, but Wells shook him off.

"I'm fine, but I don't have much time. I need to ask you about—"

Your ring.

The words were right there on his lips, but Simon's hands were still outstretched, and in the dim glow of the iron and antler chandelier overhead, his signet ring caught the light.

Wells felt as though the ground were very slowly tilting underneath his feet, and Simon stepped forward again.

Flinching back, Wells raised his eyes to his father's. "I thought you gave me that ring," he said, and Simon looked at his hand.

"Ah," he said, flexing his fingers. "And I see you're not wearing yours." Simon nodded down at Wells's hand. "Someone already catch wise? They're a quick lot, I'll give them that. But never mind it, boy. I take it the thing did its job."

Simon was already turning away, and Wells felt frozen in place, blood whooshing in his ears.

"It *was* you," Wells said, and he hated that he sounded surprised. Hated that there was still some part of him, somewhere, that had wanted to believe his brothers were wrong about their father. That he was a better man than this.

A better *father* than this.

Simon's brows drew together as he looked back at Wells, his hands folded in front of him.

"What, did you think someone else cursed a ring that brought pain unto our enemies?"

He gave one of those huffing laughs, the one Wells had heard himself make and vowed never, ever to make again.

"You . . . you gave me that ring so that I could drain the power of the Joneses," he said, still not wanting to believe it even though it was so clearly true.

"Yes, but I didn't think you'd be caught out so soon. It was meant to be a slow drain, take months, maybe even years."

"It took a few weeks," Wells said, lifeless. "And it only took power from one of them."

Simon's eyebrows rose. "Then you must've gotten very close to that one indeed. The spell works on proximity, so the more you were around her, the more you took. Well, *I* took, to be fair." He thumped Wells on the shoulder.

"Stronger than I've been in years, which is a good thing because returning our magic to that town is going to take some work."

"You used me," Wells said. "You knew that night when you came into the pub that I'd volunteer to go. That's why you came. Had to let me think it was all my idea because I never, ever would've been a part of this knowingly. But good, dutiful Llewellyn. Couldn't resist the chance to make you proud."

"Don't act so wounded, boy," Simon said, voice gruff. "I did what needed to be done. Besides, how do we know those sad excuses for witches were even telling the truth? Gryffud Penhallow was a powerful warlock. He'd have had no need to take magic from a woman like Aelwyd Jones. Barely more than a hedge witch from what I've read. No, all of this was merely some sort of scheme by those Jones women to wrest control of our power, and—"

"Stop it."

Wells didn't shout the words. He'd never been one to raise his voice, and he certainly had never raised it to his father, but he'd also never interrupted him, never looked at him the way he knew he must be looking at Simon now.

And maybe it was that look or maybe it was something in his voice, because Simon fell silent even though his scowl deepened.

"Rhys was right," Wells went on. "The spirit of Aelwyd Jones was right. Gryffud had magic, yes, but he took hers as well, and the Jones family has just as much a right to the town of Graves Glen as we ever did. More, given that they made it their home. What you've done is—"

"It was necessary," Simon said, and Wells knew then that there was no coming back from this for him.

He thought again about Gwyn's face in the candlelight, closed off to him, her eyes hard.

Every time he'd been near her, touched her, kissed her, he'd been pulling magic from her veins.

The shame was enough to nearly choke him.

He knew he would never forgive his father, but more than that, he didn't think he'd ever forgive himself.

"Well, it's failed," he said now. "Gwyn may have lost her power, but her mother will still have hers. So will Vivi. And Rhys will never speak to you again after this. Bowen, either. This . . . this was too far."

Simon waved that off. "You've all turned so bloody dramatic," he said, and if Wells weren't feeling quite so shattered, he might have retorted that those were bold words from a man currently wearing sorcerer's robes.

"In time," Simon went on, "you'll understand. You'll know what one has to do to preserve the legacy of this family."

"Nothing about this family is worth preserving," Wells replied, and he turned away, heading for the door.

"Where are you going?" his father demanded, and Wells stopped, turning around to face this man he had once been so desperate to please.

"I don't know, honestly," he replied. "But I'm not staying here. Not for one fucking second more."

Simon's expression went thunderous. "Don't you dare use that language to me, boy."

But Wells was already walking away.

IT HAD BEEN over a week since Wells had disappeared from the storage room of Gwyn's shop.

Over a week since she'd learned he was the reason she'd lost her magic.

Over a week since she'd felt like smiling. Or laughing.

Or getting out of bed.

But the thing was, the world didn't stop when your heart broke. She'd always told herself that, always bounced back from breakups quickly before, and she told herself that's what she'd do this time, too.

So she *did* get out of bed every day, and she made breakfast and fed Sir Purrcival and ran the shop, and worked on finding ways of undoing what Wells had unknowingly done.

And she did it all feeling like there was a bag of shattered glass in her chest.

That part was new. In the past, getting back to normal as quickly as possible had been her own personal brand of magic, clearing the pain of heartache away better than any spell.

But not this time.

Why wasn't he back? She could admit that she'd frozen him out that night, but when you found out the man you thought you might be falling for was the reason you'd lost your magic, you were allowed to take some time to process that.

And yes, it had pissed her off that he'd been so quick to defend his father, but she'd known Wells was loyal, and hell, who wanted to believe their dad went past "kind of a dick" and straight into "power-hungry monster"?

Still, it had hurt. In that moment, she had wanted him to believe her, and he hadn't.

Or hadn't been able to.

In any case, she'd still expected him to show up at her door later that night, and then he just . . . hadn't.

Had he gone back, discovered the truth, and assumed she'd never want to see him again?

Was his father missing, and Wells was searching for him?

Or—and this was the kind of thing that only sneaked into her mind late at night, whispering when she couldn't sleep—had it all been a plan? Had Wells known what he was doing after all, and, mission accomplished, fucked off back home?

Gwyn knew in her bones that that couldn't be true, but the longer he was gone, the louder that voice was getting.

We were supposed to be a team, she'd thought to herself a million times since he'd been gone. *We were supposed to work this out together.*

And that, really, was the crux of it. When things had gotten hard, gotten messy, he'd bailed, and now, as she sat behind the booth she'd set up at the Fall Festival, her eyes kept being drawn to the empty spot where the Penhallow's booth should have been.

She could still feel his arms around her as they'd stood there in Something Wicked, teasing each other about sorcerer's robes; she thought of how happy she'd been, how good it had felt to stand there with him, joking and kissing and making plans.

How impossible it seemed that only a heartbeat later, everything would change.

The memory made her eyes sting, so she shoved it away, turning to a customer approaching her booth with a smile.

This was her place, after all. This is what she did, and she was damn good at it. Wells Penhallow was not going to spoil Fall Festival for her.

So she straightened her witch's hat and sold the hell out of some tarot cards while the evening breeze sent the lights strung overhead swaying, and the smell of autumn filled the air.

When there was a lull in her line, she checked her cell phone—she tried not to have it out at things like this, technology really killed the Witch Vibe she was going for—and was surprised to see she had a missed call from Sam, two from Cait, and one from Parker.

That was weird.

But maybe they'd heard something about Wells.

Gwyn was just about to call them back when she heard someone shouting her name.

"Gwyn!"

Glancing up, she saw Morgan making her way over to her, not nearly as severe as usual, decked out in an orange blouse, black pencil skirt, and orange-and-black-striped tights.

Smiling, Gwyn put her phone down. "I see you're embracing the theme!" she called out, and Morgan struck a pose, arms raised.

"When in Graves Glen!" she replied, and Gwyn gave her a thumbs-up.

"Actually," Morgan went on, coming closer, "can I get a hand with something? I found a painting in all that stuff in the attic that wasn't actually magic *or* terrifying, so I thought I might donate it to my friend Charlotte's booth."

Gwyn vaguely knew Charlotte, a non-witch in town who ran a small gallery just down from the Coffee Cauldron.

"Sure," Gwyn said, coming out from behind her booth. This side of the fair was quiet right now, most people in line for food at this time of night, and she could use the chance to stretch her legs.

Morgan walked quickly, and even though Gwyn was pretty long-legged, she had to jog a little to keep up. Overhead, the sky was dark, clouds stretching across it, and Gwyn shivered as the sounds of the fair grew fainter.

"Did you park in North Carolina?" she asked Morgan, and the other woman laughed, the sound high and a little strained.

"Sorry, it's just a little farther."

Gwyn shrugged. "I see why you wanted help," she called to Morgan. "It would be a real pain to lug a picture all the way back from out here."

Morgan didn't reply, and Gwyn felt her neck prickle.

The grass was taller here, damp against her ankles as she stopped, looking around her. It wasn't just the night chill she was feeling, she realized.

It was magic.

A lot of it.

"Morgan?" she called again, and Morgan turned around then, her arms folded over her chest, her lips tilting up into a smug smile.

"You know, it's a real shame you don't have any more magic, Gwyn," she said, and out of the corner of her eye, Gwyn saw a dark figure approaching.

She turned and there was another. A third. A fourth.

"Lucky for us, though," Morgan continued, walking forward, her hands in front of her, fingers crackling with power, "we don't need your magic. We just need your blood."

CHAPTER 33

After a week of staying in Bowen's shack far up in the mountains, Wells was beginning to understand why Bowen was the way he was.

For one, the bloody thing was miles from any kind of civilization, and also bloody hard to find. Wells had spent days searching for him, even with the Traveling Stone. Turned out, Bowen had enough enchantments around the place to send any witch on a wild-goose chase. But Wells had been determined.

If anyone knew how to fix what Da had done, it would be Bowen, up there in his hut, doing whatever strange and esoteric magic shite he did, and Wells was now single-minded: He was going to undo this.

And if that meant scrambling up the wrong mountain for three fucking days, so be it.

By the time he'd found his brother, he'd felt almost feral with worry and anger, and had clearly looked it, too, because Bowen had let him in with only a grunt and a "Fuck happened to you?"

By the time he'd told his younger brother the whole story, Bowen's fists were clenched, his jaw set, and he'd gotten to work.

The hut was small, barely furnished except for a couple of camp cots, and there was an outhouse situation Wells hoped he could eventually wipe from his memory, but what Bowen lacked in amenities, he made up for in magic.

If there was a book about it, Bowen had it. If there was a spell ingredient, it was tucked away on a cubbyhole bookshelf that, as far as Wells could tell, contained an infinity's worth of cubbyholes. Everything in the hut was pared down in the service of magic, and within a few days, Wells hardly minded the lack of indoor plumbing.

He barely ate, he hardly slept, and Bowen was at his side for all of it, the two of them paging through books, testing out other rings, other stones, anything that might work.

Bowen thought they were close to something now. Once he'd learned that Simon's spell was a combination of two spells, he reasoned that the same would probably be needed to reverse it.

"It's tricky," he said now to Wells as they stood over the one solid piece of furniture in the hut, a massive table covered in spells, books, pieces of paper. "But that's magic, eh?"

"This also seems to call for . . . my blood?" Wells said as he read over what Bowen had sketched out, and his brother clapped his shoulder, a hint of teeth appearing in all that beard.

"Love is pain," he said, and Wells grunted in reply.

Christ, he'd clearly been around Bowen too long.

Still, he held out his hand and let Bowen slide a silver blade in a quick stroke over the meat of his palm, wincing as the blood dripped into a small mother-of-pearl dish.

"Where do you get all this stuff?" he asked his brother, trying to distract himself as he bled.

"Here and there," Bowen replied in his typical Bowen way.

"Thank you," Wells said. "As always, you are a font of information, overflowing."

One corner of Bowen's mouth lifted. "Shops," he clarified. "Other witches. Some humans deal in magical artifacts, and I know one of them."

"That sounds danger—ow!"

Wells glared at his brother as Bowen slapped some kind of salve on his cut. It stung like a bastard, but whatever it was healed the cut almost immediately, and Wells studied his hand, reluctantly impressed.

"How soon do you think it can be ready?" he asked, and his brother shrugged as he turned away.

"Never can say with this kind of stuff," Bowen replied, heading for his cabinet and setting the dish of blood inside. "When did you tell her you were coming back?"

"I didn't."

Bowen paused. "What?"

"When I left," Wells said, distracted as he read over the spell, "I just left. And once I'd learned the truth from Simon, I knew I had to fix this, so I came straight to you."

"So you . . . buggered off. After she found out our father was the reason she'd lost her magic."

"If there's a point here, Bowen, now would be the time to approach it."

"Ever occur to you she might think you were in on it, then? That you flew back home to Da, job well done?"

Now it was Wells's turn to pause.

"I . . . I couldn't go back without a solution," he said because that had been the dominating thought in his mind. He had caused this, and he wouldn't return until he could restore her magic.

"Still, maybe a phone call?" Bowen suggested. "Text message? 'Hi, really sorry my family's so fucked up, I'll be back as soon as I've unfucked things'?"

"Shit," Wells muttered now, running a hand over his beard. It wasn't quite as shaggy as Bowen's yet, but it was definitely getting there. "I should have done that."

"Yeah, you should've," Bowen replied, then shook his head. "How is it that I stay up here all the bloody time, no woman in sight, and yet *I'm* smarter about this shite than you *and* Rhys? Fucking riddle me *that,* mate."

"Because being in love makes you insane and also quite stupid, I think," Wells said, his stomach still sinking.

Did Gwyn think he'd left her for good? Or, worse, that this was all part of his father's plan?

"Look, we need to get this spell working as soon as possible," he said, turning to Bowen. "I've got to get back to her, I've got to—"

One minute, he was looking at his brother.

The next, Sam, Cait, and Parker were standing there between him and Bowen, their eyes wide, their mouths open.

"Ohmigod that was so scary," Sam said, and from behind them, Bowen scowled.

"Who in the hell are you and how did you get on my mountain?"

"Werewolf," Cait whispered, staring at him, and Sam's eyes swung around before settling on Wells.

"Oh, thank the Goddess!" she yelled, and then all three of them were rushing him, babbling at once, and he was so surprised to see them that he couldn't even make sense of anything they were saying, until he heard, "She took Gwyn!"

"Enough!" he barked, his voice a sharp crack, and all three of them went silent, their faces pale.

"What," Wells asked, trying very hard to stay calm even as his heart threatened to beat out of his chest, "is going on?"

"Morgan took Gwyn!" Parker blurted out, and Wells stepped back, confused.

"Morgan?" he asked. "What are you talking about?"

He could tell they were all about to start talking at once again, so he pointed at Parker, delegating them. "You. Tell me everything."

Parker's eyes darted nervously around, but they nodded, licking their lips. "So after you left, we kept looking for ways to reverse your dad's spell. And when we were looking through Gwyn's stuff, we found Morgan's file."

"That file didn't tell us anything," Wells said, and Parker nodded.

"I know. But I used this on it."

They pulled out that coin they'd had the day Wells had taken the file. He remembered it, the spell that was supposed to absorb what was written and write it out somewhere else. Wells hadn't used it, though, he'd just taken the file, and now Parker added, "I was just messing around, waiting for Cait to finish with the book she was looking at, so I ran it over the file, just seeing if it worked. But when I put what was in the file on another piece of paper—"

"The file was enchanted," Sam said, thrusting a sheet of paper at him.

Wells took it, his eyes scanning, and there, where on Morgan's original file it had given that vague thing about "inappropriate magic," now a much different—much darker—story was spelled out.

"Bloody fucking hell," Wells whispered.

"They almost killed a student," Cait said. "Like, drained her of blood, vampire-style, all because I guess her ancestor had been some powerful witch. The only reason the college didn't go further was because the girl had volunteered for it."

"Apparently she thought she was gonna get all powered up, too, but they were just using her," Sam added, and Wells was pretty sure his own blood had just been replaced with ice water.

"And you think Morgan's taken Gwyn?"

"Her booth was empty at the Fall Festival, and someone said they saw her leave with a dark-haired woman and not come back.

And when we went to Morgan's house, there's a major magical-force-field-type thing around it. We couldn't get in," Parker said.

"And we didn't know what to do because Vivi and Elaine are still gone, and we're not powerful enough to take on a bunch of dark witches, but then we remembered there was a Traveling Stone in the back room at Something Wicked," Sam went on.

"And, like, we're mad at you and stuff, but we didn't know who else to go to, so we just thought of you, and then *poof!*" Cait summarized.

"Wait, you *poofed* onto my mountain? In one go?" Bowen was staring at the three with a mixture of suspicion and interest, but Wells was already moving, gesturing to the spell on Bowen's table.

"Finish this. Quick as you can. Then meet me in Graves Glen."

Bowen nodded. "Go help your girl."

"Can the three of you get back all right?" he asked Sam, and she pulled out the Traveling Stone.

"I think so. Should be easier going home than coming here."

"Good."

Wells pulled out his own Traveling Stone, trying not to think of Gwyn, magic-less, helpless, at the mercy of Morgan and her coven.

Bringing her face to mind, he squeezed the stone tight and thought one word.

Home.

CHAPTER 34

Gwyn was no expert on dark magic, but she was pretty sure nothing good ever came of being tied down on a black stone table with a bunch of people in scary robes standing around you.

Her head still woozy from whatever spell it was they'd used on her, Gwyn tested her bonds, but given that they were silver chains, she wasn't surprised to see there wasn't much give there, and she flopped back onto the table with a sigh, fighting to keep the panic down.

If ever there was a time to panic, surely this is it, she reasoned, but if she panicked, then she couldn't think, and if she couldn't think, she couldn't get out of this, and she really needed to get out of this.

"So I guess all that stuff about getting kicked out for glamours was real bullshit, huh?" she called out, and from somewhere behind her head, she heard Morgan chuckle.

"We got lunchroom duty for the glamours," she said. "It was the blood magic that got us kicked out."

"Yeah, they're really strict about that kind of thing," Gwyn said, rattling her chains. "Can't imagine why. Although to be honest, I never saw the appeal. I mean, might you get a little more power? Yes. Is it *also* icky and super evil? Another yes!"

"We wouldn't expect you to understand."

That was Harrison, down near her foot. They were in the attic, Gwyn realized now, seeing the looming shape of the iron maiden behind him.

Great.

"There are limits to what magic can do," he went on, "but if you're willing to go further, to bleed, those limits disappear. Anything becomes possible. Building entire cities out of nothing, creating universes."

"Right, but you're not going to be the one to bleed, are you?" Gwyn asked.

"No," Rosa said, stepping forward, her dark eyes surprisingly compassionate as she looked down at Gwyn. "But then, none of us have a powerful witch like Aelwyd Jones in our bloodline."

"I was sincere about wanting to help you get your magic back, Gwyn," Morgan said. "It would've been better if you'd had it."

"Which is why you invited me to come hang out in this fucking attic," Gwyn said, remembering their conversation outside the town hall.

"I did. But then Harrison realized we'd need to do the ritual before Samhain, and we were running out of time. It had to be now, during the new moon."

Morgan gestured to the dark sky beyond the attic window. "And while your magic may be gone, it's still Aelwyd's blood in your veins. When we spill it, her power becomes ours. Graves Glen becomes ours, and with an entire town to draw from?"

She spread her hands wide. "We're unstoppable."

"I really don't think it works like that," Gwyn said, and Morgan frowned now, her dark eyes sharp.

"I think we might know better than you on this, Gwyn. We've all spent the past ten years steeping in magic while you've been here, hocking toys to tourists. I've collected some of the most powerful talismans in the world, all for this."

Gwyn lifted her head just enough to look around, taking in the paintings, the thumbscrews, all that other terrifying shit she and Wells had seen. So that's what that was all about. These things were infused with dark magic, strengthening Morgan's own evil powers.

"If you want, we can enchant you first," Rosa offered. "So it won't hurt."

Gwyn almost laughed at that. Or maybe sobbed. "Right. Like I'm at the dentist and not . . . whatever the hell this is."

Morgan laid a hand on her forehead, her skin clammy and cold. "It will be over quickly, I promise," she said. "We don't take any pleasure in causing pain. But we learned last time that too little blood might as well be none. So we're going to need all of yours."

The fear Gwyn had been trying so hard to keep down squirmed back up now, making her tremble just a little. Even with her magic, this group might be too much for her, but without it?

Closing her eyes, Gwyn took deep breaths as Morgan and

the others began moving closer. Whatever enchantment Rosa had promised her was clearly starting to work because she could feel a kind of heaviness slipping into her limbs, her brain going cloudy.

She thought about Vivi and Elaine, and Sir Purrcival and her Baby Witches.

She even thought about Wells, about seeing him there behind the counter at Penhallow's, and in her bed, and by her side, and she clenched her fists, gritting her teeth.

Morgan was chanting something now, the others joining in, and Gwyn could feel the pull of magic in the room getting stronger.

Darker.

She was going to die all so some jacked-up witches could play at being gods while wearing dorky robes.

The hell I am.

The thought was so strong it made her eyes snap open, the lassitude Rosa's spell had created suddenly draining out of her.

Gwynnevere Jones was not going out like this.

The chanting was still happening, and Gwyn concentrated with everything she had, wiggling her fingers.

There was an answering spark.

Tiny, almost insignificant, but *there,* and Gwyn fought back a grin as a fierce joy spilled through her.

My magic is not something anyone can take from me, she thought, her mind clear. *It is* mine. *And it's still there.*

And so it was. She could feel it now, racing through her, summoned up out of her very blood, and this time, when she moved her fingers, there wasn't just a spark.

There was a fire.

WHEN WELLS SUDDENLY appeared in the field just outside Morgan's house, his stomach gave a sickening lurch.

It wasn't the Traveling Stone this time.

Whatever sense of magical wrongness he'd felt before had gotten stronger now, a rot that seemed to pulse, making him grit his teeth as he staggered forward.

It was dark, and when he looked at his watch, he saw it was nearly three A.M. here.

The witching hour.

Despite the pain in his head, Wells made himself move, and just out of the corner of his eye, he caught sight of Sam, Cait, and Parker, stumbling onto the ground. "Stay back!" he called.

They hadn't lied about the magical barrier around the house. It was strong, and Wells tried to focus, mentally testing for weak spots, gathering up a magical blast that might be strong enough to blow a hole in it even as his brain kept chanting, *Hurry, hurry, hurry, she's in there, hurry.*

He'd just about summoned up enough power for a decent blast at the barrier when there was a loud crash, the sound of broken glass, and he looked up in horror as a gout of flame flared out a window at the top of the house.

Wells had no memory of how he got through the barrier or into the house. One moment he was staring at that flame, the next he was inside the house, his feet pounding up the attic stairs, flinging the door open.

The first thing he saw was Gwyn, gorgeous glorious Gwyn, blessedly alive and standing on top of some kind of black stone table, her hands glowing as she held them out in front of her, and he almost fell to his knees with relief.

Then he realized she was facing off against that bloody Harrison arsehole, currently swinging a Morningstar in her direction.

The blast Wells had been preparing to shatter the force field was nothing compared to the one he sent flying at that man, and as Harrison flew backward, hitting the wall, Gwyn turned, seeing him.

And she smiled.

Wells felt that smile in every part of him. A sunrise could not be brighter than that smile.

But he didn't have time to admire it because Rosa was coming toward him, some terrifyingly medieval sword clutched in her hands, and he dodged, trying to gather up enough magic to push her back.

He was exhausted, his time away having taken it out of him more than he'd realized, his relief at seeing Gwyn alive and whole distracting him, and he was so focused on Rosa that he didn't see Morgan behind him until he heard Gwyn cry out, "Wells!"

It all seemed to happen in slow motion. Morgan was reaching for him, her teeth bared, her eyes wild, a silver dagger in one hand.

I think she's actually going to stab me, he thought, almost like it was happening to someone else, and then there was a blast of light, and Morgan reared back, clutching her arm as the knife clattered to the ground.

Gwyn was at his side, her hands still outstretched, and Wells could see the edge of Morgan's sleeve was singed, the skin of her hand red and cracked, and she glared at Gwyn, stumbling back.

As she did, she bumped into one of those trunks lining the attic floor, falling hard against it, the rusted lock giving way and dropping to the floor with a heavy thud.

For a moment everything was still, the only sound Morgan's pained breathing, and then the lid of the trunk suddenly flew open with a howl.

Wells heard Morgan scream, and it was like there was suddenly a hurricane in the attic, a fierce wind that had him shutting his eyes, pulling Gwyn tight against him as the howling went on and on, his bones practically rattling with the force of it.

And then the trunk snapped closed, reminding Wells of nothing so much as a large jaw.

The attic was quiet. Still.

And Morgan and the others were gone.

CHAPTER 35

H onestly, this whole thing is a very valuable lesson in why you don't keep scary magical shit just lying around your house," Gwyn said as she walked away from Morgan's house, Wells next to her, Sam, Cait, and Parker clustered around her. "I really hope you three take that to heart."

"So it just . . . ate them?" Parker asked with a shudder, and Wells sighed, putting his hands in his pockets.

"Not exactly. I believe what Morgan had was what's known as a Soul Catcher. Sucks people into other dimensions, holds them captive there. Nasty bit of work."

"Not as nasty as being eaten," Sam said, and Gwyn had to agree with her there.

"Why didn't it take the two of you?" Parker asked, and Wells shrugged.

"Soul Catchers tend to feed on negative energy, from what I remember, and there was an awful lot of it in that coven's souls. Once it had all of them, I suppose it was . . . full."

Gwyn couldn't repress a shudder at that, even after all Morgan and her coven had tried to do.

"Well," she said, trying to joke, "good to know that my soul is still relatively untainted despite that year I went to Burning Man. Oh, and the year I cut my own bangs. Actually, all of the years 2011 to 2014."

"But big news is," Cait said, practically skipping across the damp grass, "is that your magic is back!" Turning to Wells, she asked, "Did your brother get the spell to you in time?"

Gwyn paused, looking over at him.

Wells looked . . . well, he'd be handsome no matter what, there was no escaping that bone structure, but he was clearly exhausted, dark circles under his eyes, his beard shaggy, and now he met her eyes with a weak smile.

"No," he told Cait. "She did that all on her own."

"God, Glinda, you're so badass," Cait said, and Sam and Parker nodded, Sam slipping her arm through Gwyn's.

"Best witch mom ever," she said, and Gwyn laughed, tired but happy, leaning her cheek against Sam's bright hair.

"I still ought to ground you for running into danger like that. Morgan and her friends were not fucking around. Promise me you won't do something like that again."

"We promise," they all chorused, but then Sam gave Wells a sly glance.

"We also went to Wales. With *magic*."

"And met Wells's scary brother."

"And he didn't say it, but I think he was really impressed that we magicked ourselves there."

The three of them kept talking over each other, filling Gwyn in on their adventures, and she listened and smiled in the right places, but her eyes kept drifting over to Wells, and his to her, and she wanted to smack him and kiss him and ask just where the hell he'd been, and she swore she'd do exactly that the second she got him alone.

But when, thanks to the Traveling Stone, they appeared at the foot of Gwyn's porch steps, she realized that was going to have to wait.

"Gwyn!"

Vivi came flying out the front door, Elaine on her heels, and Gwyn thought her heart might burst out of her chest as she ran up the steps to fling herself into their arms.

"What are you two doing here?"

"We knew something was wrong," Vivi said.

"Both of us. Practically at the same time," Elaine confirmed, reaching out to smooth Gwyn's hair, and Gwyn leaned into the touch, tears stinging her eyes.

When she'd thought about them there on that awful table, they'd felt her. They'd known she needed them, and they'd come back for her.

"It's been a long night," Gwyn said, "and it's an even longer story, but I can tell some of it, and Wells—"

But when she looked behind her, Wells was gone.

IT WAS THE right thing to do, letting Gwyn have time alone with her family, Wells thought as he sat in his dark living room, alone.

She'd missed them and had so much to tell them, and he didn't want to sit there, an awkward presence, while she explained what it was his father had done.

So yes. He was being gallant.

Noble.

"You're being a fucking idiot."

Sighing, Wells turned toward the front door. The porch lights were on, and he could see a figure standing there, a figure who now rattled the doorknob and called out, "I know you're in there, feeling sorry for yourself, you ponce. Now let me in."

Wells knew from experience that Rhys would not leave until he'd had his say, so he got up to unlock the door.

His youngest brother pushed his way in, looking annoyingly well rested and happy, and Wells glowered at him. "I'm not feeling sorry for myself. I'm giving Gwyn some space."

"Did she tell you, 'I want space'? Or are you doing that thing you do where you just assume you know better than *everyone* all the time forever?"

"I did not miss you at all, let me just say for the record. In fact, I think you and Vivienne should take a second, much longer honeymoon. Possibly *to* the actual moon."

Rhys grinned then, slapping him on the arm. "And miss this kind of excitement again? Never."

There was a clattering from the dining room, and both he and

Rhys turned to see Bowen standing there, swaying a little on his feet, but otherwise his usual grumpy self.

"Rhys," Bowen said, and Rhys pulled a face, tilting back on his heels.

"What the hell are you doing here? Wait, is this some kind of intervention? Are we doing an intervention on Wells for being a sad bastard, and no one told me?"

"Shut up, Rhys," Wells and Bowen said in unison, and then glanced at each other before looking back to their youngest brother.

"I don't think the three of us have been in one room in five years," Wells said, not sure he was sorry they were breaking that trend.

"Calls for a drink," Bowen muttered.

In the end, it called for several. Not only did they have to talk about their father, but Wells had to catch Rhys up on exactly what had happened while he'd been gone, everything from Morgan's appearance to a (very edited) explanation of where things now stood with Gwyn, and by the time he was finished, the last of their father's good scotch was nearly gone.

"I knew Da was a prick," Rhys said with a sigh, "but I didn't think he'd do something like this."

"I think losing the town affected him more than we knew," Wells said, turning his glass around in his hands, and Rhys reached over, patting his knee.

"I'm sorry, mate. Me and Bowen, we never really got along with him. But you two were close. Had to hurt."

"Hmm," was Wells's only reply, but he thumped Rhys's leg in return, and his brother smiled at him.

"So what now?" Rhys asked. "Can sons disown their father?"

"Maybe not in the law, but certainly in the spirit," Wells said, grim.

He'd loved his father. Maybe part of him always would. If we could stop loving people, life would be so much simpler, but Wells knew it didn't work that way.

But there was no place for a man like Simon in Wells's life, and he had made peace with that during that long week on Bowen's mountain. He had his brothers, absolute wankers that they both were, and that was enough.

Well, almost enough.

He could deal with that later, though. For now, his father was the issue.

"Da, *Simon,* is more powerful than ever right now," Wells reminded them. "And even if he can't take this town back over, I'm sure he has some other plan in mind. The pub, maybe. The ancient Penhallow magic still there."

"I'm going to need, at the very least, a nap and another stiff drink before I declare war on Da," Rhys said, "but I'm willing if you are."

Wells nodded, but to his surprise, Bowen drained his drink, standing up. "You two have shite to fix here," he said, then pointed at Wells. "'Specially you."

"St. Bugi's balls, but I love this new world where Wells is the one everyone wants to get-it-to-fucking-gether already, and *I*—"

"Shut up, Rhys," Bowen and Wells said again, and then Bowen put his glass on the coffee table with a thunk.

"I'll deal with Da," Bowen said, and Wells had no idea what exactly he meant by that, but having seen Bowen's hut, he had no doubt his brother was well up to the task of any kind of magical battle.

"Good," he said, and Rhys made a disbelieving sound.

"What, no lecture? No reminder of what Bowen should and should not do? No random insult to me just for kicks? You *have* changed."

Wells flipped his youngest brother off, but he was smiling, as was Rhys.

Even Bowen might have been smiling beneath that metric fuckton of hair on his face.

"So that's Da handled," Rhys continued. "And I for once have no cock-ups to fix except that we were in such a rush to get back here that I think I *might* have magically sent our luggage to Georgia the *country* as opposed to Georgia the *state*, but Vivienne will understand. And as for you . . ."

He gave Wells's leg another thump, and Wells sighed.

Yes, as for him.

Reading his thoughts, Bowen nodded toward the door and, Wells assumed, Gwyn's cabin. "So she just got her magic back on her own, then. No spell needed."

When Wells nodded, Bowen grunted.

"Never heard of such a thing."

"You've never met Gwyn Jones," Wells said with a small smile, and Rhys laughed, leaning back.

"Ah, the sound of a man completely clobbered by love. I know the feeling well."

Wells didn't bother to argue. He loved her, was completely mad for her, and surely that was obvious to everyone by now.

Everyone, he suddenly realized, but the one person who mattered most.

CHAPTER 36

G wyn figured being nearly ritually sacrificed gave a girl an excuse to sleep in, so it was nearly noon by the time she made her way to Something Wicked the next day. Elaine had told her not to bother going in at all, but staying home would've just made her feel restless, and that was no good.

What she needed was a return to normalcy, and nothing felt more normal to her than her store.

Downtown was fairly quiet given that it was a weekday afternoon, and she slid a glance at Penhallow's as she unlocked her door.

The *Open* sign hung in the window.

So he was still here, then.

After Wells had disappeared last night, Rhys had gone after him, and when he'd come back to the cabin, he'd confirmed Wells was still there, in his house just up the mountain.

That was something, at least.

He'd come back for her, too. And according to Cait, he'd been working on some kind of reversal spell with his brother, so she'd been right. He hadn't wanted to return to Graves Glen until he could fix things.

Which was just . . . so annoyingly Esquire.

And now he would undoubtedly stay away, assuming she didn't want to see him, which was also annoyingly Esquire. He'd wait for her to make the first move, a gentleman to the last.

Well.

Gwyn was good at first moves.

Turning away from Something Wicked, she marched across the street to Penhallow's, already planning what she'd say to him. How she'd missed him, but how it had hurt when he'd left, how this self-flagellation thing was not going to work for her, and how he didn't get to decide if she should be angry at him or not.

The walk was a short one, but Gwyn had had plenty of time to work up a head of steam, and she flung open the door to Penhallow's, the bell ringing loudly.

"Okay, so we are not doing this—" she started, and then every bit of the truly spectacular rant she'd composed in her head dissolved like a mist.

Wells was standing in front of the counter in long black robes. Formal witch's robes, the kind she'd teased him about wearing.

Those were formal and traditional, but what was *not* was the hat he held in his hand, a dark blue pointy thing with silver stars printed on it, the sort of thing she sometimes sold in Something Wicked.

His eyes were bloodshot, and they widened to see her standing there, the two of them silent as they took each other in.

"You're wearing robes," Gwyn finally said, frowning, and Wells glanced down at himself, the pointy hat still in one hand.

"Yes. I . . . I realized I missed the Fall Festival, and we'd talked—well, we'd *joked,* I supposed—about me wearing robes, and Rhys said that a big gesture might be required, so I was going to come over to your store like this. The hat was . . . well, the hat was meant to be funny? And slightly humiliating, which I assumed you'd enjoy as mocking me does seem to be one of your great joys in life—not that I mind it—and oh! I, I also bought this."

Reaching for the counter behind him, Wells pulled out a very familiar-looking velvet bag, and Gwyn felt her cheeks aching with the need to smile.

"So I was going to come over to your store in the robes and the mockable hat with the edible bath glitter, and after a groveling apology for my father being a monster, and for not believing that could be the case at first, and then *also* for fucking the fuck off without letting you know I was coming back—the apology portion was going to take up a fair amount of time, I can assure you—*then* I was going to offer you the Pixie Licks and deliver a witty and devastating riposte about how, while you might still be furious with me, if you ever needed an excuse to kiss me again, I could provide such a thing."

He was breathing a little hard now, the tips of his ears scarlet, and Gwyn tried to school her face into a very solemn expression as Wells continued:

"Except that when I got the robes on, I realized I looked like a *bit* of a tit, and then it began to occur to me that a plan formulated when one has not slept in twenty-four hours and is running solely on tea and the bone-rattling relief of finding you alive and all right might not be the wisest of schemes. And then I began to think I'd never listened to Rhys in my life, so why was I taking his lead on this, one of the most important moments of my life as I try to win back the woman I love, and it was about three seconds after that epiphany that you walked in," he finally finished, punctuating that amazing speech by throwing his pointy hat onto one of the wing-back chairs.

Gwyn blinked, and Wells stared at her, his chest heaving up and down, his fist propped on one hip, his hair a wreck, and, she noticed, he was wearing one black shoe and one navy one, and if she hadn't already fallen in love with him sometime between the night he'd found Sir Purrcival and the moment she'd walked into this shop on the day of the Gathering and seen him frantically making cups of tea, those mismatched shoes would've done it.

"You are a disaster," she told him. "Like, not just in this moment, but maybe on a fundamental level."

Wells nodded. "I am. I hide it well on the whole, I think, but yes, Gwynnevere, absolute wreck of a man."

Her heart beating hard, Gwyn moved a little closer. "And here I thought you were the responsible one."

"A sham. A cover-up of immense proportions."

Gwyn laughed even as she watched his eyes warm and darken the closer she came. "Is it weird that I'm kind of into this version of you? I can't even call you Esquire when you're like this."

"You can call me anything you like," he told her, and there was such naked longing in his face that her throat went tight.

"Wells, Esquire, That Dickhead Who Works Across the Street. Anything," Wells went on, and Gwyn swallowed hard, letting one hand reach out and just barely brush against his, their fingers briefly tangling together.

"And if I wanted to call you mine?" she asked, her voice low, and Wells's grip tightened on her hand.

"I'll be that until I die."

Lifting her head, Gwyn looked into his eyes. "So I guess you meant it, then. That bit about me being the woman you loved."

Wells winced. "I did mention that in the middle of my completely unhinged rant, didn't I? Fucked up both the apology *and* the declaration of love, well done, me."

But Gwyn only shook her head. "No, this was better," she said, and then grinned. "I mean, I want that groveling apology later because what girl doesn't love a good grovel? I think I'll even film it on my phone."

Wells made a sound that might have been a laugh, and Gwyn took a deep breath, bringing their joined hands between them. "It's been a while since I've heard someone say they're in love with me. Even longer since I've said it back."

Wells was very still now, watching her, and somehow that made saying something that had once been so hard for her as easy as breathing. "But I love you, Wells."

His fingers flexed in hers, his throat working, and Gwyn reached up with her free hand to tug gently at his beard. "And this is what I want," she told him. "Not big gestures. Just you. All of you. The disaster bits and the parts that say words like 'henceforth.'"

"I have never said that," he protested, and off her look amended, "to you."

Still smiling, Gwyn ducked her head, kissing his knuckles. "I want the man who finds missing pets and makes me soup and may sound like he's auditioning for *Masterpiece Theatre* but will also make love to me in the back of a pickup truck."

His free hand came up to stroke her hair back from her face. "I want all of you, too," he told her. "The powerful witch and the woman who loves nothing better than to take the piss out of me when I deserve it. The woman who inspires loyalty in talking cats and Baby Witches and everyone she meets because her heart is the only thing more impressive than her magic. I want you, Gwyn Jones."

"Then that's all that matters," she said, sunlight in her veins, in her heart, flowing just as powerfully as her magic ever had.

His kiss was magic, too, slow and thorough, a promise and a declaration and an apology, and Gwyn accepted all of it, her arms coming around him, her body melting into his with the rightness of it all.

A sudden thumping noise had them breaking the kiss, looking toward the front window of the shop, and there were Sam, Cait, and Parker, their faces practically pressed against the glass as Parker thumped their fist next to the painted letters, Sam whooped, and Cait swooned.

"Heathens," Wells grumbled, but he was smiling and Gwyn laughed even as she shooed them away with a wave.

"Love me, love my Baby Witches," she said, and he looked back at her, smiling.

"The first part is the easiest thing I've ever done. The second may take some practice."

"You better start now, then," Gwyn replied. "I think those three will be a vital part of the Jones and Esquire Empire."

Still smiling, Wells brushed his lips against hers again. "Penhallow and Jones."

Gwyn kissed him back. "Jones and Penhallow, final offer."

"We'll talk about it at home," Wells replied, and as he kissed her again, Gwyn realized she didn't know if he meant her cabin or his haunted mansion, but it didn't really matter.

Wherever the two of them were together, that was home.

Acknowledgments

I've been doing this writing thing for long enough now that you'd think I'd remember the ancient writer proverb that Second Books Are Always a Beast. And yet! But given how stubborn both Wells and Gwyn are, I guess I shouldn't have been surprised they'd give me such a fight on their way to a HEA.

Luckily for me, I had powerful forces on my side in the form of my brilliant editor, Tessa Woodward, and my fabulous agent, Holly Root. Tessa, your patience and support with this book meant the world to me, and Holly, if there were a gold medal for Talking Authors Off Ledges, you'd probably have an entire room in your house full of those things by now. So much of publishing comes down to working with good people, and I am so fortunate to get to work with The Best in you two!

Thank you to everyone at Avon/HarperCollins both for your support of these books and your general Excellence.

As always, I couldn't do this without the support of my family and friends, a powerful coven indeed.

Lastly, it's been so delightful to see Sir Purrcival become The

Star of these books (AS HE WAS MEANT TO BE!). He's based on my own two black cats, a pair of brothers I adopted from my local humane society in 2018. They're truly magical little guys, but black cats still have trouble getting adopted due to all kinds of factors ranging from superstition to the fear that they won't photograph well (although a quick look at my Instagram would prove that one wrong!). So if you're considering adopting a cat, I hope you'll think of Sir Purrcival when you stop by your local shelter and bring home your own Witchy Kitty!

ERIN STERLING, who also writes as Rachel Hawkins, is the *New York Times* bestselling author of *The Ex Hex* and *The Wife Upstairs*, as well as multiple books for young readers. Her work has been translated in more than a dozen countries. She studied gender and sexuality in Victorian literature at Auburn University and currently lives in Alabama.

ALSO BY
ERIN STERLING

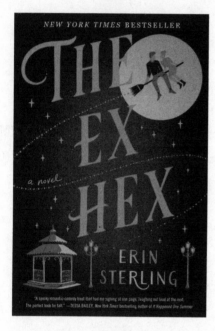

THE EX HEX

New York Times Bestseller

Erin Sterling casts a delightful spell with a spine-tingling romance full of wishes, witches, and hexes gone wrong.

"A delightful and witty take on witchy mayhem."
— Popsugar

Nine years ago, Vivienne Jones nursed her broken heart like any young witch would: vodka, weepy music, bubble baths...and a curse on the horrible boyfriend. Sure, Vivi knows she shouldn't use her magic this way, but with only an "orchard hayride" scented candle on hand, she isn't worried it will cause him anything more than a bad hair day or two.

That is until Rhys Penhallow, descendent of the town's ancestors, breaker of hearts, and annoyingly just as gorgeous as he always was, returns to Graves Glen, Georgia. What should be a quick trip to recharge the town's ley lines and make an appearance at the annual fall festival turns disastrously wrong. With one calamity after another striking Rhys, Vivi realizes her silly little Ex Hex may not have been so harmless after all.

Suddenly, Graves Glen is under attack from murderous wind-up toys, a pissed off ghost, and a talking cat with some interesting things to say. Vivi and Rhys have to ignore their off the charts chemistry to work together to save the town and find a way to break the break-up curse before it's too late.